SUBTERRANEAN CONFRONTATION!

It was not a man, although it possessed superficial aspects of humanity. One might write, as did Bleek, of a head, and arms and legs attached to a trunk, but there the illusion of kinship ceased. Pale it was, like a cave worm, fearfully thin and wiry, with very long limbs bent at multiple joints. It stood upright like a man, yet when it advanced from the yellow arch it seemed to scuttle as might a crab or spider. There was nothing manlike in that locomotion. Its hairless head was little more than a distorted, lopsided skull over which the skin was tightly drawn, with holes for ears, noseless nostrils, a small red mouth filled with many tiny, pointed teeth. The small, dark round eyes gleamed from deep sockets and greenly reflected light as would the eyes of animals, yet there was cunning in those beady orbs, a steadfast, malign intelligence. They regarded Bleek evilly, and as the wizard gazed back at them a third, previously invisible eye unsealed above the other two in that grotesque skull, a moist red eye which possessed even more mocking intellect and malevolence than the others. The figures on the benches rose and stood to attention, a row of dreadful, silent, skull-headed horrors.

From "The Search for Maltheus the Wise"

Science and Sorcery: Fifteen stories of obsessed researchers, power mad wizards, bold adventurers, and hapless victims of lunatic fate.

SCIENCE AND SORCERY
A Collection of Alarming Tales

by Jeffery Scott Sims

Published by the Press of Dyrezan
Copyright 2013 by Jeffery Scott Sims
ISBN: 978-0-9899322-0-2

CONTENTS

An Introduction, Intended to Enlighten

Science and sorcery; what, reader, an impossible combination? Can, or should, Frodo meet Einstein? Easier accomplished in a collection of short stories, perhaps, yet the road Lovecraft confidently strode, that others have since uneasily ventured upon, shows that it can be done too within a tale. Many of my well received stories recounting the fantastic adventures of Professor Anton Vorchek take this route, melding aspects of science fiction with outright fantasy, and such stories form the backbone of the current selection. Jacob Bleek, wizard of a past age—lovably hateful hero of my recent novel, *The Journey of Jacob Bleek*—knows a thing or two about science as well, and while his appearances in this volume focus on morbid magic, he remains ever the keen-minded, analytical scholar.

Vorchek and Bleek provide the framework for this book, though since a story collection can promise variety, I've kicked in some choice one-off pieces as well, providing spice to the mix. As the subtitle indicates, all are meant to alarm; no warm fuzzies here, at any rate, rather an assortment of the weird, the macabre, the thrilling, and the terrifying. Several aren't actually fantastic in nature—call them strange or disturbing, relations of events that just possibly could happen in a crazy world—but the rest, hopefully, offer unnatural or supernatural chills by the bucketful.

I don't wish to scare off anyone—at the moment, remember, I intend only to enlighten—however, the dedicated reader deserves forewarning. Allow me to tantalize by hinting at what awaits grim perusal:

If approached in order, commence with "Subject No. 249," one of my paranoia pieces, akin to such previously published tales as "The Man in the Globe," "The Nasty Club," and "Critical Information." Secretive evil stalks our world, for reasons of its own, as the hapless 249 learns to his dreadful cost.

"The Book of Jacob Bleek" presents the first prose reference to that spooky fellow of yesteryear, and to his equally ominous tome of insidious, oft sought lore. While Bleek himself doesn't appear in the

i

story—not exactly—he surely haunts it.   The lurid discussion of Xenophor marks the first of several references to that awesome Lovecraftian entity.

"Realization: a Tale of the True Theory" introduces none other than Professor Anton Vorchek, but in a peculiar variant, quite unlike his conventional appearances. One may choose to write him off in this as a crank, whose manic scribblings blast the mind of the tormented narrator.

"The Discovery of the X Force" showcases another odd Vorchek sighting. Not really a Vorchek story, I call it a gloomy futuristic fable. If necessary, think of this, with "Realization," as glimpses into an alternative universe.

Ah, but "Canyon Diablo" exhibits Vorchek in his glory as persistent (and cold-blooded) seeker after the strange, hunting for prehistoric survivals with the aid of his feckless graduate student. The story, while not utterly fantastic in content, inaugurates his "Weird Arizona" series, which includes the remaining Vorchek adventures in this collection.

"The Beneficiary" falls afoul of one of my most paranoiac puzzles. Here I experiment with a villain unknown, unseen, his motives forever a mystery. As the beneficiary discovers, only the final result counts.

"Cathedral Rock" tells in fable-like form the grotesque history of a famous Arizona landmark, as investigated by Professor Vorchek. It's a capsule version of more to come.

Another fable, "Jacob Bleek on the Mountain" describes the climax of the determined sorcerer's quest for ultimate knowledge and boundless power. I'm sentimentally fond of this very short piece, as it comprises the original kernel of what became the aforementioned novel, *The Journey of Jacob Bleek*. Readers of that long work, especially its final chapter, will experience some deja vu here.

"At the Bottom of Montezuma Well" is quintessential Vorchek, setting the pattern for others to follow. Accompanied by Theresa Delaney, his beautiful if querulous assistant, the professor probes the lethal menace lurking beneath the waters of another well known Arizona site. Vorchek derives much of his background information from antique Indian lore, and achieves a resolution which he, at least, finds satisfying.

Back in action, Vorchek and Theresa wander amidst the perils of "A Nature Scene," a companion piece to the foregoing. Nature run riot, of course, nature stirred and perverted by mysterious cosmic forces; what else?

"The Search for Maltheus the Wise" discloses such creepiness that even Jacob Bleek can scarcely face the revelations. In the enchanted east he seeks the famed mage, learns of his tragic death. Not the end of the story, however, not by a long shot. Similar conceptions of the loathsome deity Blug have appeared in previously published tales, notably the Vorchek adventures "The Man Who Sought Blug" and "The God in the Machine."

"Vorchek's Vacation" leads him and the delightful Miss Delaney to Oak Creek Canyon, the jewel of Arizona, where more horrors await. Dutiful Theresa finds herself the chosen victim of ancient nastiness reaching through time and space. Can Vorchek save her, or is that really his first item of business?

Jacob Bleek relates "An Eastern Tale," one ripped from the pages of his monstrous *Black Book*. This true sequel to "The Search for Maltheus the Wise" covers some of the same ground—the exotic city of Elibama, the shunned Valley of Voltakis, the hideous demons—but the greedy hero of this one proves in no wise as savvy as Bleek.

"Under the Natural Bridge" sums up the weird aboriginal lore underlying several of the previous Vorchek stories, as it takes the professor, Theresa, and a callow graduate student to still another famed Arizona locale. Vorchek, like Bleek, craves cosmic knowledge, confronts a tricky situation his august forbear would appreciate. Indeed, the "Messengers" with whom the scientist treats in this tale hark back to those faced by the sorcerer at the conclusion to *The Journey of Jacob Bleek*.

Saved for last, I indulge my penchant for old cinema with the tasty morsel "Late Night Movies," conceive them intruding in harrowing fashion into the real world. What's going on here? What does it mean? Who's next to suffer an unendurable fate? All historic film references are fictionalized, but the astute aficionado can figure them out.

Well, enough by way of preparation. Experience now the stories—with a bite of the lip, a grit of the teeth, a shudder when circumstances demand—and enjoy.

Jeffery Scott Sims
July 3, 2013, penned at dawn atop the eastern rim of Oak Creek Canyon

Subject No. 249

My Dear K___:

I'm grateful that you were willing to swing this assignment my way. Given my past performance, and my seniority, it was only reasonable that the Department cater to my preferences, in the spirit of cooperation, getting the job done right, and all that good stuff. It's not like I was asking for a great deal. I simply choose to work with intact families, for I find the results so much more striking and personally satisfying. Broken homes offer elements of interest, to be sure, but I consider them most useful, in the main, to operatives who are just starting out. They constitute an excellent training ground for new recruits. On the other hand, the members of splintered socio-personal relationships are normally under stress already, and at my level of expertise, pushing them over the edge doesn't count for much. Give me a rock-solid situation, and let me go at it hammer and tongs.

As I understand it, G___ takes on the other assignment. Well, that's good enough for him. Don't tell him I said so.

***

K___:

I've collected the basic facts on Subject No. 249. Roger Allen Willis, age 42, head architect at the old and prestigious firm of Benson and Nielstrom. Married to a young and beautiful wife, Rhonda, age 34. Two children: Allen, 12; Emily, 8. They live in a spacious brick home (remodeled Victorian, done by you-know-who) at 125 Monroe Terrace. The best part of town, naturally. Manicured lawn, with extensive gardens, more like a park than a yard. I've got pictures of all this. Three cars, one of them classic (a fully restored '57 Chevy), and a 40-foot catamaran stored in a shed by the back drive. I must say, this fellow seems perfect. Kudos to S___, who I'm informed developed this lead.

Right now I have before me on my desk a mass of pertinent papers: copies of credit card receipts, doctor and dentist bills, licenses, tax statements. I'll sift it a couple more days, but I'm getting a feel for the man. Putting it all together, it looks like our Mr. Willis is managing just

1

fine for himself.

***

Dear K___:

Surveillance have finished the preliminaries on Willis. A church goer, dines out with the family once or twice a week (usually at the same place), member of the neighborhood golf club. He often plays with potential clients. The wife is active in community organizations, where she is highly regarded. She collects antique dolls. The children attend the best private school. The boy is into track, with an excellent record; the girl takes piano lessons from a professional tutor.

I'm ready to test the waters. I'll toy with him a bit first, to find out how he deals with minor annoyance. The psychological insight will be valuable.

***

K___:

Through the Liaison Office, I arranged two events for No. 249. First, his taxes have been audited. Those fine folks put him through the wringer, as promised, giving him grief and generally offering him less respect than he's accustomed to receiving. They found nothing noteworthy, of course, but they behaved at all times as if they expected to do so. It should have been a frustrating experience. Also, Operative 12 posed as a would-be architectural client to whom Willis had been recommended. They met over lunch, and the next day discussed business while golfing. The subject must have been surprised when, between strokes, 12 became verbally abusive and condemned, in the most hostile manner, all the suggestions made to him. The game ended abruptly as 12 stalked away in feigned disgust.

How did Willis react? One of my stringers overheard the family's conversation at their favorite restaurant later in the week. The subject was puzzled, perhaps a little out of sorts, but he laughed off everything. G___ suggests that I reel the man in for a while longer, but I reject his advice (which I'm sure isn't kindly meant; G___ is no friend of mine). You see, Willis is a fellow essentially without problems. All his life he's been indoctrinated in the notion that life is basically fair. Passing aggravations won't get to him. It's time to hit him right between the eyes. I'm in touch with Planning.

P.S. They just came through with the entry permit. For this move no holding facilities will be required. All systems are go.

***

Friend K___:

SUBJECT NO. 249

In the matter of 249, I've struck home, and hard. Planning set it up, while Acquisition did the deed. It happened like this:

At 3:45 P.M. Wednesday last—having ascertained that only the chosen target was at home—a four man unit invaded the Willis house and extracted young Allen. Our men were dressed and made up as seedy types, in case they were seen by outsiders. They went in through a rear window, leaving clear evidence of break-in, and acquired the boy with minimal violence. The whole operation, from entrance to exit, took less than two minutes. They drove away, ditched the car (stolen), changed vehicles, then proceeded to a safe haven. There Allen was trussed tightly and uncomfortably—turkey style—beaten to death and emasculated. The body was then removed from that place, transported to a farm road beyond the northern precincts, dumped in a dry ditch. The unit checked back in within the hour, reporting no complications.

The first news items are coming in. Standard fare. Corpse found, dastardly crime, no leads as of yet.

***

K___:

Willis stayed home from work today. I thought he might. At this point I can tell you that his office is a-buzz with the story. He left quickly late yesterday afternoon, with something on his mind, but no sign of panic.

More news reports, one from TV useful. Reporters questioned Willis in his front driveway. His wife stood behind him, to the right, seeming subdued. Not our man; he was angry and forthright. He denounced "the cowards who perpetrated this despicable act," and swore that he would do whatever it took to "bring them to justice." He emphasized what we've already heard, that the police are doing everything they can, will leave no stone unturned; "those animals won't get away with it". He assured the gathered throng—perhaps this is important to him—that no motive has been established.

Willis is a tough boy. Evil, as he would define it, has intruded upon his life, but he doesn't falter. He actually grows stronger in the face of adversity. At this stage he, and others, are treating the event like a random bolt of lightning. Such suffering must be borne, and overcome in manly fashion. What may we deduce from this? 249 isn't taking it personally, and therefore is incapable of sensing a direct threat to his well-being. Not to worry, however. I accorded this response a probability of 73%. I tell you, I know my man. The plan incorporates this psychological contingency.

3

As to the question of escalation, I intend to give the subject breathing room, allow him to take up some slack in the line, before I hit him again. I'm desirous of observing the patterns of his subsequent activities. G___ complains, saying I ought to strike while the iron is hot. Always overkill with him. I disapprove of his methods; all flash and superficial show, the worst way to achieve deep and lingering results. If you ask me, G___ possesses a sadistic streak. He's far more interested in enjoying himself than in doing a good job. Could you talk to him, get him off my back?

***

K___:

Life at the Willis' has resumed a semblance of normality. He has returned to work, amazingly quickly. If he suffers, he suffers nobly. The wife also seems fairly chipper—considering—although she hasn't rebounded to the same extent. Her social obligations have been curtailed. Indeed, I wonder if her intuition isn't leading her to take measures, for reasons which she may not have consciously formulated. For example: it's been brought to my attention that she no longer allows her remaining child to ride the bus to and from school. Instead, Mom drives sweet Emily everywhere. If asked outright, could Rhonda explain her actions? Probably not, but it's a sign. There is tension in the Willis household; unspoken fears, perhaps, which must be made reality.

Their minister has paid several visits. He must have been a great help to them during this trying time.

I've arranged to mail flyers, to Willis and other randomly selected addresses in the area, which allude to the pressing issues of missing children and child safety. It's the typical "what you can do about it" request for money... From a real, private organization, for what it's worth. Not quite to the point, I admit, but it may generate further unease. After it's been delivered I'll wait about a week, and then get on the ball again.

***

Dear K___:

Concerning Willis, this next phase will present greater practical difficulties, obviously, since there is some greater awareness now, but all can be arranged to our liking. As I see it, snatching the girl isn't the problem. I'm tantalized by the psychological angle. She should be taken at school, where the mother will expect to find her. I've got two clever ideas: take her right in front of Mrs. Willis—the sudden shock—or shortly before pick-up time, which will foster mounting dread on the part

4

of the mother, as she begins to realize that something is amiss. You can guess which way I'm leaning. Which ever way we go, the action will be carried out on Thursday, barring last minute complications.

***

K___:

It's done. The scenario played out to perfection.

I took one step beforehand which we hadn't discussed. I placed an order, through Procurement, for a concealed camera to record the scene, especially the aftermath. My view is that such documentary material can provide information of value to trainees, as well as to old hands. I'll preview the film when it comes back, let you know what I think. One thing bugs me, however. I received the bill for camera and services from Surveillance. Good sir, surely that should be routed to Administration? Thank you for your attention.

Enough said. Our boys acquired the package very close to the designated time of 2:30 P.M. Emily stood on the concrete walkway below the steps leading down of the school, in the company of a few female friends. No adults were immediately present. Our team halted their vehicle directly in front the girls, rapidly seized the target, threw her in the back seat and raced away. Long before they reached their destination, the girl had been asphyxiated. They immediately stripped and dismembered the body, but will hold it on site, preserved, until the next act of the drama. We should make great strides now.

***

K___:

I watched the film, which arrived promptly this morning from Processing. The camera angle was just right, hiding nothing. I won't bore you with the whole thing (you may choose to watch it yourself)— the grab, the flight of the little girls, the brief appearance of a teacher who scanned the scene, then ran back inside—so, I will focus solely on the arrival of Mrs. Willis, scant minutes later. She gets out of her car, her manner casual. She waits, pensive. The teacher, an elderly woman, reappears, slowly approaches, converses. I should have allowed for a sound hook-up, but gestures tell the tale. The wild motions, the wide and fast mouth movements of the terrified mother, speak plainly. She dashes into the school, not to emerge for some time, and when she does, she is being supported by a male of grandfatherly aspect, most likely the principal. Shortly thereafter police vehicles swarm the parking lot.

The news slant is predictable. A second tragedy strikes the family, authorities suspect a personal motive, fate of the child unknown. I

5

predict a 91% chance of a personal public appeal. I'll hold off sending this memo until word comes in.

Morning: Willis made the appeal, televised, once more on his front lawn. He feels comfortable there, doesn't he? The wife wasn't in evidence, although she's definitely at home. His request to the kidnappers to return his child unharmed was rather touching. I appreciated the slight trace of tears. Note the power of uncertainty; all the harshness, the bravado, the moral righteousness, is gone. "I beg you, in the name of our common humanity..." That is good stuff. He speaks to the unknown assailants as a supplicant. The wheels turn fast. We've almost got him where we want him.

G___ advocates dangling hope before the subject. Says a ransom note would stir the pot. He's joking, right? No way. Dead silence until the genuine pay-off. I'll hold firm as long as the story is front page news. Then, as soon as public interest and sympathy begin to slip...

***

Dear K___:

Package returned to sender. Shortly after midnight a large, heavily soiled burlap sack was deposited onto the Willis lawn. You've already heard the initial reports. Horribly mutilated remains, positively identified as those of Emily Willis. Officials shocked by the cold-bloodedness of the unfathomable crime. No doubt now that these "outrages" are the work of "psychotic" person or persons bearing a grudge. They couldn't be more wrong, but of course they would say that.

Operative 9, posing as a reporter (with valid credentials, in case anyone asked), sought an interview with Willis at the offices of Benson and Nielstrom. Turned down, naturally, yet in the process learned what I wanted to know. Subject has accepted indefinite leave from the firm; not expected back anytime soon.

I had an idea to send out another mailing, purporting to be a promo for a family vacation tour outfit, which I thought might intrigue Willis. I'm informed that the current budget crunch, and the necessary cost-cutting measures, won't allow it. Nothing important, just one more turn of the screw, but a shame nonetheless. It isn't right.

***

My Dear K___:

It's all over but the shouting now. Willis is a virtual recluse, having totally withdrawn from business and social contact. The only visitors he allows in the home are police representatives, who can offer him nothing

6

but syrup. I conclude that he's holding on solely in hopes of a break in the case. Nothing else matters to him anymore. Something will break, and fast; not, however, the criminal case.

The wife constitutes the last remaining weak link in his world, the final target of opportunity. I'll wrap up our case by zeroing in on her. At the moment she is hospitalized, under care at a "private clinic." I won't wait for her status to change. As it is she's providing him no support—he is truly alone—but we can do better. I'm setting in motion an action to remove her from the facility.

I got word of G___'s transfer to District 4. Way overdue, if you'll pardon my saying. He assumed that Mrs. Willis would be terminated—I'll almost miss him, for his amusement value alone—but I have no such intention. No, we can't risk our man becoming inured to hardship, as might occur if we hit him again in the exact same fashion. This will require finesse. It's critical that the third stage finish Willis, irretrievably. I'll take no chances. Instead, my plan is to hand her over to the Special Team for sustained sexual abuse. A week will suffice, during which time the subject will be crumbling psychologically, the last cement of his soul disintegrating. Then, the denouement: her return, alive, along with her hair-raising story of what atrocities have been perpetrated upon her. Shattered in mind and body, just enough of her left to tell the tale, hubby should hear enough detail to drive him over the edge. I assure you, he won't be able to cope with her revelations, not if the Team live up to their reputation.

I predict that the conclusion of our program will lead, with 100% certainty, to the complete nervous and mental breakdown of Subject No. 249. The collapse should be rapid and permanent. My secretary is filing the closing paperwork. The final report will go to you as soon as the desired goal is achieved.

I'm absolutely confident that all will develop as stated, so much so that I'm already losing interest in this one. It's always like that; getting them there is the real challenge. Any hints on the next assignment? I'll keep an eye on this one, but I'm keen to get started on No. 250!

The Book of Jacob Bleek

At last I've acquired it—I've held it in my hands—and finally read the infamous, irreproducible, priceless book containing the complete works of the reputed dark sorcerer Jacob Bleek, who delved into every secret of the universe, and about whom such strange stories have been whispered since his mysterious death. What a beautiful volume this is, with its weighty, unadorned leather binding, or perhaps I should say something like leather. I have peculiar suspicions about that. The rough, frayed covers exude a faintly acrid aroma, the mustiness of age maybe, or something more unusual. The yellowed, heavy parchment pages, hundreds of them, are hand sewn with artful crudity into the sturdy binding. Did old Bleek weave them in himself? I see in my mind the image of that terrible wizard, patiently fabricating his magnum opus long ago in the wee hours by the flickering of a curiously scented candle.

In jotting down these rough notes—which I fully intend to form, in time, the basis of professional publication—my goal is to illuminate general aspects of the manuscript. There is much of interest to students and connoisseurs of occult lore. Only I can do this. As far as I've been able to learn, via extensive inquiries, no one until now has read it in its entirety other than the author. The various copies of Bleek already in quiet circulation or locked in guarded archives all appear to be fragments of his complete writings, often altered by "improvers," or carelessly transcribed by speakers of foreign tongues.

Bleek composed his great work in English (not his first language, I presume; grammar, syntax, word choice are often complex or clumsy, and I've strained to convert these into something comprehensible), but for the benefit of any wandering eyes shielded his work behind a primitive code of his own devising. Based largely on simple letter substitution, it should have been unbearably tedious to translate, except for the sheer pleasure of seeing the clear text come into view like a developing photograph. Such was my joy when the heading of the first page so appeared: *Jacob Bleek—His Black Book—Collected Wisdom—And a*

9

SCIENCE AND SORCERY

Catalogue of Truths Revealed to Him. I expected a great deal from a volume
with a portentous title like that. I wasn't disappointed. The preamble
well sets the tone:

> I, Bleek, determined seeker of the true
> Here set down as my life's culmination
> Knowledge gleaned of this awesome creation
> Presented in meticulous review.
> The great and the small have I analyzed
> Evil facts and peculiar mysteries
> Revelations of forgotten histories
> Reality such as none have realized.
> Where far-seeing worthies pointed the way
> I have hesitated not to follow
> Where I gained advantage on my fellow
> I brought forth vast truths to the light of day.
> Beware, all ye who would come after me
> That ye be blinded by what now I see.

Imagine my fascination at discovering that Bleek was, in addition to
everything else, a dedicated poet. The whole mammoth volume is
written in poetic format, something akin to the scholarly treatises, often
covering unbearably mundane topics, once written in verse by the
Classical Romans and Greeks, a practice maintained by their imitators
well into the Renaissance. Nothing in Bleek's educational background,
or what I can discern of his mental make up, prepared me for this. I can
only speculate that his zeal for his subjects, his sense of their bigness,
drove him to create a literary epic of heroic proportions, and he
composed in what he considered a fitting style.

I can't be sure, for so little is really known of the author, and much
that has come down to us is so entangled in myth as to be hopelessly
suspect. Many others have attempted to gain access to his knowledge,
both during his lifetime and later, but if the stories are to be believed—if
even a fraction of them can be accepted—such attempts have been
fraught with peril, usually leading to grotesque results. I can't say much
about that, but can relate how I came to possess this document. For
some time I'd been aware that portions of Bleek's writings had found
their way into other hands, intellectual appetizers as it were, only hinting
at the magnitude of the whole. Bleek had disseminated these enticing
morsels to lesser colleagues, perhaps to taunt them. Craving the original,
which studied deduction assured me must still exist, I sent a hired man to
the historic Bleek House to confiscate the document before somebody

else beat me to it. That man didn't return. I never heard from him again, nor has he ever turned up in any of his regular haunts. Fearing the worst, I took drastic action, renting the forsaken old house from the seedy realtor, making it and its contents temporarily mine. Following a lengthy search throughout the dreadful place, I discovered the manuscript in a locked drawer located in a hidden room, behind a bricked up door, deep in the dank cellar.

So I've come here, ensconced in relative comfort in the highest chamber of the creaky, leaning tower of the Bleek House, with the marvelous dead wizard's *Black Book* before me. Here I shall carry out my research, encouraged by the fitting surroundings.

The first part or chapter of the book, headed "The Saying of Words," consists of a series of spells, many of them commonplace charms, which the author gathered from old sources or, in some cases as he assures us, devised himself. I quote a portion of description by way of illustration:

There is a method which the wise may use
To gain favor over another's mind
To alter his thoughts from callous to kind
And compel him to perform as ye choose.
This power, like all others, is a tool
To be employed with care, judiciously
Whether for the good, or maliciously
Think well before acting, play not the fool.
By such means I have preserved my standing
In this quaint village, where none care for me
Left well enough alone I ask to be
That and trifles, nothing too demanding.
The incantation which follows will serve
The cunning and cautious, as he deserve.

So much for that; the spell may actually work for all I know. I ought to try it sometime. All kinds of magic formulae are covered. There is even one having to do with a love potion! What sort of love potion would such a single-minded, obsessive fellow concoct? I shudder to think. This kind of stuff, however, doesn't justify Bleek's lurid reputation. More to the point is something like this:

In concourse with the infernal powers
'Tis safer, and often necessary
To employ an intermediary
A FAMILIAR, who walks in the dark hours.

11

SCIENCE AND SORCERY

From whence these creatures spring I can not say
Though they arise via incantation
Are they called up, or is it creation?
Whatever the source, use them as one may.
For they're only inferior beings
Living a while on the blood of their host
Then thrown back to the darkness they love most
Dying or sleeping when the dawn bell rings.
If one must keep them around for a spell
Feed them on others, then send them to hell.

The spells include not only the precise words to be employed but also the necessary material ingredients, some of which sound rather sensible, while others are of a most alarming nature. That magnesium tetrachloride, for example, might possess a worthwhile chemical or alchemical benefit I presume not to doubt; but what is one to make of such requirements as the pulped brains of infants, the living flesh of the extinct auroch, or a type of organic dust which, we are casually informed, can not be found on this planet at all, but only on a dead sun in the constellation Orion?

Of interest, I think, are the occasional bits of biographical information scattered throughout this section of the text, much of which may have been composed early in his oddly long life. I gather this youthful Bleek carried something of a chip on his shoulder, which comes through in his writings before he attained his later mastery and self-confidence. I observe such nuggets as these, which I present in no particular order:

For then the spirits of air run amok;
At the university I spoke thus
The dense professors kicked up such a fuss
No such argument could their brains unlock.

***

Smug, pompous Granville craved these final notes
Even dared steal them when my back was turned
He laughed hard, but not long, for he soon learned
Death stalks the craven, wearing many coats.

***

I gave Bjorn much, got nothing in exchange
So I sent him a visitor for free
A sweet deal for Bjorn, privileged to see
What won't kill, just permanently derange.

12

THE BOOK OF JACOB BLEEK
***

I've journeyed to that mysterious land
And beheld that grim face in the mountain
Stood on the spot where the spheres do fountain
Above the stones carved by no mortal hand.

From elements such as these, and other allusions of a more prosaic nature, it may prove possible to put together the framework of a Bleek biography, after a fashion, one of these days. I doubt there would be any money in it, nor would devotees of the occult find much to amuse them.

The perils of residing in an old, long abandoned building: I've been distracted by ominous, furtive noises from below. Is it true what they say, that Bleek still walks? Of course not; I've seen his grave, a time-sunk mound of earth, scarce adorned. I've now been throughout the house, armed with a flashlight, checking doors, making certain no scholarly rival or other larcenous type has slipped in. This place is bigger than it looks. There are the three main floors, apparently never fully used by the original occupant, where he lived out his solitary life. No electricity, of course; I work by oil lantern. Then there is the cellar, an expansive two-level complex, the upper floor paneled like the rest of the house, the lower of solid granite slabs, incredibly thick. I could swear that region is hollowed out bedrock; it almost resembles a cave. There are ugly signs— antique instruments, complicated machinery, suggestive stains—that in the past it's been the scene of nasty business. Finally there's the tower, to which I've returned. No marvel of construction, but thrilling in its own way. This slender needle, hardly more than a spire, rises the equivalent of two additional levels. One ascends a rickety spiral staircase of groaning wood to the high chamber. It's quite a large room—I wonder if it's architecturally sound—plain, containing only a long desk, single uncomfortable chair, and a cabinet. That and the desk are empty. It's probable that any more useful finds, when I set aside time for further search, will also be made in the cellar.

This room has two windows, neither of which affords a view of the surrounding landscape. The major one is a rectangular skylight, with a zig-zag fissure running through it, directly overhead in the blackened ceiling. The second, smaller one, puzzles me. It's more like a portal, round, and faces nearly, but not exactly, due north. It points about two degrees from the true, yet still offers a decent view of the polar sky. It looks like it may focus on a particular dim star beyond Ursa Minor. I wonder what that signified to Bleek.

13

SCIENCE AND SORCERY

Well, back to him. The second chapter of the manuscript bears, in the upper left margin, the phrase "Sources of Power", which I've found to be a kind of alternative physics text. I don't know what a modern scientist would make of this. Bleek largely ignores the standard convention of the four universal forces—electrical, atomic, whatever—in favor of what he with grandiloquence refers to as *extra-cosmic forces*. His argument appears to be that our universe is nested within larger cosmic structures, that the laws emanating from those unfathomable realms exert a more determinative sway over man and the natural order than anyone has previously realized; anyone prior to Bleek, of course.

Commonplace matter is a latticework
Which molecules and atoms can explain
Yet miracles and mysteries remain
When natural law breaks down, run berserk.
Higher law lies not within but without
A power which from beyond intrudes
And slipping throughout each substance extrudes
The unified force I discourse about.
Those who fail to take it into account
Must forever by this world be puzzled
And with their cracked brains so sorely muzzled
Learn nothing useful in any amount.
Attend to what follows and know the all
Of every worldly facet, great and small.

This constant sneering at the "cracked brains" of other thinkers is a tiresome feature of Bleek's writings. Axes to grind—some personal bitterness—a crank's certainty? Most likely the latter, for the author makes every attempt to justify and support his bizarre claims.

The density of the material
Is what determines conductivity,
In proportion to relativity,
Of the flow of forces ethereal.
Light materials are of little use
While crystals and heavy elementals
Are the sorcerer's prime fundamentals
For the channeling of powers abstruse.
Energies, which from the ignorant hide
Generated from above, infiltrate
Entering our world and reckoning fate
Along the smooth planes of crystals they slide.

14

THE BOOK OF JACOB BLEEK
He who would master mortal flesh and bones
Must collect and keep rare metals and stones.

It's difficult to make sense of this section (and I'm quoting the clearer parts, leaving out the incredibly tedious technical stuff), but I think I see what Bleek is driving at. These "Sources of Power"—by which the author can only mean *magical* power, that which is of special benefit to a wizard—reside in outer realms beyond the universe of normal matter, yet at the same time they dominate this universe and can affect every action within it. Coming from outside, they require a medium through which they must function for full efficiency. If I'm rightly understanding Bleek's jumbled terminology, that medium is the planar surfaces existing between material units, or atoms. The forces slide along these angles—think of them as being greased—thus weave themselves about all aspects of the cosmos. The idea fascinates, because it suggests that such supernatural entry is actually a natural property of matter, and can occur randomly; he refers to events unexplainable by science, which simply crop up on occasion. He is more interested, I gather, in the possibility of intelligently utilizing such powers for his own gain.

The more dense the substance, then the stronger the planes, and the more conductive of power they are. He mentions metals, but it is crystals which have traditionally been considered "power stones." Bleek offers a pseudo-scientific basis for this. The perfect angles of gems and semi-precious stones provide a perfect surface along which the outer forces may "infiltrate" the universe.

*****

I wrote that paragraph late last night. It is now the following afternoon. I had a most unusual experience, surely the product of over-tiredness, but nevertheless unnerving. Having digested the key passages, I entertained myself with a cache of crystals which I'd noticed earlier in a lower room. Fine specimens they were, of every color, carefully chosen. I realized that Bleek must have used them in his alchemical delving, and wondered if I might try them myself. Not expecting anything, I recited as best I could a spell which had caught my attention in the first chapter. "An Incantation of Raising" he called it, especially eye-catching because the author had drawn a thick red circle around the whole page. Difficult it was to speak the words properly—these were decidedly not English— but I did the best I could. Well, obviously nothing really happened, yet the recital gave me an uneasy feeling, as if the room had suddenly warmed, and I heard... nothing, just nothing. There are so many sounds in this old house. A squeaking board toyed with by the wind might have sounded like a distant laugh.

Bleek concludes his discussion of weird physics with a jarring description of the prime mover, or First Cause, of these all-encompassing forces which surround life and being. His general statement begins with the following, on page 346 of the manuscript, which includes his first reference to an exceedingly ominous term:

Man's finest brains devised his universe

Deeming it orderly or chaotic

But ever the truth drives him psychotic

There's belief, and that which is so much worse.

Scholars choose to play with reality

While knowing nothing of the Utter Mind

The world's a toy for amusement designed

The plaything of controlling Entity.

A King reigns, who is His own dimension

Dreaming the fabric of nature in sleep

From restless stirrings does existence seep

As well as its ultimate suspension.

Harken to the Great One who came before;

We're the imaginings of Xenophor.

I suppose Xenophor is a metaphor—see, I'm learning from Bleek—standing for the pan-universal natural laws postulated in the text. There is something humorous in the departed mage's old-fashioned, conventionalized approach to the question. In the end, like so many famous philosophers before him, Bleek conceives the universe as the creation of a god, an anthropomorphized cosmic mind operating with goals and desires. He blandly accepts the easy out by insisting that mind comes before matter, that the world is a thought—the dreams—within a great brain. There's nothing remarkable in this conclusion. That being said, Bleek's choice of metaphor is rather alarming. No major, overt religion has ever been willing to embrace a concept quite like Xenophor.

There is boundless, eternal Mind without

Sanity or reason any vestige

Though dormant now It still sends Its message

To the world which once trembled at Its shout.

Void of thought, yet It creates in Its dreams

The structure of time, substance, and space

16

THE BOOK OF JACOB BLEEK

Each mental vibration sets in its place
Each atom with which the universe teems.
Xenophor, the final cause without cause
Sees all around Him with His sightless eye
Overturns the earth and brings down the sky
Mutters to Himself and changes the laws.
He neither thinks, explains, or understands
But He rules from here to the farthest lands.

Xenophor; I know that word. Deriving from primitive myth, it traditionally signifies the supreme evil which underlies the world, a mindless, hungry, unconquerable evil. As embodied in legend, Xenophor is the insane deity who created the universe and populated it, solely in order to have victims to torment and destroy; creation for the sole purpose of sadistic annihilation. I once made the mistake of reading Johnson's monograph on the subject; disquieting material it is. The object of worship by degenerate pagan peoples (thankfully extinct), it is argued that underground cults still carry on the devotion to him. It's pretty clear to me that Bleek made contact with such charming characters, and took them very seriously. To be blunt, he must have become a worshiper himself, for he presents the information from the standpoint of a true believer rather than as a dispassionate reporter. How else to explain the last piece in this section, separated from the rest on its own page, composed in a different style, and headed "The Song of Xenophor:"

Xenophor the Mighty formed the world from slime
Xenophor the Glorious rules all space and time
He is the world and the world is Him
At the mercy of His every whim.
He knows nothing, but knows all
He sees nothing, but sees all
He hears nothing, but hears all
He feels nothing, but clutches all.
Xenophor created, and when done He grinned
He laughed at the way His miserable creatures sinned
He teaches nothing, but still from Him they learn
Life's a game He plays, and in the end they'll burn.
He knows nothing, but knows all
He sees nothing, but sees all
He hears nothing, but hears all
He feels nothing, but clutches all.

17

SCIENCE AND SORCERY

Live not as you're told, but for Xenophor's joy
Amuse your master, thou art only His toy
Whatever your evil, you'll die like the rest
So do as thou wilt, friend, all life's but a jest.
He knows nothing, but knows all
He sees nothing, but sees all
He hears nothing, but hears all
He feels nothing, but clutches all.

What a kick it would be to set that to music! I mustn't be too hard on old Bleek, though; a lifetime (especially one as long as his was reputed to be) spent immersed in such warped lore would be enough to addle the soundest brain. I'll have to remember that, if I don't want to end up like him.

I am working too hard, keeping such late hours doing nothing but reading and writing. Now I'm seeing things. While diverting myself with that silly song—even muttering it aloud, to a foolish jingle of my own devising—I found myself suddenly dazzled by an intense flash of light, which for a moment completely obliterated the image of the room around me. I recall only the brightness, not the color, which I couldn't make out at all. Blinking, with my eyes watering freely, I traced the source—the apparent source—to that odd astronomical portal in the ceiling. Perhaps somebody is signaling to me. It's past time for bed.

*****

Whether or not the dreams of the Great One create reality, there can be no question that my current reality gives rise to dreams. Having nodded off shortly before dawn, in what passes for a bedroom on the third floor, I imagined the entry of a visitor. I seemed to wake, lying motionless on the sagging bed frame upon which I'd thrown a sleeping bag, staring into pitch darkness. Then, without apparent cause, a lambent bluish glow seemed to pervade the chamber. Suddenly a dimly seen figure loomed over me. I could barely make out his features—the piercing eyes, hawk nose, tight-lipped mouth; iron-gray at the temples, clipped goatee—and the old-fashioned attire which called to mind a sooty, anonymous oil painting I'd noticed in the hall downstairs. I knew, with the absolute certainty of dream logic, that I beheld none other than Jacob Bleek. He stood tall, glaring down at me, and spoke, English with a harsh accent, just these words: "And what will you do with my knowledge? Are you the one, to dare carry on my work?" Then it was late morning, with the sun filtering through the ratty curtains, and I was

18

truly awake if groggy, as if I'd never slept. I felt the need to get out of this place, so popped down to the village to stock up on supplies of food and oil. I entertained the notion of leaving for good—the influences here aren't wholesome—but by the light of day such concerns seem ridiculous. There is too much work to do, I can learn a great deal here... and, after all, I have paid for the accommodations.

I once again examined the painting, this time with care. It is very like the man in my vision. In the dream there wasn't so much cruelty about the mouth. It was more like contempt.

The third, the longest, and by far the most fascinating section of Bleek's work is that portion simply entitled "Mysteries." It reads, on first perusal, like a grab-bag of every weird claim and legend ever recorded by mankind, from the earliest times to the author's present. Bleek assures us that he's personally investigated every tale which finds its way into his scrapbook of the strange, though I can't fathom how he'd manage that in ten lifetimes. Furthermore, several of these items were obviously collected from the works of known authors. On the other hand, our friendly neighborhood sorcerer has a knack for infusing into each such account his own unique twist, as if he really does possess special knowledge of these matters beyond that of the original writers. I also note that he writes with easy familiarity of the locales involved, as if he's visited every one. If there be any truth to this, it means that Bleek must have been a great traveler in his day, belying his reputation as a manic recluse; a reputation otherwise borne out by several statements in the text. At this point in time, who can say? Perhaps his wanderings were restricted to the years of his long lost youth.

Below I've culled two derivative fragments, to show how Bleek handles classic sources:

Through the balmy Ethiopian nights
Creep the misshapen men called troglodytes
Who crawl from caves to feed the ancient way
As acolytes of Blug, Lord of Decay.

***

The Minamora dance by moonlight still
In honor of the spirits of dead kings
But what join them instead are loathsome things
That feast until sated on human swill.

Bleek borrowed the former from Herodotus, of course, but has inserted the insidious reference to "Blug", a deity I've never heard of outside this work. I'm not aware of any other traditional source which bears on the matter. The latter tidbit, it appears, is lifted straight from *The Golden Bough* (I should say from Frazer's repugnant Egyptian source), but it's left to Bleek to assure us that the ancestor worship of the Minamora brings real results, however baleful.

Here's one more, in which the reader is expected to believe that the wizard has seen with his own eyes what he has to tell us:

> Caesar writes of the city beyond Khem
> To which he was led by a priestly guide
> There he spoke with those who must always hide
> For the fair sunlight is poison to them.
> I once endeavored to visit the spot
> Far west of the Nile, in the stone desert
> And this is the truth which I now assert
> Caesar didn't tell all, but he lied not.
> Bare ruins remain, yet there is the vault
> In which dwells still the blind, all-knowing seer
> My companion looked once and blanched with fear
> He perished miserably, as well he ought.
> I'm pleased to say I got what I went for
> I gained wisdom from my squamous mentor.

The famous description in *The Commentaries* forms the basis of this passage. Archeologists have long considered the story told by the literary general to be a fake, as no trace of such a desert city has ever been unearthed. Bleek would have us think differently. I'm constantly torn by my reactions to this stuff. I'm convinced there is something to it all, always have been, and I truly believe that this man can impart knowledge of the secret world I suspect to exist. There is a path to genuine enlightenment, which I choose to follow. If only Bleek didn't go so far! The wildness of his vision repels me. When I eventually get around to publishing my study, I don't want to be written off as a kook just because I'm willing to make use of documentary material like this. It's easy to acquire a mountebank's reputation in this business. What a trump if I pull it off, and still retain scholarly respect.

To the best of my knowledge, most of these pieces are Jacob Bleek originals. If he didn't make them up—or dream them (right about now that seems a likely answer)—then his research on the dark side must have been monumental. Sometimes it isn't so much the story he has to relate that gives me a shiver, but rather his creepy claims as to how he acquired the information, as in his take on Caesar. Here's another snippet:

20

THE BOOK OF JACOB BLEEK

Though too long dead, and crawling with vermin
My informant feebly struggled to tell
Of the doom which upon the Mayans fell
Rotten-tongued truth I couldn't determine.

The narrator goes on at repellent length about how he finally does determine the secret, no thanks to his pitiful informant, for whose suffering Bleek seems to feel little sympathy; sweet fellow. The impression I derive of the poet's character, from reading all this, is that of a man driven, perhaps to the point of madness—certainly beyond any normal or wholesome human emotion—by his quest for knowledge in the pursuit of his goal, a goal which means everything to him... and yet it isn't altogether clear to me what that is! I detect no great desire for personal gain after all, or glory, or fame; often quite the reverse. Bleek was more than a connoisseur of the weird. He was up to something, on the track of big ideas, and it ought to be possible to puzzle them out. His second chapter suggests that there's structure to his research, for it goes far toward justifying the spell chapter. Is this third and greatest section a mere addendum, however thrilling, as it does appear at first? I think not. I shall dig deeper.

At this stage I see apparent formlessness. Horrid items of an unbelievable nature are thrown up in profusion. Dreadful things which walk or crawl, fly or burrow, share this world with us, and perhaps it is more theirs than ours. The author conceives menaces and marvels from unknown spans of distant space, and from speculative regions farther away. Throughout all times and places these things have existed and continue to do so, normally lurking just beyond the ken of the unimaginative. Occasionally poor souls stumble across such horrors, but seldom in a worthwhile fashion. Only the educated, deep-thinking seeker has a chance to make sense of such discoveries.

What troubles me most is the vileness of it all. These conceptions are profoundly different in nature from those which animate most occult scholars, not to mention the layman. Most men, I suppose, are drawn to such studies by a desire to reinforce cherished beliefs—the existence of God, the truth of the afterlife, the reality of a higher, happier world beyond our own—and selectively go after material which supports their preconceived notions. Philosophers, theologians, and speculatists present sugar-coated mysteries. I've tried hard not to fall into that trap myself, but it isn't an issue in this case. Bleek, flaunting what he pretends is a scientist's sober objectivity, brings forth debased, perverted versions

SCIENCE AND SORCERY

of such ideas.

In the mountains of Santa Clara walk
Dead ones, dear departed who shun the grave
Believers in life who too little gave
Offerings to hear the island priests talk.
Now they do naught but stagger and stumble
At the beck and call of priestly demand
Driven to obey by brutish command
To which they assent with nod and mumble.
The natives aver their souls live within
Those carcasses which do move while they rot
They inspire terror, but sympathy not
Useful they are, so how can it be sin?
As long as flesh and bone together hold
They labor tirelessly through heat and cold

***

A wise man of Prague has seen past the veil
Which divides the mundane world from the next
Nor blessed is he, rather by knowledge hexed
For he reports a scarce uplifting tale.
The dead do live, as he surely relates
But there's no lasting reward for the good
For their hapless souls are served up as food
To predators which determine their fates.
Evil or virtuous, it's all the same
To these scavengers who burrow like moles
Through the hereafter seeking juicy souls
Snapped up without regard for earthly fame.
Achemides assures me man is prey
To the creatures lurking beyond the day.

Dreadful stuff, and there is much more, for it is in this section that Bleek really lets himself go and conjures up the extremes of cosmic horror. Note how the following segments bear no relation, at least directly, to man and his conceptions. It's almost as if the writer has tired of us, desires to move on to more worthy subjects. In the case of these materials, the author is surprisingly reticent about his sources of information. That may be a blessing.

Deenos, geographically imprecise
A lost world of another time and place
Dead, in the universe of ultra-space

THE BOOK OF JACOB BLEEK

The scene of the ultimate sacrifice.
Its inhabitants, proud and wise
Garnered wisdom to the final degree
The purest essence of truth did they see
Which sight caused their immediate demise.
On the day they made their knowledge complete
Their cosmos unraveled, torn asunder
All existence foundered and went under
Life and mind erased in utter defeat.
Deenos, planet of flickering black light
Feebly beckoning through the brilliant night.

I ask myself whether a tale such as this one provides a key to comprehending Bleek's strident morbidity and hatefulness. Here is a man who devotes his life to the pursuit of ultimate knowledge, yet he tells this story. What is he trying to say? And they get only worse, so much worse.

*****

My situation has deteriorated alarmingly. It's no longer clear to me that I'm going to survive my sojourn here. Such a pity; I'm sure I only needed time. Somebody must disagree. Not long ago—assuming I've kept track of time properly—I detected unmistakable sounds of intrusion from far below. I naturally hesitated, then eventually climbed down to investigate. It took some time, for the muffled noises had ceased, but in the end I found what I sought in the cellar. There, on a large plank table, were laid out a series of tools of torture, all now cleaned and polished. Of course I quickly vacated that room, all thought of fame and scholarly endeavor forsaken, and headed straight for the exit and the sane world beyond. I never arrived there. As if in a fell dream—after a sensation of interval, I know not how long—I awakened to find myself scaling the last steps up to the tower chamber. I realize it is no dream, nor has it ever been. I'm trapped, like so many others who must have come before me. Once again seated at the desk, I haven't stirred from this spot for an indeterminate period. It seems that much time has passed, yet the windows still reveal only darkness. Not even stars are visible.

I try to absorb the message of Jacob Bleek, clawing at random through these yellowed pages for the answer. I feel that I have failed the test, but I still don't know what was expected of me; I never figured out the rules of the game. I know now that somebody else was writing them, and I'm pretty sure who that is.

23

Movement again, louder, from various locations beneath me. A gathering is in progress. Apparently I'm supposed to join them, but I'll sit it out while I can. The festivities will begin soon enough.

Is it the pointlessness of striving that matters, in a universe of ugly chaos? Must there be a penalty to pay for seeing, through the darkly crystalline mind of Bleek, into the infinities of cosmic reality? Perhaps it would have made a difference if I'd seen it his way... but why would I want to do so? Why did he choose to do so?

This meaningless compound of dust and clay
Rears on hind legs to gaze upon a star
Seeing nothing, believing he sees far
Into the night which never becomes day.

Jacob Bleek, the morose, cynical genius, penned those words. I wearily close his *Black Book*. The commotion recommences. Heartless laughter, movement below—approaching—the sound of many heavy feet. The flaring radiance of my lantern dwindles out, yet there is light, weak but steady, dripping down from the round window. Nothing remains for me to do. I wait patiently. From without the door that harsh voice calls my name. Impelled, I must beckon him, and his dreadful companions, to enter.

Who knows? The next man who dares open the book of Jacob Bleek may discover a sonnet dedicated to me.

Realization: A Tale of the True Theory

Wise men assure us that true reality is the objective background upon which all rational thought and endeavor is based. We are informed that the scholar dedicates his life to uncovering the facts of which this universe is composed, while the philosopher ascertains the laws of logic which illuminate these facts. This they assert, and can provide, when called upon, compelling arguments to support their case. They point to our knowledge of history, derived from a vast mass of documentation, and to the discoveries of science, the fruit of patient observation and careful analysis. This is what the world is, they insist; this is how it is; this is why it is. To the extent that our facts suffice, there can be no other way. They grant, in their benevolent wisdom, that mistakes may creep into their formulations, as a result of inadequate understanding of reality where evidence is weak or lacking, but the revelation of error spurs them on to ever more sober, clear-minded investigation, so that the intellectual fault may be examined and discarded without regret, and the truth made known at last.

In the mind of the rationalist, there can be no toleration for alternative world views founded upon non-rational mental strategies. Thus belief systems, embedded within frameworks of intuition, populism, and moral certainty, must be disputed; in fact, the totality of the corpus of conventional, vulgar understanding ought to be rejected. Belief sidesteps reality. Instead of being rational, objective, and evidentially connected, it is irrational, wishful, and logically disconnected. The worst form of belief is that which not only negates its own facet of actuality, but reaches out imperialistically to degrade other facets of knowledge; non-truth which spreads like a cancer, absorbing, dominating, and destroying every sane, healthy, and wholesome thought in its path.

Continuing in this line of argument, it necessarily follows that the most pernicious of all forms of illogical belief is that which the learned style CONSPIRACY THEORY. This is the sole intellectual system, of which it can be said, that it violates every rule of objective reason. Nay, one must go farther: such a theory, by definition, is designed to subvert the rules of reason. That is the purpose of its existence. One adheres to the belief in conspiracy because the facts in the case do not lead to a desired, cherished, subjectively chosen result. Objectivity, so the savants say, is the arch enemy of all such schemes.

Conspiracy theory may be understood as a systematic, comprehensive formulation postulated to explain or to justify the lack of evidence for a conclusion which is known, *a priori*, to be correct. Given the conclusion, the failure to evidentially support it is rendered sensible only on the subsequent assumption that an intelligent design is in motion to suppress the facts. Once this certain conspiracy is deduced, its apparent substance may be fleshed out to the extent required to establish the original conclusion, which need not, at any point in the argument, be itself supported.

The broken or absent chain of evidence is the key, not the mere claim of conspiracy itself. After all, conspiracies do exist. The annals of history are replete with verified instances in which secretive combinations of men come together in order to further their furtive plans. So common is this practice that, to a fair degree, one may suggest that it is the standard lot of mankind. Two criminals spy jewelry in a shop window, and converse in low tones as to the best means of making away with the loot; that is conspiracy. Minor executives in a corporate office meet after business hours in order to discuss ways of embarrassing a rival; a conspiracy has been established. Then, of course, on the national or international level, the realm of kings, presidents and generals, political or military conspiracy may be considered a necessary fact of life. Action undertaken in the open, for good or ill, may stand no chance of success (perhaps because others, in the know, will cunningly unite against it), while the addition of the element of secrecy may lead to triumph. A nation which launches a war with a well-prepared surprise attack stands to gain a permanent advantage over its victim. All genuine conspiracies, however, no matter how well concealed, may be proven, at least in principle, via the ordinary mechanisms of logic and detection. The thieves may be apprehended with the jewels, and their trail followed back to the smashed pane; the company officer who finds himself squeezed out during a crucial board meeting knows all too well that his colleagues have betrayed him; the movers and shakers of the world are prone to subsequent boasting of their exploits, if others do not condemn them for same.

REALIZATION

In the foregoing instances, as in all cases of true, verifiable conspiracy, it is determined that an event has occurred, making use of reason and the rational analysis of evidence and historical documentation; and only then, after the truth of the event has been clarified, can one honestly posit a conspiracy by way of explanation. If the explanation prove valid, it eventually passes from supposition into recognized history. Fact always precedes argumentation, and the latter must remain dependent upon the former. One need not be the great detective of Baker Street to reason in this manner. Large minds or small, if they be sane and healthy, perceive the world that way.

The brain of the conspiracy theorist functions within a crude, primitive, quasi-mystical realm of flickering light and shifting shadow, an unreal tableau in which associations can be made or unmade at whim, and the most gigantic conclusions erected upon the slightest of perceived or suspected clues. It is the intent of the theorist to justify his fantasy, to convince others of its reality. The hard-core type, of whom we speak, can not tolerate living in isolation; he must propagate his beliefs to the masses at all costs. The theory, however originally devised, becomes central to his sense of self. To deny its validity is to deny himself, his own worthiness. All such formulations must needs partake of extreme paranoia (in our enlightened age, mental diagnosis is often deemed as helpful to understanding as analysis) directed against argumentative opponents. The more logical and consistent the debunking, the more ferocious is the counter-response. Any attempt by others to introduce structured debate induces sustained hostility. If the nay-sayers be not fools, then it seems, with mounting certainty, that they are in league with the enemy, those lurking behind the murky shades, the sinister syndicate which the theorist has devoted his life to exposing.

Every logical flaw is cheerfully accepted if it serve to sway the minds of others. Straw men are stuffed to bursting, the vertebrae of reason are snapped and scattered with abandon. The iceberg of scientific method, with its carefully ordered conclusion atop a vast base of data, is overturned to reveal its dark side, in which a mountain of facts are heaped precariously upon a crumbling claim. While there is seldom uniformity at the level of detail, it can be stated that all conspiracy theories must incorporate the three classic analytical errors of failure to proportion cause to effect, a tendency toward selection of evidence, and an inability to accept the principle of falsifiability.

1. The conspiracy theorist invariably starts with a known effect, and develops his claim in an attempt to surmise the cause, a procedure not

27

unknown in more rational circles. The theorist whose personal bugaboo is the military catastrophe at Pearl Harbor, for instance, begins with the assumption that a great deal concerning that event requires explanation. So far, so good; he and the true historian stand, to that extent, on equal footing. Furthermore, both may agree that an unusual disaster of that sort implies the need for an unusual explanation. It is even possible to imagine the conspiracist, in his obsessive quest for documentation, uncovering usable material which may aid the researches of worthy scholars. Alas, such is seldom the case. The theorist can not grasp the beautiful intricacies of the Humean dilemma. He rarely proves capable of contributing quality knowledge, for in his shameless theorizing he knows not when to stop.

Who (to continue with the above circumstance) was responsible for Pearl Harbor? The historian calmly identifies the culprit as the Japanese. He lays out for his readers the elements of a real-world conspiracy: the grand geopolitical designs, the decision to initiate force, the secret preparations for military action, the spying, the bland diplomacy employed to lull the victims into lassitude, the undertaking of incredible precautions and the acceptance of great risk as the fateful moment nears. This series of actions legitimately makes up the bulk of the cause necessary to produce the historical effect, the annihilation of the American fleet. Given all this, what remains to be understood is the failure of the chosen targets to discern what is coming; an interesting story in its own right, an illuminating study of harrowing mistakes and smug hubris but, given the known facts, hardly remarkable.

Unfortunately, it is this latter issue which excites the irrational theorist and leads him to find, within the recesses of his own mind, an imaginative conspiracy piled atop the real one. Without intellectual justification, he concludes that the genuine scheme is insufficient to account for the facts as they are known. Knowledge from the heart, rather than from the head, tells him that the cause is insignificant compared to the magnitude of the effect, and therefore he must seek sinister designs among the very victims of the outrage. They, or some of them, must have been parties in subtle collusion to the overt attack on the naval base. American leaders, the "real" conspirators, withheld vital evidence or suppressed information—with definite evil intent—which might have forestalled the tragedy. To the dedicated theorist, there are no honest errors.

The conspiracy-minded misunderstand, or have never heard, of Occam's Razor. In their zeal to promote their arguments, they multiply entities beyond all necessity. Each pointing of the finger of suspicion requires the acknowledgment of still further skullduggery; every unsupported claim must be extended by more, and still more, *ad infinitum*. There is no end, no proportion, no logic.

2. The trained researcher, confronted by an ostensibly factual claim, immediately sets out to amass all of the pertinent evidence—any datum which may bear upon the matter—in order to properly assess the claim. Given sufficient information, what scholars call the "weight of evidence" will eventually tip the scales for or against the argument. It is critical that all known factors be taken into account prior to the moment of judgment. Only this will lead to a mature, reasoned result.

The conspiracy theorist sees it differently. He is not a researcher, but rather, an advocate. His goal is, in practice, not the advancement of wisdom but propaganda. Like a writer of fiction—very much so—he sets out to tell a story, and all of his skills are bent toward furthering the plot. His employment of the evidence constitutes no exception to this rule. He evaluates the evidence most carefully indeed, but unlike the scholar is concerned solely with its utility. If a datum supports the thesis, or appears to do so, it is considered worthy of merit; if it does not, it is treated as invalid, or even as nonexistent.

This selection of evidence, as it is termed, can lend superficial strength to any theory, no matter how absurd. It creates the illusion that all known facts lead inescapably to the desired conclusion, when it may be wiser to adjudge that very few do, and those only when taken out of context. Seemingly good evidence, shorn of intellectual balance, becomes worthless, and the most ridiculous of claims may appear extremely convincing to the ignorant, when absolutely no contradiction is allowed.

3. For years scientists and historians have attempted, with growing impatience, to explain to the increasingly irrational layman that no theory about the real world can be taken seriously unless it can, in principle, be shown to be false. It is not only the various pseudo-s (-scientists, -historians, -theorists, etc.) who have trouble with this concept. At first blush, the notion of a *non-falsifiable* hypothesis is immensely comforting. Imagine a theory which has not been contradicted by any available fact, and which has been so constructed that it can not be contradicted by any possible fact. Surely, one may ask, must not such a theory, by its very nature, be correct? The answer, unfortunately, is a resounding "no". The theory carries no argumentative or intellectual weight because it can not be tested, because it can not be shown to be false, even if it should

be so.

Consider the simple hypothesis, "There are trees in Antarctica." This is a perfectly valid scientific claim. It certainly could be true—trees grow in all kinds of unlikely places—and it might be false—there are known geographical regions without trees. What is important is that the claim is objectively testable; a quick trip to Antarctica, failing all else, would settle the matter.

The conspiracy theorist, as previously noted, cares naught for William of Occam's simplicity, and would not be keen to leave the Antarctic claim at that utilitarian level. If this world be so ordered as to logically prohibit trees in Antarctica, the inability to find evidence for them would not be taken as proof of absence, but as proof of a black-warmhearted attempt to conceal the truth. Government agencies might be hiding the trees—perhaps shuttling them about the ice flows in specially constructed military vans—or the trees could be invisible, a fact which powerful financial conglomerates would, without doubt, wish to hide. Needless to say, if such arguments were allowed, the matter could never be settled to the satisfaction of all. There is no end to the imaginative fecundity of the conspiracy theorist.

This craving to render theories untestable lies at the heart of all conspiracism. It is mother's milk to the flying saucer kook, who, almost from the beginning, perceived enemies lurking in the shadows, stealing away his precious evidence; and to the neo-Nazi revisionist, convinced that the whole world has combined to smear the memory of his great hero; and to all the others who quest after marvels, yet who smart from the jeering laughter of a universe which refuses to yield up that which they seek. The desire for moral certitude, at whatever intellectual cost, is an addictive drug which may crack the soundest brain. In the end, the believer is enslaved by the phantasms of his own mind, and he can not rebel against their tyranny. The truth is out there, he cries, even if it never be found, and no one will ever prove him wrong.

So the wise tell us, and there was a time when I agreed with them. The foregoing conventional presentation, it is hoped, lays the basis, establishes the background, which will lead to an understanding of how I came to be in my present predicament, and of the tragic fate which befell my good friend and colleague, Martin Holbein.

I had devoted my life to science. Youthful enthusiasm had given way to an adult pursuit of knowledge which transcended hobby and became vocation. As a trained anthropologist I soon settled into the joys of academia and the endless rounds of research and paper presentation.

REALIZATION

I was the living embodiment of man's eternal quest to know and understand the nature of reality. And almost from the moment of my arrival at the university, I found a kindred soul in the person of Martin Holbein, the chairman of the department. A noted psychologist, Holbein had interested himself in all facets of the human experience, a useful attribute for a man who oversaw all the social sciences at a small but highly esteemed college. Immediately impressing me with his intellectual acumen, I felt that this was a man I would appreciate working with, for we seemed to share much in common, and before long he took pains to make clear that he felt likewise.

During my long years of advanced education I had developed a fascination for the mental vagaries of the human race, especially as they manifested themselves in the strange, yet oddly entertaining, constructs of pseudoscience and pseudo-history. Many of these popular issues touched upon aspects of my chosen field, which provided sufficient justification for my devoting considerable time and effort to these fringe themes. I wrote and lectured at length about such unusual matters as ancient astronauts, lost continents, and creationism, always taking a hard-line, rationalistic approach to the subjects. I would present the claims in all their wildness, maintaining a severely objective, even-handed style, then submit the genuine data derived from scientific findings in the relevant fields. Having done this, in each case I proceeded to demolish the bizarre hypothesis, concluding with congenial, yet often facetious, debunking of the imaginative genre. I composed and published several such essays, which were eventually collected into a book—*Challenges to Anthropology*—which received excellent reviews, and even sold fairly well.

Dr. Holbein assured me that he fully approved of my tangential labors (my formal area of expertise centered on the Indian prehistory of the Southwest), and let it be known that he had long entertained work along similar lines. As a psychologist, he had pondered with dismay the nature of popular manias, and for some years had been quietly collecting evidence for a comprehensive work of his own. His tastes complemented mine—while I pursued matters of deep history, he was drawn to timeless themes, or questions of recent note—and despite different initial interests, he insisted that my talents could be useful to him. I accepted his earnest flattery, and soon we had embarked together upon a mammoth research project.

The result, a heavy volume entitled *Popular Myths and Fallacies*, quickly became the most highly esteemed work of its kind in scholarly circles, and developed some substantial influence among the wider public, too. Our amassing of the facts was first-rate, our logic pristine, our arguments unbeatable. Our chosen targets received no mercy. We shattered the dreams of the flying saucer chasers, skewered the fantasies of the ESP nuts, scoffed at the ramblings of New Age gurus, gave no quarter to the hackneyed history propounded by the conspiracy theorists. Analysis of the latter constituted well over half the book, and I could tell that Dr. Holbein went after their lunacies with great zest.

My friend—for so I considered him—possessed the remarkable ability of tackling any or all of these disparate subjects, in many cases the only connecting link among them being the curious psychological states which made such ideas attractive. Most of the topics we exposed lay far beyond his realm of expertise, but he had a knack for digging out their logical roots and revealing their weaknesses which suggested that he might have excelled in any academic line. As far as I could tell, he was never unsure, never doubted himself; his mastery of the human mind made him the master of all things.

I was not like that. Away from my own turf, the familiar preserve of anthropology, I often found myself shaky on the ground, and forced to rely on him for much of the higher level analysis. Some of the wilder themes with which we worked—fabulous monsters in lakes, bizarre supernatural oddities and the like—gave me much trouble, but I contributed significantly, tending to follow his lead. It was the conspiratorial claims, often more prosaic in nature, that utterly mystified me. I had no feel for that kind of mental spookiness at all, and without, I trusted, being too obvious about it, I allowed him to handle the bulk of that material. In the end, while pleased by the enhanced reputation this work had brought to me, I considered it a mixed blessing, one which left me in some disorder of my spirits, for I had a secret, one which I had hidden from Dr. Holbein and anyone else whose opinion counted with me.

I suffered from the dreadful affliction of gullibility. My mental make-up incorporated a species of naiveté which, to others, might have seemed charming at times, but which led me time and again into error. In my dealings with the world I had always felt unsure of myself, always inclined to accept others at face value.. It had been so throughout my life. My grade school years I looked back upon as an eternity of horror; I fell for every schoolboy prank, could be made the butt of every practical joke. There were my teenage dealings with girls; suffice to say, I never understood what they were really driving at, until I had made a complete fool of myself. In my initial semesters at college I blandly absorbed everything taught to me, at least until I noticed how often they disagreed with one another; I finally figured that out, for even I wasn't that stupid. During these unpleasant epochs of my life I was what would be styled a "true believer," although I would have died rather than admit it. I bought into every crazy claim ever promulgated on television or in paperback books. I knew no way to evaluate such arguments, nor did it ever occur to me to try.

Looking back on it all, I've wondered if I didn't choose a career in science as a desperate, last-ditch attempt to break the shackles of gullibility, to join the ranks of an intellectual fraternity which would give me the answers I craved, and a belief system to live by, of which I could speak in public without embarrassment, to which I could cling without spiritual agony. If so, it worked for a time. By immersing myself in one, narrowly defined scientific discipline, I found solid ground and a semblance of certainty. I convinced myself that I had put behind my youthful weakness. With better luck the rest of my life might have thus continued.

Terrible to relate that it was the good Dr. Holbein who destroyed my brittle defenses. One would assume, surely, that he didn't realize what he was doing to me. He presented himself as the stereotypically hard-nosed, no nonsense man of science, and I had no reason to doubt him then. He questioned without fear, analyzed with calm assurance, dived into any subject without hesitation. Apparently he read his own character into me, and throughout our labors considered us of one mind. I envied him, but a creeping bitterness toward my friend began to gnaw at me. Without, presumably, any ill intent, he exposed me once again to so many of the strange and perplexing ideas which I had hoped never to face again, and which I had studiously avoided for years. To him they were objects of research; to me, they were torments.

After the success of our joint book venture I fervently wished to lay such matters to rest and return to my scientific refuge. Dr. Holbein, however, had other thoughts on the matter, which were ostensibly sound. If we had together triumphed once, why couldn't we do it again? As he pointed out to me, on increasingly frequent occasions, we had hardly scratched the surface of the available material. There was much more work to be done along these unusual lines—exposing the crackpots festering within our society—and it was our good fortune that we—this dynamic duo of the mind—should be universally regarded as the best men for the job. I disagreed, violently, but I dared not reveal myself to him. Instead I chose delaying or attritional tactics, pleading an excess of private research, and a desire not to be professionally typed as an expert on the weird. I raised the necessity of concentrating on my students, who I falsely claimed had been sorely neglected during the period of our project. He responded with his own style of attrition. After his fashion—always sincere, always considerate, always the gentleman—he wore me down at conference meetings and faculty parties. He corralled my other colleagues to urge me on. He reminded me, ever so subtly— this could have been my imagination, but I believe now otherwise—that he was my superior, responsible for approving grants, the life's blood of modern scholarship. At length, I gave in.

What he proposed was an entire volume devoted to the specter of conspiracy theory. At first I couldn't believe it; it was as if he were striking for my jugular, seeking out the critical flaw in my psyche. Of course his particular interests were already known to me, so there was no excuse for surprise, but this development did not lighten my mood or endear me further to the scheme. Another big book, with chapter after chapter devoted to one clever, preposterous, seductive theory after another, each one especially designed to prey upon my gullible nature. How could I stand it? How would I survive through the long months— months at least—necessary to sift the evidence and prepare the manuscript? It could not be borne... and yet I must bear. I would go through with it. At this stage, to do otherwise would risk my standing and my place. Therefore, I would go through the motions—agree to everything—make no trouble—keep myself in check—and then, when it was all over—this I swore—never put myself through such an ordeal again.

Having steeled myself with these firm resolutions, I embarked upon what proved to be my final scholarly odyssey with Dr. Holbein. The source materials piled up on my desk in rapid profusion. At home, the coffee table in my den groaned under its burden of glossy magazines, crudely duplicated pamphlets, and skinny paperbacks. The heftier hardcovers I took to bed with me. I lived and breathed in the world of enticing cranks. Therein I was exposed to ever more revelations from the Pearl Harbor fanatics, the frenzied neo-Nazis, exposers of communist penetration into unlikely sectors of society, watchdogs of freakish big business frauds, and those in-the-know on every government secret conceivable (and then some). I learned—to the authors' satisfaction, certainly—that the Germans had sent all their Jews to swanky resorts; that Marx was a maligned prophet, really the sweetest fellow; that automobiles could run on corn syrup, but the oil companies bought up the patents; that every government in the world (especially our own), throughout time, was concealing, for no readily obvious reason, just about everything that made the world really interesting.

Good Lord! but what did Holbein expect me to do with this stuff? Sneer at it, I supposed, after a proper analysis of the shaky, cracked foundations upon which all these claims were built. What else? It wasn't easy, though. Try as I might, I could not elude the force of their propounders' pathetic earnestness. These men *believed*. Their simmering hostility against the world which denigrated them, hostility liable to explode into full-fledged, hate-filled paranoia, should have repelled, but instead infected, me. Could all of this manic certainty be completely untrue? To my ever so brilliant partner that was a question unworthy of being asked, but I could not refrain from asking.

How, in a lifetime of research, could I ever prove all of these hypotheses wrong? I know, I know; that is never the point when testing a new and unusual claim. As I have been told, untold dreary times, it is up to the advocate to persuasively advance his case. I know that, I don't need a lecture. The problem was that I just could not see it that way. I would say aloud to myself, "So-and-so has not entirely succeeded in establishing his point", while an insidious demon within would ask, "How can you be sure?" I argued back, but the demon would laugh and respond, "What if he is right?" During that awful period my psychic state altered: my temper sharpened, my manner became abrupt, even surly; perhaps my health suffered. As did others, Holbein noticed the change and—all smiles and goodness—advised me to slow down, take a break. He expressed enormous pleasure in the undeniable fact of my extreme dedication. Toward him I could scarcely maintain a veneer of civility. It was in this mood that I happened across that damnable manuscript of Anton Vorchek.

I know not whence it came (nor, if I may anticipate, did I ever learn more of its provenience; its origin remains unknown), for the messily typed autograph copy, with stapled leaves, which came into my possession without covers, contained only a partial, torn title page, sans date and location. There I read, *The Machinations of Our Visitors*, by one Professor Anton Vorchek. Beyond that lay the body of the manuscript, through which it was an incredible chore to wade. While not an important point, I may note here that conspiracy theorists and other pseudo-spinners are seldom great stylists. Many are mere literary hobbyists, and it does show. It did in this case, although what I had in hand may not have been intended as camera-ready. The pages were unnumbered (I counted them: 146), single spaced, without one paragraph break or chapter heading from beginning to end.

Professor Vorchek recounts an ominous tale which incorporates the standard, stale themes of extraterrestrial invasion and high official conniving, but which goes far beyond both. As he tells it, the space aliens exist, have arrived, are among us in force, and have come with ominous intentions. For reasons which have never been clear to me, he precisely dates their advent to the Gold Reserve Act of 1933, "that decisive turning point in all of history." Their goal is subversion and conquest, their method, infiltration.

These highly advanced creatures from a distant planet (located in the Spectra Galaxy, "millions of miles from Earth") possess the awesome ability to change their shapes into any forms they please. Thus they may walk among us as men, with few the wiser, as they formulate and advance their schemes. Being vastly intelligent, it is a simple matter for them to enter occupations and acquire positions of authority which serve their purposes. When necessary, they are quite capable of replacing genuine human beings, destroying or spiriting away the originals, leaving in place seemingly perfect duplicates. It is just possible to spot the phonies, if one is aware of the telltale signs. Professor Vorchek, as a result of careful observation over many years, has noted their common attribute of small, bright, narrowly focused eyes, a distinct tendency toward slender build, and a certain ungainliness in the proportions of their limbs. He speculates on the repulsive differences which may lie beneath their clothing.

Ultimately, once they have attained numerical superiority, the invaders seek outright domination, but until that time comes they plan to sap our strength via social disruption. If they have their way, the enfeebled relics of *Homo sapiens* will be incapable of resistance when the intruders strike. "Essentially, the Spectrans so operate as to unravel the bonds of culture, to pit races and groups against one another in fratricidal competition, to break up personal relationships—man to mate, parent to child, teacher to student—to lessen the fires of the will—to spread diseases of the mind, and those physical ailments which are the sure products of induced, unrelieved stress. By stirring up turmoil and confusion they can break us, rendering us impotent, a prey to their horrid mercies."

What most fascinates about Professor Vorchek's theory is that it explains everything: there is no fact in the world, once the premise is accepted, which can not be incorporated into his musings; he has constructed for himself a perfect logical box. Any sign of tension or unease, any display of apparent foolishness or stupidity, is proof of the aliens at work. Occasional flashes of wisdom or insight, wherever found, are evidence of the rare loner, in the know, who is on to the Spectrans' game and hopes to thwart them. The author claims that he has corresponded with several others who, like himself, have arrived at a true understanding of the desperate state of terrestrial affairs. He concludes by exhorting his readers to organize, "to combine against the Invisible Peril while time and life remain to us."

This I read, as I had read so many before, and I can say that my initial reaction was to laugh. Give me neo-Nazis and One Worlders, any time. This latest fragment of rubbish made me tired, and I had perused it at the end of a long, dreary day, and all I could think was how glad I was to put it behind me. Tomorrow I would check a few points, write up a summary paragraph, forget it, and move on. *Prière de ne pas deranger!* The sooner I got this wretched book over with, the better for my peace of mind.

That is not how it happened. The next morning Holbein proved singularly unhelpful when I asked him for background information on the writer of this novel thesis. He claimed to know nothing about Professor Vorchek or his manuscript, nor even how the latter had come into his possession. Presumably one of his many scholarly correspondents had sent it—Holbein received such material in batches—but since the papers had been removed from their envelope or mailing package, he was not immediately in a position to trace their source. I would never have committed that kind of error. At any rate, he knew nothing about it, and did not see the sense in wasting much time on such a tendentious, derivative argument, when we had so much with which to work.

Perhaps, but now the mystery had peaked my curiosity. There was one thing I could do on my own, which was to look up the bona fides of the author. The document itself contained no personal information of any sort, but there could not be too many Professor Vorcheks around. To my intense disgust, my efforts to learn more about the man were a total failure. I could not locate him on any academic listing published in this country, and I eventually checked them all, going right back to 1933. Despite his ready grasp of idiomatically American English, it of course occurred to me that, given his unusual name, he might reside in a foreign land. I checked everything, without success. Intrigued, increasingly determined, I gave a great deal of attention to this matter. Whatever I tried, then or later, proved to no avail. The entirety of my objective knowledge concerning Professor Vorchek, at the present time, still derives only from his written work, of which I may own the only extant copy.

As I have written, dealing with any conspiracy theories left me cold, but something about this one generated qualms within me that would not subside. First I had to wend my way through the author's frantic certainty—always troubling, but nothing new—which should have consisted of little more than noting his inability—nay, lack of attempt— to support his key point. Then I should have established the chain of howling logical flaws embodied in the manuscript. Maybe I should not have given it any thought at all—who had heard of Anton Vorchek?— yet the mystery captivated me. I found myself, instead, falling into the trap, like never before, of trying to refute his subsidiary conclusions, on the assumption that the main tenet were true. How does one refute lunacy? To the mad, it is no different from denying truth.

Going back over the material, this time with greater absorption, I was struck by its lurid air of insinuating persuasiveness. Truly, in the one hundred and forty-six yellowed pages of *The Machinations* the unknown (self-styled?) professor had covered all the bases. The framework of argumentation was internally logical, reasonable, and sound; given A, then B, and so on. I sought a weakness which I could declare with soothing triumph. I found none. There were many strange aspects to this world, unusual events and personalities and ideas, which might well demand further explanation than common wisdom would allow. At various difficult moments in my life I had idly wondered—not always so idly—if something was happening behind the scenes which, if I only knew about it, would make sense of things, clear away the petty mysteries that plagued me. What if—I say, what if—there was a grand, unified, explanation for everything, an answer which, once known, would cause all facts to fall into place? Was not that the nature of the true scientific theory?

The mess of the world situation, with its continual horrors; that could not be accident. The wreckage of our society, the debilitating cultural miasma, the soulless acceptance of same; surely elements of design could be discerned in that picture. Someone, or something, was marshaling the forces which brought all this about. Nor could I absolutely ignore the lower key, seemingly trivial disappointments of my personal life, disquieting occurrences which I had never understood, and which were never due to any actions of my own, but which I had long noticed were invariably instigated by others. Viewed separately, they meant nothing except, possibly, bad luck, but when treated in unitary fashion a pattern emerged, a clear, definite pattern. Pattern implied intelligence, a guiding hand at the wheel. These things were *made* to happen. There could be a sinister power loose on Earth—it fit—the indications were there—the facts fell into line—such a power existed!

At the moment of comprehension I felt an inner warmth, a searing heat, sensed an ambient glow of shimmering light which might have been actual. I was blind, but now I could see; I was lost, but now I was found; and yet it was not mere revelation, the uncovering of the hidden; it was that, but more: REALIZATION, the unknown made real at the moment of discovery. This was not fantasy, but rather the underlying truth of all human reality. I knew it now—I had joined, at long last, that holy brotherhood of the wise—and my life would never be the same again.

I continued, sporadically, my work on the project, to the extent that I was able—my mind was a whirlwind, a torrent, which made it difficult to concentrate on unimportant matters—but I cleverly concealed from Holbein my new awakening, my mounting obsession with the papers of Professor Vorchek. My so-called partner was the sort who might be inclined to appropriate and take credit for ideas not his own. Furthermore, I could not be sure with whom he was in communication. At this stage, caution equaled wisdom. The Spectrans were out there, perhaps watching us, and I was by no means sufficiently savvy at this time to identify them. What might they deduce from an alteration in my behavior?

Despite my cunning, Holbein did discern something discordant in my attitude. We began to have words on the subject. He remonstrated with me on my sudden lack of drive. He reminded me that much research remained to be completed. He made a point of urging me to drop "the Vorchek crap!" How did he know about that? I had committed a single *faux pas* one afternoon, in class, when a stray reference to my secret studies caused my bored students' eyes to flash in surprise; some of them more brightly that I might have predicted. Had Holbein heard about that? He did not say, nor did he make mention of the copious notes I had been taking, and which a cheap snoop might have come across. I feigned a chummy air and good-naturedly laughed off his worries, but I was more careful after that.

Then came the dream. I could not doubt now that there were many paths to knowledge, so I took seriously this episode. Surrounded by utter darkness, the black absence of presence, Professor Anton Vorchek sat hunched, leaning forward in an uncomfortable, unpadded wooden chair, illuminated as if by a searchlight. I saw before me an elderly man, well dressed, his black beard shot with gray, his noble brow beaded with perspiration. He spoke earnestly and rapidly with a slight Central European accent, directly to me, only to me. His words were not quite those of the manuscript, but like them, and he seemed desperately eager to finish what he was saying, as if time were pressing. Once he turned sharply and glanced back into the nothingness, then hurriedly continued with his tale. In this nightmare recital he offered clinching, detailed proof which mesmerized me (but which I could not quite recall afterward). Presently the impenetrable gloom began to lighten, and I could dimly see beyond the Professor a vast room curving upward, an auditorium with fixed leather-backed seats, all occupied. At first I could make out little of the occupants; my attention was diverted, however, by tiny, twinkling scintillas of light scattered among them, resembling motionless fireflies. As the murk lifted further I saw row after row of identically dressed, lanky men, with grim, intent faces, each distorted by coldly glowing red eyes. They, too, listened to the Professor speak, with evil interest. He attempted to carry on, started to turn round again, froze, then looked at me piteously and covered his mouth with his hands. At that precise moment the audience *blurred*. For a second I could not focus properly; then every one of those men began to change into their true, hideously unbearable forms. The Professor moaned and cowered, and I turned away in sickened revulsion, and then I saw no more.

That morning I sat in my office at the college, *The Machinations* and related papers on my desk, pondering the meaning of the dream and the probable fate of the missing Professor. I felt empty, drained, crushed by the mental burden of these conceptions, wondering how to go on. Then Holbein entered, without knocking. Saluting me, he was about to launch into routine chatter when his gaze took in the mass of precious material. Then he sat down opposite me—unbidden—and with hands clenched before him began to lecture me severely on the mess I was making of my reputation and the danger of my attitude. Danger? He spoke of more than he knew! With an air of strained patience he informed me that our colleagues were fully aware of my late "peccadilloes," and that I stood on the verge of becoming a permanent laughing stock. He wanted to help me if he could—if he could!—but it was necessary that I talk to him as I used to do. That got my attention. On a sudden impulse I cut him off and blurted forth the entire story of my recent advancement, from first inklings to final realization. I held back nothing. I laid bare, in perfect, logical, connected form, the findings of *The Machinations*. I demanded action against the Spectrans, pleaded for help in locating, if it still be possible, the Professor. When I finished, minutes or hours later, I paused, nerved to a fever pitch, awaited his reaction. He smiled—a silly, degrading smile—shook his head ever so slightly, as if in disbelief, then abruptly barked a booming laugh. His close-set eyes flashing brightly with merriment, he congratulated me on my *parody* of the very "morons" we were engaging to analyze!

What was this? As much as I despised him, I knew he wasn't such a fool as this palpably false reaction suggested. Even a skinny, long-armed fellow like Holbein ought to be able to understand me. So he did. The last pieces of the puzzle fell into place. He knew that I spoke truth; he knew all too well. Shortly he would find an excuse to leave, a casual exit, and then he would race to report me to his masters... or to his comrade infiltrators. Unless, of course, I prevented him.

I acted quickly, without need for coherent, conscious thought, but the operation involved more noise than I anticipated. Scarcely had my fingers left his neck than iron-gripped hands were hauling me away, and now I am a prisoner in this cell within what they call a hospital, though I fear it is in reality a secret dungeon established by *them* to hide away the questing minds they can not otherwise contain. Most of them speak to me as Holbein did—poor Holbein, they call him—seeking to probe what they refer to as my sense of guilt, but their words are vapor in my ears. I know that I can never escape their clutches, so I feel no reason to pretend. Also, there is that one datum I must not ignore, however they try to weaken my brain: that last sight of Holbein as he slipped to the floor, that non-human limpness and discolored flabbiness of face. There is no question in my mind that he, with whom I had worked while I thought him a man, was beginning to change.

I have written this narrative for my own sake, presenting the facts as I understood them at the various stages, and expressing my views as I remember them from those past times. Though I am doomed—perhaps already replaced—I imagine to myself fanciful methods of smuggling my words to the world. Suppose not all of the staff here are Spectrans; suppose I could make contact with a real human being, one rightly puzzled by the mystery of my case, and determined to get to the bottom of it? A slim hope at best, but stranger things have happened. While life remains, I will not flag, I will not surrender.

By now they must have destroyed my copy of Professor Vorchek's expose. I am told that they retain it for "clues to my condition," but they will not let me see it, which is in keeping with the machinations of our visitors. Though one copy has been suppressed, I pray that there are others out there, somewhere. The Spectrans may erase me out of existence, as they did him, but the truth shall not die. Get hold of the Professor's manuscript, however you can. Read it, learn it, know it in your bones. Spread the word, by any means. Gather like minds, combine against the alien conspirators. That is the only chance for us.

"We face the end of times, yet if we join hands and come together to confront our enemies, we stand on the threshold of the new," the Professor assures us. It must be so. I will not live to see it, but I dream of the day when men like myself, true, stout-hearted men, will unite and rise up to wipe these monsters from the face of the Earth.

The Discovery of the X Force

Professor Anton Vorchek, the respected elder statesman of science, first announced his great discovery in the prestigious *Journal of Advanced Astro-Physics*. In his groundbreaking article, "Confirmation of the Existence of a New Universal Force," he presented, at great length and in great detail, the fundamentals of his theory. Beyond gravity, he wrote, beyond electro-magnetism and the strong and weak nuclear forces, their lies a fifth universal force, which underlies all the rest, which underlies and sustains all previously held conceptions of matter, energy, and reality. This force, which he provisionally designated "X," is the ultimate building block and, at the same time, the ultimate power source, for every universal process from the beginning of time to the present. According to Vorchek, what he had done was to reveal the long sought "Grand Unifier" of Einsteinian physics, which makes final sense of the operations of the natural world.

The X Force, he showed, is the substratum lying behind the hitherto understood or recognized elements of nature. The Force exists within its own hyper-dimensional realm, beyond space and time, yet permeates—nay, forms—the basic fabric of the space-time continuum. Vorchek asked his learned professional readers, as a thought experiment, to imagine the universe as viewed from the standpoint of the Force. In its timelessness, the Force is, at the same time and at all times, the creator, the builder, and the preserver or sustainer of all things, now and forever. The eternal "X" brought the universe into being, provided its development and structure, and laid the groundwork for the laws which govern all physical interactions. The Force itself is infinite and changeless, can not be divided, diminished, or transformed in any way. It is what it is, always, regardless of the particular historical variations of common substance. It is always there, composing yet transcending the ordinary.

Professor Vorchek, in the conclusion to his treatise, posits the following: "At present the X Force appears a marvelous mystery, a great unknown, beyond the mere fact of its existence. We predict that this situation will change. The Force shares, we may surmise, one attribute in common with the four standard forces: it may be utilized, bent to the will of Man. Our findings promise the possibility of new applied and practical uses of supreme benefit. We may derive from the Force vast sources of power, limitless and virtually free. The equivalent of a single sub-atomic particle contains within itself an endless amount of "X," and, therefore, if the means of extraction be discerned, will give to us utilitarian power which will transform human civilization, and potently affect the destiny of the human race."

Such, in outline, was the publication of Professor Vorchek. He presented his premises, offered the logical steps leading to his conclusion, provided a battery of tests by which his theory could be explored by others. He made clear what gigantic results he expected to follow from his discovery. It might be worthwhile, in another forum, to discuss the reasonableness of his expectations, but from this point they are no longer pertinent. What follows is what actually happened.

Vorchek made his case to the world in the most erudite and technically forbidding professional journal in the world. For all of its credentials—and they were beyond reproach—the *Journal of Advanced Astro-Physics* was read by no more than a few hundred cloistered scholars, and even fewer of them could keep up with all of the crystalline ideas found within, and all of the ramifications of, "Confirmation of the Existence of a New Universal Force." The people of the Earth, of course, did not read that journal, nor had they even heard of it. Many laymen first became aware of the new theory as a result of a publication in *Modern Living*, a Sunday newspaper insert. An article was rushed into that supplement, penned by a lesser regarded colleague of Professor Vorchek. That man, a Doctor Mark Hodges, not well known in his field, had not participated in the discovery; in fact, he had questioned it from the first, and belittled every step of the earlier investigations. Now, sensing major developments and seeking notoriety, professional or otherwise, he leaped upon the bandwagon after his own fashion and charged to the forefront with the first and most influential popular article on the subject.

Under the heading "Final Proof of the Nonexistence of God," Dr. Hodges argued that the X Force, now an established fact of the cosmos, completely obviated the long presumed necessity of believing in the need for a universal Creator. That primitive superstition could now be dismissed once and for all; why accept God, when we had X? X possessed all of the logical attributes of the mythical deity, without any of

His illogical baggage. Although the newly discovered power transcended nature as conventionally understood, it was nonetheless part of nature, not a separate entity. The timeless X Force was the very engine of creation, in and of itself, with no requirement for mind or purpose underlying reality. Everything could be explained in terms of X; there was nothing left over which demanded any hypothesizing of additional factors, no matter how traditional or cherished those might be.

"We may thank Professor Vorchek," wrote Hodges, "for the inestimable service he has performed for humanity. Never again will it be necessary to debate or wonder, to hope or pray, to agonize over a question which once seemed itself as immortal as the trivial concept of godhood which has disturbed and confounded our race since we crept from the caves."

Everybody read that article, everybody talked about it. The literate people of the world began to scream, in their millions, and the less literate, in their more overwhelming numbers, soon joined in when Dr. Hodges began hitting the television talk shows. He turned up everywhere, always hammering home the same thesis, snidely brushing aside the clumsy counter-arguments of his hosts. Soon others got into the act, the scholars and the intellectuals, and those not so scholarly or intellectual, all eager to expostulate their views on what quickly became known to the public as the "Hodges Theory."

It took the world by storm. It was the sensation, the craze of the day. Everyone wanted to discuss, to explicate, to praise or to condemn, the Hodges Theory. Nothing else mattered. Also, the strangest thing happened: somehow, in that mysterious realm of the public mind, the Hodges concept utterly triumphed. Of course there were opponents and nay-sayers. There was that old saw often employed against uncomfortable ideas in the past, that it was "only a theory." For some reason, perhaps the steady drumbeat of propaganda, the old saw didn't cut it. There were authoritative types, representatives of many denominations, who suggested that the X Force was itself a manifestation of God. However it came about, people would not buy that. As Hodges and others explained it, that didn't sound right. There were others who simply stuck their heads in the sand. Well and good, but nobody paid attention to them.

The facts of the Hodges Theory swept the world and the collective mind of Man. Within weeks the first noteworthy effects of the new discovery became evident. Church attendance plummeted. In every civilized country on the globe—every country where regular folk had a chance to comprehend the news pouring out of their TVs, their magazines and newspapers—the old-time believers dwindled and the churches closed. There just wasn't any point in all that effort; people may do the oddest things, but there were not many willing to go down on their knees and worship the X Force. Dr. Hodges, its discoverer, and a flock of other clever chaps had told them how silly that was.

Politicians began removing references to deity from their public discourse. They didn't want to sound like idiots. There was a lot of loose, if earnest, talk about "fresh modes of thinking" and the "liberating effects of genuine knowledge". Henceforth, forthright and practical men would base their actions and philosophies of the true and the known, the tangible and the real. In the universe of "Hodges' Force," that was the only sensible solution.

The other effects of the new view began to multiply. For no good reason that anybody was willing to accept or face, moral breakdown ensued. The X Force might be an absolute, but nothing else was, and increasingly large numbers of people began to behave accordingly. At first it didn't seem a big deal; there had been problems of the kind before—talking heads in the media had long debated disturbing trends—this might be only a difference in degree. Came the moment that the authorities realized they were dealing with a difference in kind, and they didn't know what to do about it, nor did they show much inclination. Their powers of analysis and action, it appeared, were paralyzed by "X."

The citizens of the great nations behaved oddly, and destructively. Crime rates soared; every conceivable form of crime. Murder became the major cause of death within a matter of weeks. Robberies, rapes, vandalism, and other wanton species of nastiness, became regular facts of life. There was no sane dealing with people any more. "Why did you do it?" the police would ask of a previously law-abiding citizen who had run wild and committed unspeakable atrocities. "Why not?" would come the bland reply. Indeed, that proved the rallying cry of the era. "Why Not?" was emblazoned on the bumper stickers of cars, on signs in yards. In one notable case it was written in smoke above a major city by skywriters. All those who spoke publicly deplored these actions, and yet none were quick to condemn, nor did any do anything about them.

Local governments were the first to disintegrate, but they soon had bigger company. It was bad enough that the police, the firemen, and the like social servants shirked their duties or even contributed to the mayhem. The situation turned catastrophic when the army went on the

46

rampage. They did it, they said, because they could. They were right; they could, and did. Panic, devastation, slaughter, the burning of cities; the conflagration raged unchecked. Dozens of groups formed in response, to add their sniping and bomb throwing to the melee. From all sides came demands and pleas for justice. No one remained who was capable of defining the term.

Why was this happening? "Blame it on the X Force!" the new battle cry. The contagion spread from one country to the next, like wildfire. There was no checking it. Backward nations sealed themselves off and retreated to the safety of a new Dark Age, the only apparent solution. Elsewhere, madness and chaos reigned.

Ultimately, the popular fury must expend itself, and the survivors would pull themselves up out of the debris of their world and wonder what they had done to themselves. Many would curse Dr. Hodges, whom they formerly called the "Great Discoverer," while others would vainly insist on praising him for his gigantic, if double-edged, contributions to science and philosophy. They would honor him posthumously, however; he had been taken out by a car bomb, casually devised by a twelve year old boy who employed readily available household products. In the midst of the societal confusion, Hodges had been on his way to receive an award, to be presented by the remnants of the American Association for the Advancement of Science. Instead, the conference delivered fitting eulogies.

Only one reporter, who worked for a small independent daily newspaper, thought to contact Professor Anton Vorchek and ask what he thought of it all. To be sure, by that time travel and communication were necessarily restricted, but one would think others might have remembered Vorchek. He was, after all, the man who—objectively speaking—had actually discovered the awesome X Force, and had predicted the countless marvels to be derived from it. Sad to relate, the good professor, that titan of his field, when his opportunity finally came, had little to say. "I do not understand," he exclaimed, "I do not understand it at all. I do not know what is happening to people. The things they say, these absurd ideas; none of that has anything to do with me. I can tell you about every aspect of physical reality, yet you ask me of morality and mental states. You want me to explain all this to you. For the love of God, my friend: explain it to me!"

Canyon Diablo

"These are the Badlands," said Anton Vorchek, motioning before him as he and his companion rested atop the steep, crumbling slope. "Weathered lumps of sandstone and limestone, cut by ragged ridges of granite, a primordial wasteland, without life or the capacity to support life. Nothing lives here, nothing ever will; perhaps nothing ever has. This is a strange and ancient territory, the result of countless eons of pitiless geological forces. To the east lies the Petrified Forest, a once living land which still preserves a mockery of the flora which flourished there when the world was young; to the north lies the Painted Desert, a region seemingly as dead as this, yet where a few pathetic creatures continue the struggle against cosmic entropy. To the west—I tell you this is so—may be found Canyon Diablo, the semi-fabulous goal of our search."

"I find it hard to believe, Professor," replied Leonard Kartch, "that anything could survive out here. I've never seen a place so suggestive of death. This soil is so sterile; acidic in one spot, alkaline in another, most of it incapable of supporting life, even when the rains do come, which is seldom enough, I take it. It appears to me there's simply nothing out here." Leonard picked up a pebble and cast it down the near vertical slope, shaking his head as he watched the object bounce and then fall out of sight. "I'm impressed by your ideas, Professor, and I can't tell you how pleased I am that you've asked me along on this expedition—it's a big opportunity for me, I know—but I'm not yet ready to accept that we'll discover anything in this wilderness, much less what you seek."

"Be patient," advised Vorchek, who always spoke precisely and heavily, with a trace of an unplaceable accent. "All will be revealed to you, Leonard, in good time. You possess the typical impatience of the graduate student, always eager to complete the project now. This is the gateway to where we are going, not the destination itself." He rose, dusting himself off. As Leonard imitated his actions the Professor added, "And it is my pleasure to bring you with me. I have a special need

49

for your presence, and it has been my experience that graduate students have their uses."

"I'm glad you think so, but my grades haven't been that good, and I hadn't given much thought to pursuing this line of research. I've even debated dropping out of the program and getting myself a regular job, times being what they are. I guess you require a witness to back up your findings, if they pan out, but why me?"

"You are perfect for my purposes," Vorchek said abruptly. "I considered the matter carefully, and I chose you. Feel as honored as you like. Now, collect your bags and let us get moving."

They did so, Vorchek carrying his assortment of notes, writing materials, camera and recording equipment, actually a light burden; Leonard carrying everything else, the food, the water, camping gear, a hefty bundle indeed. They slowly made their way down the slope, slipping and shuffling at an angle as they descended, until they reached the plain below and set out across the Badlands, trackless wastes which motorists might admire briefly from a distant overlook, snapping a picture or two before they shrugged and passed on, but into which few would ever deign to venture. The professor and his student trudged between the multicolored mounds—this one gray, that one pink, there a blue one, here a vivid red, farther on a heap of coal black—picked their way along rocky ravines, pushed their way through ancient beds of silicate dust. Overhead the interminable sun blazed, painful to the eye and to the skin, out of a sky whose blue seemed harsh and leaden by comparison with the pastel landscape below it. On the whole, they marched in silence. Vorchek appeared to know where he was going. He consulted a compass on occasion, thereupon directing their steps in slightly different directions, even cresting the disintegrating mounds if necessary. Leonard, who felt the urge to complain at the extra effort, held his tongue. He didn't know where they were, he didn't really know where they were heading, but he presumed faith that his guide, to the necessary extent, knew what he was doing.

"As you know," Vorchek began presently, "it is the standard body of anthropological lore which initialized my research. I started from the scientifically known basis that such a people existed in prehistoric times, leaving their monuments and the stories that the descendants of other peoples told about them. So far, so good; an interesting line of investigation, but little more, one which others could and have pursued before me without my aid. Even in that mass of material, however, there were indicators, stray relics and curious tales which most chose to ignore or to explain away.

"Another of my lines of research—an entertaining sideline—appeared to connect certain dots, to weave a cohesive picture not quite like any that had been deduced before. Consider the known: Navajo informants have told us much concerning the mysterious foreigners who entered their tribal lands in the old days, those marvelous and terrible invaders from the north whom the Navajo styled the 'Anasazi', commonly translated as the 'Evil Ones'. Imagine my thrill when I discovered, during the course of a comparative language study, that the term is more appropriately translated as 'Eaters of the Dead'.

"The Navajo always relate their tales as if from a distance, speaking of people known of but furtively shunned if at all possible. The stories told by the historic Hopi, a people whose basic life ways somewhat resemble those of the Anasazi, are more detailed and more remarkable. Their term for the intruders into their antique lands is 'Tonipah': 'Eaters of the Living'. Do you begin to see the pattern, my boy?"

They made camp at dusk on the far edge of the Badlands, where the bleak, weathered mounds gave way to a featureless plain of harsh, rasping grasses and thorny shrubs. Life retained a precarious foothold in this region. Ugly, scrawny black birds squawked and flitted between the dry bushes. Lizards darted from one patch of ragged shade to another. Small mammals, most likely gopher rats, stood up on their haunches to survey the new arrivals, then dived into holes. Somewhere, away on the thin, hot wind, wafted the howl of a coyote. From elsewhere another coyote answered.

Leonard started the campfire, while Vorchek keenly examined the darkening western horizon. From his attitude he might have been looking for something, or wondering whether something was looking for them. Eventually he joined his compatriot and they ate heated soup from a can, and dry biscuits washed down with warm, metallic thermos water. Afterward they relaxed and sipped coffee before the two-man tent, which Leonard had erected.

"Of course the Anasazi once existed," Leonard granted. "Everyone knows that much, even tourists. I was already aware, as well, about some of the weird stories told about them, although I didn't realize anybody took them so seriously."

"Very seriously," replied Vorchek. "Turner has uncovered unambiguous traces of their former practices. He was not the first, but he certainly carried such studies to a higher level. There is no scientific dispute; cavils come only from those who imagine prehistory as a kind of Eden, a naturally harmonious world of balance and warm, fuzzy thoughts. The facts reveal a distressingly different picture."

"I guess, but it's one thing to posit the occasional practice, in time of great need and privation; it's quite another to admit the possibility of an entire culture based on the systematic... well, utilization of such resources."

"The Aztecs would have argued that point," Vorchek noted. "That fearsome tribe were not freaks of nature but, rather, a people employing one of the many means this world allows for human survival. There have been other, similar, episodes throughout time. The Anasazi constitute one more.

"Cannibalism," he continued, after setting aside his empty coffee cup, "is an unusual practice, but really a clever one. Whatever the shortages of other protein sources, there is always one in good supply. Man may always live on Man, if he can get away with it."

"That's the problem," shot back Leonard. "He can't, not routinely, not forever. The livestock, shall we say, tend to object, and unlike cattle, may be in a position to do something about it. The system generates inherent conflict. It can't last."

"And so the system crashes," agreed the professor, "when the victims revolt. That is, pretty apparently, what happened in the case of the Anasazi. We have the legends of the Navajo, the Hopi, the Sinagua, the Pima, and other tribes whose descendants have survived into the historic period, when scholars could record their beliefs. Such stories are interlarded, unfortunately, with useless and cumbersome mythology, which hinders factual analysis, but a surprising level of consistency remains. They have all passed on accounts of their meetings with the intruders, the conflicts, the horrors observed or suspected, and the eventual struggles—successful or not, in any given case—to throw off the brutal shadow which had shrouded their world. Then, of course, there is the archaeological evidence."

"I know something about that," said his student. "The Anasazi have left some fancy ruins. I stopped at one once, during spring break, on the way to a class party."

"In that case I give you an 'A' for effort, Leonard. Well done, sir! And you wonder why I brought you along, when you make it so obvious. You are quite an expert, after your own fashion. I could not have done better.

"We have the physical evidence they left behind," Vorchek went on, after a snort of amusement, "across a broad swath of the Southwest; the evidence of their dwelling places, always tucked into remote, inaccessible areas, many of them blackened by the fires of their final destruction; we have the ruins of their temples, the remnants of their communal dining rooms, the debris of their abattoirs. We have all that, the tumbled stone, the crumbling mud cement, the pottery shards, the dusty beads and discarded shells of their ornaments. Then, too, we have other, very different, kinds of physical remains, which offer clear indications as to the unique life ways of the departed Anasazi.

"We have the bones, my friend, the relics of their culinary artistry, the human bones, chopped, hacked, splintered by crude tools of feldspar and chert; we have the tell-tale marks of the butcher's shop on those bones, bones stacked in side chambers, bones heaped in garbage mounds or dumped in massive loads into trash pits; we have all this to confirm the ancestral whisperings which have come down to us through the ages, and from this we must infer a dreadful tale of savage cruelty and terror which once blighted this land, and which—as we are conventionally given to understand—vanished suddenly and completely as the result of a pan-regional social upheaval, marking the end of the Anasazi."

Vorchek paused to light his pipe. "Those are the facts, and what we can make of them. As is my wont, I have carried my studies one step farther than most. A gigantic leap, I would say."

"That's the part I have trouble accepting," Leonard said. "I just don't see how your latest theory could be true. I mean, after all this time—"

"Later, my boy. Soon all will be revealed, and you will know as I know. For now, let us sleep. We cover much difficult ground tomorrow."

They slept, Vorchek easily, Leonard after grumbling at their primitive circumstances, within the little tent. They were up at dawn, were underway in the early coolness before the sun became hostile again. They trekked across a featureless, scrubby landscape, an unimpressive realm of dust, crackling-dry bushes and fleet lizards, on a journey which, to one of the party, seemed endless. Leonard made clear that he disliked the hike, hated the heat, was bored by the unvarying terrain. He openly questioned Vorchek's ability to chart a true course, despite the compass; what did it serve to know the cardinal points, when the destination itself was an imaginative mystery? The professor calmly indicated certain faint landmarks on the distant horizons: a couple of well spaced cinder cones, the hazy eminence of the San Francisco Peaks far to the west. Professor Vorchek kept a careful eye on those features, as he assured his dubious colleague, and through regular consultation of his notes would see to it that they did not wander astray.

Just about at the point when Leonard felt the urge to cry "Hold, enough!"—although he might not have given vent to his feelings with those precise words—the stark landscape began to change. It grew rocky and uneven; they left behind the windy plain, plunged into a series of rocky washes cutting between jagged hills. When a choice of ravine offered itself, Vorchek spent precious minutes calculating and measuring angles, noting the evidence of compass, sun, and landmarks, before rushing down happily into his choice. They walked many miles (Leonard was chagrined by the estimated number) before the sun dipped low and the professor called a halt.

"This will be our last camp," said he, and they repeated the chores of the previous evening. This time Vorchek scanned the western horizon with binoculars. When he joined his companion for their simple meal, he did so with evident satisfaction.

"Do you see that largish gap, between the big hills, just to the right of the sun?" He pointed at the spot. "There; do you see? I tell you, son, that is the entrance to Canyon Diablo."

"It doesn't look like much," Leonard mulishly muttered.

"It is everything to me. That nondescript fissure is the mouth of a lost and forgotten world. It shall speak."

"So you say," came back the short reply. Leonard moaned. "I've never cared for chicken noodle soup. I ate too much of it as a kid."

"Now that you are an adult," Vorchek said with a grin, "you crave man's food. Is that it? Such ideas intrigue me, in this place."

"I don't see anything special about that canyon. Who calls it that, anyway? I wonder that it has a name."

"The tales of Canyon Diablo," said Vorchek, "are my own contribution to ethnographic lore. I stumbled across them purely by chance, without prior expectations. The Navajo knew nothing of them, and since they are the prime source of traditional information on the Anasazi, the stories long escaped professional gaze. I spent some weeks among the Hopi, and it was they who furtively hinted at their darkest legend.

"Think of it: they told to me these frightful tales, tales of a contemporary nature, headlines from a modern oral newspaper, if you will, of children and lone wayfarers being snatched away in the dark of night by unseen assailants; 'just like in the old days,' they said. They spoke, under their breath, of pathetic cries heard in the wee hours, of ugly traces found, come morning, at the scenes of the disappearances. They spoke of an age-old fear that has never completely died. They suggested to me that, within a hazily known, vaguely circumscribed territory, certain patterns from prehistoric times still linger. That got me thinking, thinking quite a lot."

"It's just a story to scare the children."

"I allowed for that possibility, until I interviewed Yotipai. In the meantime, however, I consulted tribal and police records. Documentation is not what it should be on these vast, largely empty Indian reservations. People tend to keep to themselves, minding their own business, and then too, the locals retain an ingrained distrust of government bureaucracy and the paid keepers of official, written records. No, it was not easy for me, but I eventually unearthed the supporting clues. Do you know, could you have imagined, that the disappearance rate among these people in this area, for a thousand square miles around us, is seven times that of the national average? I learned that, I suspected, and then I talked to Yotipai, and I understood. You recall my mentioning the name?"

"Some old drunk, wasn't he?"

"Please, none of that. Maintain good humor, Leonard, and a sense of proportion. Whatever transpires, you are taking part in scientific research of the highest caliber. Hold on to that, no matter what happens. Any man of an intellectual bent should be pleased in this situation."

Leonard laughed sarcastically.

Professor Vorchek hunched forward over his coffee and resumed his running lecture, ignoring the interruption. "Yotipai is my finest source on the tales of Canyon Diablo. Though not a Hopi himself, he has imbibed their traditions, and those of other tribes as well. He is an old fashioned medicine man, a 'shaman', whose job it is, among other things, to retain the collected wisdom of bygone and, supposedly, better days. There is not much call for a man like him anymore, but his type still exists, and he is a fine specimen of his kind. He tends to keep his own counsel, but he can be cajoled, flattered, and reasoned with. I got the whole story from him, as best he knew it.

"For a nominal sum he told me all. Yotipai described to me a shunned, forbidden region—this Canyon Diablo—where dwell still the Evil Ones, survivors of a despicable race, who maintain a hidden foothold in our world, surrounded by the descendants of their ancient sworn enemies, who manage to remain out of sight of the skeptical authorities and powers of our day. In this last stronghold of the Anasazi, so he assured me, these awful people still practice their grim arts according to their old code, allowing no one to enter their realm unbidden, and—as a matter of course—seeing to it that no stranger leaves their territory alive. From his account I gleaned the fact that Yotipai spoke from certain and personal knowledge; he was not passing on a twice told tale, but had actually been there, in his prime, with a youthful companion, a sort of apprentice shaman, and together they had met the Evil Ones face to face, observed them in action, and noted the location. Despite the passage of years he was able to recall the location with precision—more, perhaps, than any other living outsider could boast—and it was he who furnished me with explicit directions."

"A cock and bull story," Leonard grunted. "You've been taken in by a drunken Indian, fishing for whiskey money. It's a crock."

"I do not think so, my friend."

"The story gives itself away. There's a contradiction: no one can visit Canyon Diablo and live, but what's-his-name has been there, and he's alive, and he'll tell you everything for, I guess, ten bucks. Professor, that's ridiculous. Why can't you see it? And that story is what dragged me out to this God forsaken hole!"

"Your manner aside," replied Vorchek, "you make a cogent point. If that were all, I might agree with you. Yotipai, however, explained to my satisfaction his continued health and well being. The solution—one to which I paid serious attention—revolves around a primordial custom of the Anasazi, one which was widely practiced in the days of their hegemony, and one which Yotipai proved is still efficacious today. Thanks to my aboriginal informant, I have an ace up my sleeve. I know how to deal with those people!"

"What's that, Professor?"

"It is simple. I want something from them: to observe their ways, to record that priceless anthropological information for posterity, or at least for my own intellectual benefit. In return, I must offer them something they want. I shall make a trade."

"Something in particular?"

"Not so fast, Leonard. You know my methods; I prefer to husband my secrets until the proper time. That comes very soon. In the morning, when we reach Canyon Diablo, you will learn all. I guarantee it."

Vorchek spent another night of restful slumber, happily anticipating the morrow. His hapless graduate student suffered through another troubled night of rough bedding, ominous sounds, and pestering insects. He wondered aloud (though the professor didn't stir) whether they would make better time on the return journey, after they got this nonsense over with. He wasn't especially convinced that they would find much of anything in this so-called Canyon Diablo.

They did, however. Vorchek got them going before dawn this time. A sliver of crescent moon hung over the eastern horizon as they embarked upon the last march to the west. As the sun first peeped they reached the mouth of the fissure, which had grown during their approach to a respectable gorge. Into it they went, and the walls rose higher and higher as they progressed. It was easier hiking here, where the towering walls screened the direct heat. They spied a few more desert animals, then came upon a little stream, bubbling up from a spring in a rocky cleft, choked with green riparian plants. Beyond that they found the three totems.

These were poles of ironwood hammered into the hard soil, topped with black and white feathers and one browned, polished human skull apiece. These items fascinated Vorchek. Leonard balked.

"This looks serious, Professor."

"So it is, Leonard."

"We should turn back."

"Such foolishness! So near the goal, boy, and you wish to run? We are minutes away from a scientific marvel. Let us hasten."

"There could be trouble."

"I am not afraid; I expect no difficulties. Remember: I have something they want."

The spooky canyon (as Leonard perceived it) narrowed almost to a tunnel, through which the clear stream tinkled, then widened into a large bowl-shaped hollow. Within the two men gazed upon a sight that staggered them, even Vorchek: an old-styled Anasazi town of antique make, a collection of geometrical stones and mortar forming a series of once fashionable pueblos. Not ruins were these, but whole, maintained, and inhabited dwellings, built out from the opposing cliff face and sprawling into the center of the hollow.

The natives were present, perhaps three dozen of them, watching expectantly. The men wore loincloths of tanned leather, the women, shapeless leather shifts. All were dark, moon-faced, solemn. They seemed unfazed by the arrival of the intruders, as if they had known outsiders were coming. As the two men stood there, several husky young fellows appeared from the sides of the hollow to join the others.

"No sudden moves," Vorchek advised his companion in a whisper. "Say nothing. Let me handle this. Just keep your eyes open until I have struck the bargain."

"Bargain, with these people?" Leonard hissed. "I don't think so. Don't you see what I see?" He alluded to the ceremonial altar, or temple stone, or whatever it might be called, raised on a limestone dais before the dwellings. That terrible flat stone was stained with patches of crusty brown, and littered with splintered fragments of bones. One chunk of bone, more complete than the rest, told the story. It was a piece of skull, human, a bit of a very small human skull.

"Of course I see it, Leonard. Why should that surprise you? We could expect no less. In fact, I was counting on it. Now stand quietly, while I get down to business."

Vorchek lowered his gear bag to the ground and left his companion standing there, in his misery and fear, while the eager scholar advanced confidently across the open space, his right hand raised in presumably universal greeting. Nobody else moved until Vorchek came near and halted. Then the Indians slowly closed in around him in a semicircle.

Leonard nervously watched the entire transaction. He saw Vorchek speaking briefly, at intervals, while the Indians stood mute. Then they began to speak, also at hesitant intervals. Then it appeared that the professor was engaging in a sort of conversation. Many of them were speaking now, accompanying their words with gestures. This went on for a spell. Vorchek seemed to be urging a proposition upon them, one which they rejected, judging from their hand movements. Then he pointed to Leonard—many pairs of eyes followed his finger—and whatever argument he was currently making apparently broke the logjam. The Indians grinned and began to nod. Leonard didn't care for those grins, but Vorchek seemed altogether pleased as he rejoined his companion.

"As I had deduced, Leonard, the language barrier proved less difficult than it might have been. Of course I can't speak their language, it being a unique, unknown tongue, with no obvious parallels to other local tribes. I look forward to recording it. Fortunately, they know a smattering of Navajo and Hopi, as do I; enough to get by.

"It is all arranged. We have struck the bargain. I get what I want—the right to gather all information I can for one day and, as a special boon, the privilege of recording one of their most important ceremonial rites—while the Anasazi receive what they want most. If you will oblige me, I desire to get down to business at once."

"That's great, Professor," Leonard replied, with little warmth in his voice. He didn't care for the way the natives were watching them; expectantly watching. "But can you trust them? According to you, they're dangerous people."

"I think so," Vorchek said glibly. He was in remarkably high spirits, practically radiant. "I think I can trust them. You see, I made clear that if our arrangement succeeds this time, that I may return in the future, to repeat the process. They seemed to appreciate that. Now, if you will be so kind—"

"What can you possibly offer them?" Leonard asked. "Do you have beads or trinkets in that bag?"

"Oh, heavens no, this is my photographic equipment. I intend to record everything." With that, Vorchek extracted his camera and tripod, and began setting up for action. "Leonard, my friend, do me a favor; just go over there and join them."

"You want me in the picture?"

"It would be pointless without you. Right over there, please, on the double. I promised them we would get this matter over with first."

"I don't—I don't want—to go over there," Leonard stammered. "I don't like them. You go."

Vorchek sighed, glanced with a certain irritation at his graduate student. "This will not do." He motioned to the Anasazi. They grinned again, and several powerfully built young men approached. Leonard flinched and started back.

"What do they want, Professor?" he cried.

Vorchek replied, still intently fiddling with his apparatus, "They want you, Leonard."

The Indians seized the youth, tugged him gently forward. He resisted, so they tugged more forcefully. They were, as he instantly realized, pulling him toward the big stone. He screamed. They dragged harder.

"Professor, help me!" Leonard shrieked, struggling helplessly in their iron grip. "Stop them. They're going to kill me!"

"I dare say," drawled Vorchek, who rose as he finished his preparations. "That is the typical fate of fresh game, my boy. Do not fight them, and do not waste your emotions on useless fear. Consider this a great honor. Thank your lucky stars, Leonard, that you have been granted the opportunity to take part in such a thrilling scientific enterprise. This is a once in a lifetime occasion, and you are materially aiding the advancement of knowledge."

Leonard Kartch did not thank the stars, then or when the Anasazi hurled him roughly onto the filthy stone. He pleaded for mercy as they held him down and the painted, feathered medicine man began chanting in his weird fashion; and he begged Vorchek to save him as the razor-sharp obsidian knives pressed against his squirming flesh.

Vorchek could not be distracted from his vital work, however. He was too busy snapping photographs and scribbling in his notebook.

The Beneficiary

George Bael, stepping down from the bus and walking home from yet another long day at the job, thought for the thousandth time that he was going out of his mind. The store was a dispiriting place, his boss a brutish thug, his fellow employees a pack of tiresome fools, and as for the customers! They were beyond belief, a vermin species. Sometimes he didn't know how he stood it. Life had to offer him more than this. He wearily crunched across the gravel lot to the cheap apartment block where he hid out when he wasn't earning a precarious living. He looked inside his mail box: bills and junk flyers. Then up the outside stairs he went to the second floor, to the door of his dingy flat. He didn't see any of his neighbors, which was just as well, for they were a tragic bunch. He saw a note from the apartment management taped to his door. Oh Lord, what was it now? Perhaps they were ramming through still another rent increase, justified by more "improvements," as they had done last year with that faulty plumbing work—all those grubby men tramping in and out for days, yet the pipes still groaned and whistled—or maybe they were finally selling out, and informing him that he must vacate by the end of the week. His throat clutched at the thought. He didn't even have a car to sleep in. But no; the scrawled message notified him that a package awaited him in the office.

He wasn't expecting anything. He went inside, hungry as a bear, pushed through the debris-strewn living room to the kitchen, shedding his jacket and shoes on the way. For now he made himself a ham sandwich and heated a pot of canned soup, which he ate on the pitted coffee table, washed down with a beer. He flicked on the old, cranky television. There was nothing but nonsense on, and he couldn't see it well anyway, but he left it running. The noise was better than nothing. Presently he rose and deposited his dirty dishes in the sink. He didn't need to wash them now, for the sink wasn't filled up yet. He wondered about his package. He ought to collect it before the office closed.

He threw on comfortable clothes, trooped downstairs to the office, found both halves of the management team in. Evil, wasted old Harper—Bael hoped he didn't end up like that man—sent his ugly, crabby wife into the back room, from which she re-emerged dragging a big box across the floor. She asked Bael what it was, but of course he couldn't tell her, and for some reason she seemed to take offense, which was not at all unusual for her. He hefted the cumbersome load and staggered with it back to his room. He dumped it on the coffee table, sat on the worn sofa, examined the mailing label. It was made out to "George Bale;" he noted the inaccurate spelling, but the address was correct. There was no return address, nor anything on the outside of the box to suggest what lay inside.

He scrabbled and scratched at the thick wrapping without success, then fetched a steak knife from the kitchen and sawed through the brown paper and packing tape. Underneath he discerned the glossy sheen of a store-bought box, with words and photographic pictures. What was this thing? He dug deeper, finally extracted the contents. He could hardly get over it. This was a complete stereo music system, with a combination player for CDs and DVDs and BRs, with a built-in monitor to view videos, bulky speakers and quality headphones. It was all there, ready to go, and someone had sent it to him.

Bael—no fool he—realized that a mistake had been made. Having poked among the Styrofoam and leafed through the documentation, without finding any personal message, he could only guess that the parcel had gone astray, despite his clearly typed address on the label. Somewhere out there a George Bale was anxiously awaiting his gift or purchase. Of course it had to be that. No one in the world would send George Bael such a present, and he, even in a tipsy fit, wouldn't be so stupid as to order an expensive item of this kind. It ought to go back where it came from. He ought to send it back. That was the right thing to do.

Now, that wasn't the easiest thing to do, now was it? Return to sender was all well and good as a notion, an ethical stance, but since he didn't know who the sender was, or where he was, it wasn't something he was morally required to worry about. Bael had done no wrong, nor would he, regardless of his actions. As long as the stereo remained on his property, he would take good care of it. If the postman showed up tomorrow demanding the package, it would be here waiting for him.

On the other hand, what if the postman didn't come for it, ever? Bael popped open and swilled another beer while he turned over the possibilities. It might be that he was stuck with this fancy system, and would have to make the best of the situation. Could he tolerate that eventuality? It seemed to him that he could. It seemed most likely.

He still made do with his crummy old record player, for God's sake; a turntable which didn't always spin at the right speed any more, and therefore didn't even play his ancient, scratched up LPs adequately. Nobody listened to records nowadays. Why should he? It shamed him to be so far behind the times. That was immoral.

He couldn't shake the feeling that he was owed this prize. Though it came to him by mistake—that had to be—it nevertheless belonged to him, if for no other reason by right of possession. He worked very hard, he never got his just due, life hadn't treated him fairly, and now this arrived to balance the scales, just a little bit. That was true justice. He deserved it. It could make a big impact on his lifestyle.

Just to play it safe, he didn't touch the thing again for almost three days. Then he took a deep breath, declared the stereo system his personal property, set up the machine on top of the chest of drawers in the bedroom. He hiked to the local music store and bought himself, on credit, a hundred dollars worth of music and movies, enough to get him started. He couldn't afford them, but it was worth the splurge. It took him a while to figure out how everything functioned—the remote control with its myriad of non-intuitive buttons proved tricky—but he got the hang of it. He stayed up way too late entertaining himself. He hadn't had such fun in years.

At work he bragged about his new acquisition, for which, so he claimed, he had long saved. No one seemed greatly impressed, but it felt good to tell them all about it. He was willing to bet that none of them had such a quality system. At least they now knew he owned something that wasn't garbage.

Two weeks after the arrival of the package he returned home from work, as usual. These days he looked forward to this moment more than he used to do. Lingering concerns about a claimant for his stereo turning up had faded. In the gravel parking lot he noticed a car which surely didn't belong there: a magnificent foreign sports car, low slung, enamel black and chrome, an absolutely beautiful specimen, apparently brand new. Somebody was moving up in the world, though it couldn't be anybody dwelling in this hole. It must belong to a visitor, a smug, rich relative come to gloat at a tenant's expense.

He checked his mail, gathered the few envelopes and a small cardboard box, and went up to his room. Over dinner, listening to music cranked up as loud as the neighbors would stand, he sorted the incoming

63

mail. Some went into the trash, one he set aside for future payment, and the little carton he saved for last. It was addressed to "George Bail," with no other information provided. This could be anything, a free sample, some kind of sales gimmick. He opened it with a sense of bored indifference, picking with one hand while he used the other to spoon mouthfuls of canned chili. He saw within a wrapping of printed paper, and heard something jingling underneath that. He pulled out the paper and, with a clicking together of metal parts, two keys on a ring tumbled out.

They looked like car keys. That was what they looked like—Bael had owned a couple of cars along the way, so he recognized the tell-tale signs—but he could scarcely credit this. It occurred to him that they might be plastic replicas, part of a dealer's promotion, intended to lure him to the sales floor. The satisfying clink of metal belied this explanation. He read the inclosed document. It described him as the owner of a car, a sports car which sounded very much like the one currently parked incongruously in the dirty lot.

He didn't take action right away. He waited until it grew dark, when no one else could see him clearly, before he crept downstairs to the car. It took him forever to find a flashlight, and the batteries were weak, but it served. Despite his incredulous imaginations, he was shocked to find that the license plates matched the number on the form, and shocked further when the driver's side door yielded to a key. He sat in the driver's seat, motionless, as if in a dream, staring through the tinted windshield. Then he opened the glove compartment. He extracted the bundle of documents, leafed through them. He saw his name, correctly spelled. He snapped shut the glove compartment, exited the car with the documents, locked it, ran back to his room. He didn't breathe freely until he was alone inside, poring through the ownership papers.

No one ever reads every word on every sheet contained within a car's glove compartment, but that evening George Bael did. There was no question about it: the car belonged to him. The papers told nothing of the how and the why, but there was the official registration, made out precisely in his name. What is more, it was his free and clear; the records established that it had been completely paid off. Even the insurance was covered, for a month. He was now the astonished new owner of a new car, and such a car as he could not have expected to own in a lifetime of scrounging. It didn't seem possible.

Yet it was possible, and it was so. While he hadn't received the best education available (he attended a public school, after all), he knew a thing or two, possessed a certain native intelligence, and he was quite capable of connecting and rationalizing two similar, unusual events. This was the stereo all over again. It wasn't a mistake. He had a fairy godmother. A mysterious benefactor was buying these things for him. It was like something out of a movie, something that happened in a story book rather than real life. This was real life, though, and it was happening to him.

Had he ever done a big favor for anybody important, or powerful, or rich, somebody in a position to reward him in such a manner? He couldn't think of anyone, nor could he understand why it should be a secret. If someone owed him—owed him more than twenty bucks for beer money—why not come out and say so? Perhaps the great and the wealthy didn't work that way. He wasn't inclined to pursue far this theme; he wasn't about to look a gift horse in the mouth, and he feared the consequences of probing too deeply. Suppose he learned all, and in the process lost all? Better to accept largesse as it came, than to rock the boat.

He took the car out for a drive. He hadn't owned one in years, but he had been sporadically at the wheel, and it was like they said about riding a bicycle; one never forgot. He cruised into the darkness, through the city streets, then up onto the highway and out of town. The vehicle handled flawlessly. The engine purred evenly, regardless of his speed. His unknown benefactor had thoughtfully included a full tank of gas, so Bael was prepared to test drive right through the night. He pushed the pedal to the floorboard and rocketed onward along the empty road. Almost empty, as it turned out; flashing lights and screaming sirens informed him that he had company. Fear seized him as he slowed to a stop. Did the fairy tale end here?

He got a speeding ticket, his first in ten years, but it was all right. The policeman delivered the standard sneering lecture, and pointed his fat finger, but everything was in order. This car belonged to Bael, a fact which the authorities did not dispute. It was almost worth the sickening fine to find that out. He returned home, at a more moderate rate of speed, thoroughly contented. He was happy.

He didn't go to work the next morning. He called in, made some lame excuse, his boss took it badly, Bael didn't care. He would sort that out later. He spent the day driving. He drove everywhere. He would have driven to the bathroom if he could. By the end of that first full day he had exhausted the tank of gas. Filling up indicated to him how expensive his new toy would be. He used his credit card, and would continue to do so, until the bill came round. Then he would worry. Besides, that was a sound way to gauge the level of expense. It got him off the hook now, and it was a smart move; the best of all possible worlds.

No longer did he take the bus to work. He didn't bother trying to explain himself to his so-called colleagues. He revealed the car to them, and left them to puzzle out the fact of its existence as best they might. Some made unkind comments as to how he could afford such a splendid vehicle, suggestions of illegality. He presumed they were joking, although one could never tell with those jackals. The comments persisted beyond what he considered amusing. They were jealous, he reflected.

Bael didn't spare much reflection on the source of his rise in the world. Someone felt good thoughts toward him. Someone wanted him to find a little enjoyment in life. Someone was in a position to make it happen. Beyond those obvious conclusions he didn't trouble himself to think. He tried to imagine the sort of person who would do such things for him, but that didn't get him very far. He pictured a wizened old man, filthy rich, childless, alone in the world, a man who had dedicated all his years to acquiring money, and who, in his waning years, sought to comfort one of his fellow men. Perhaps the benefactor had chosen his beneficiary at random, out of the telephone book, or perhaps he had researched the matter, found Bael especially needy and deserving. It could be. How to tell? The gift giver could present himself whenever he chose, if that was part of the plan. Bael didn't require it. The old man might be on his death bed, desperate to spread happiness, maybe to console himself for a cold, soulless career. If so, Bael hoped the old man lingered a while longer. It had occurred to him that the material miracles might not yet be over.

One thing was certain: he felt no further qualms about accepting the gifts. It was right, it was proper to accept them. He deserved this. By the squalor of his life, he had earned these rewards. It crossed his mind that he had earned more.

Exactly two weeks after the appearance of the car Bael received an important-looking letter in the mail. He had wondered about this particular anniversary, and noted with chagrin that no package awaited him. Well, all good things have to come to an end. The letter didn't promise much; it was something official from his bank. "Please read immediately" was stamped on the envelope. Nothing from his bank could be welcome news. Either his account was overdrawn, or it had dropped to an inadequate level. It wouldn't be the first time. How much would this cost him? His monetary outlays, even off the charge card, had soared alarmingly in recent times, what with gas and more music and movie discs. He simply couldn't help himself. He finally opened the letter with his other mail.

He read what it said. His bank chose to inform him of an electronic transfer into his checking account, in the sum of fifty thousand dollars ($50,000), available for his use as of this moment. His head swam, vision blurred; the words and the figure flowed and shimmered before his eyes. It had happened again, after all. He was once more the beneficiary of unexplained kindness, on an even greater scale. The mysterious donor's generosity continued to escalate, and Bael could hardly contain himself. He felt weak at the knees, a suffering from the dread malady of gift inflation.

The bank included a copy of the original transfer authorization. It provided no information on the giver, which by this time was to be expected. He spotted the sure sign of his benefactor in operation: the transfer was made out to "George Beel." It started to sink in that the great unknown one possessed a subtle sense of humor. Or was he covering himself? If something went wrong, did the mystery man want to be able to claim a mistake? Bael wracked his brains, again, but could not fathom the meaning of it all. He did note that the transfer document got his Social Security number and account information correct. Despite the game-playing with his name, no chances were being taken.

If not for his unbounded glee, he might have felt frightened by what was happening to him. Now, on top of everything, he learned that someone had access to his private information. Only with such knowledge could his benefactor pull off this trick. Bael couldn't complain, under the circumstances, and he would keep his doubts to himself, but he did wonder. One day, when it was all over—hopefully years from now—he trusted that the full story could be told.

That lay in the future, if ever; the present consisted of fifty thousand dollars, figuratively burning a hole in his pocket. Of course he must verify the transaction, which he did the following day, during his lunch break. It was for real. Then he returned to work, told his boss exactly what he thought of him, called certain choice people every name in the book, quit with a flourish and stomped out, never to return.

That afternoon and evening he blew eight hundred bucks on a fine meal and assorted goodies which he bought all over town. He picked up a new television, a blue suit and black shoes, a tie and new underwear. He would think of other items later, but he didn't plan to run hog wild.

Though his bank account had been topped off fulsomely, he knew it wasn't a bottomless pit. The money would make an enormous impact on his lifestyle, could be liberating, if he considered his options carefully.

At a normal rate of expenditure, fifty thousand would last him for two years or more. That constituted two years of freedom during which he could better himself, break out of the iron grip of lower middle class life. What did he want to do with himself? What were his fondest dreams, the kind of dreams that most men his age surrender to the corrosive demands of reality?

All his life he had dreamed of becoming a painter. That had seemed to him a classy way of making a living, of being somebody. He used to amuse himself with the idea, even though the stark demands of necessity appeared to preclude it. Now he could do anything, for a time, with no depressing, degrading job to pull him down as it gobbled up his productive hours. He hadn't actually painted a picture—or even drawn one—since he was a kid, but with plenty of leisure at his disposal, and funds for quality supplies, he could take a stab at it. To make it work, to give himself every chance, he needed the proper surroundings. He must escape from his dump of an apartment. That place was, as the job had been, psychologically debilitating. He had long known that he could never realize his true possibilities in such a setting. So, he must find himself a new dwelling, one which appealed to his aesthetic side. The thought called forth images of another old fantasy: a house in the woods, far from crowds, a quiet, cozy spot where he could find peace, be his own man, learn to create as a bohemian artist. It was a good idea. It made sense. With the money at his command he could lease a little cabin for a year or two, live simply, prepare, study and experiment, and—if fate stood up for him—attain a goal which would unleash his talents and justify his efforts.

Bael played it safe. He didn't charge out into the wilds right away. He had to stick around for a while, as much as he longed to rip into Harper and that old bag of his, and storm away. First he had to pick up his last check, money due him, which gave him a chuckle, however. Not long ago that pittance had meant everything to him. Then he began poring through the free real estate guides available at the supermarket, looking for a choice rental property. It shouldn't be fancy, but it had to offer him the basic requirements underlying his scheme. Above all else, he felt that he must hang on for another span of two weeks, in case, as seemed likely (though he dared not speak the thought aloud, lest he jinx himself), his secretive benefactor struck again.

THE BENEFICIARY

On the appointed date, the box arrived. During the preceding fourteen days Bael had looked into several promising sites for relocation. He enjoyed driving to his prospects. Quaint little cabins among the pines tended to come dear, and he was very careful not to exceed his anticipated means. One unit, a rustic one bedroom on the mountain slopes far north of town, struck him as satisfactory on all counts. The owner seemed overly concerned about Bael's credit rating, so the would-be lessee had to emphasize his willingness to pay the rent far ahead, in cash. Also, he begun purchasing art supplies. He was serious about that, and therefore saw no reason not to stockpile paint, canvas, paper, and brushes. Those could be pretty expensive. His artistic idyll might not last as long as he wished, unless the unknown came through for him once more.

The benefactor had done so. Bael thanked the man, woman, god, whoever it was. It was a relief to know that his crazy luck still held. He hadn't been sure there would be another round. After all, what could it be? He had the stereo, the car, the money. What next; more of the same? It might be a house this time. That would be a logical extension, one that would make life even easier for him.

He received the new gift, in a square box, a little more than a foot on a side, addressed to "George Ball." There was that sly humor, that congenial playfulness. The guy must be a charming fellow, in his odd fashion. The box felt heavy as he carried it up to his room. It felt like the weight of metal. If metal, why not gold? This had to be a bigger deal than the last. That was the pattern. Gold then, something extraordinarily valuable; to keep, to sell? An ornament wouldn't help him, and his benefactor clearly wanted to help. This had to be something really good.

He tore off the wrapping. He found an interior surface of polished, lacquered wood. It opened only at the top, via a brass ring. This looked like the best yet; the anticipation was dreadful, and delightful. He crooked two fingers under the ring, and pulled. The lid of the box rose easily. Bael had just enough time to view the contents—a long second— and to understand what was inside. A sense of humor?—

The bomb exploded.

Had he survived, George Bael might have admitted that the final gift made a huge impact on his lifestyle. It is doubtful whether he would have thought it right and proper. It is altogether unlikely that he would consider himself to have deserved it.

Cathedral Rock

In the ancient times, before there were any men, in the elder days when the world was young and, as yet, untenanted by any living things, the great white flame roared down from the heavens. The vast ball of streaming brilliance crashed into the new and tender crust of the Earth, sending inconceivable masses of molten rock, debris, and gases into the thin air. When the smoke cleared and the dust settled, a gigantic hollow remained, a massive sunken crater thirty miles wide, surrounded by a titanic ring of broken, steaming mountains. Within this huge bowl, so suddenly gouged into the land, there rose only a single spire a mile high, an awesome pinnacle of ugly black stone.

Ages passed—billions of years—during which the desolate planet changed. The oceans trickled out of the heaving, earthquake-torn mantle, and from these oceans oozed the first simple forms of life. These forms developed over eons, until the Earth throve with life. It teemed, across its surface, with biological forms of incredible and increasing diversity. At one time or another, every square inch of the planet felt the footsteps of life.

Nay, for the longest time there was an exception: nothing lived or grew in the great hollow. Nothing that entered that domain could thrive, nothing that settled there could live for long. Terrible things happened to all creatures that tried. The ancient crater stayed primordially barren. Something lurked there within the violated ground which was not compatible with the fragile flora and fauna which should otherwise have flourished there.

Over countless millennia the world changed. Mountains rose, fell; the seas advanced, receded; the very continents shifted. During one forgotten era the hollow vanished beneath the waves. When it reemerged, during the reign of the giant reptiles, as the warm shallow sea dried, the age-old hole appeared with a new cap of bloody red across its northern expanse. The waters had deposited millions of tons of bright sandstone upon the hostile face of the crater. The dark pinnacle of black stone, too, had acquired a fresh covering of a startling red hue.

71

SCIENCE AND SORCERY

The world changed again, and the legendary monsters went away, and one day, long afterward, the first men appeared. In the fullness of time they journeyed to the seemingly eternal hollow, and one day they came to stay. Here they would live. How could that be, in this place where nothing could live? Much else had changed. The new layer of sandstone crust served to subdue or mask the fateful emanations from beneath. A river now ran year round through the hollow. The river induced fertility, and wherever the water flowed, there sprang green plants, leafy trees, and edible herbs. The ancient crater assumed the aspect of a verdant valley. The animals had swarmed in and found the land beneficial, and after the final age of ice so had man.

It was the red man—the American Indian, as he would one day be known—who initially colonized the valley, at first a trickle of settlement which swelled to denser numbers as the population multiplied. Generations passed, births and deaths; the Indian families grew into bands, the bands merged into a tribe who came to call themselves the Yavapai; and in time they became known, from the old stories passed by word of mouth, as the primordial masters of their valley, fated to dominate it forever.

Certain of the old stories linger from the prehistoric times, when the Yavapai dwelt in what some like to imagine a natural paradise. Paradise it was not, but prosper they did, for they lacked no necessities, and were so well settled in their home that they built permanent stone houses and reared great pueblos with granite towers, a style of life which could be termed barbarous, and yet far removed from that of their desperately roaming savage neighbors. In their moments of leisure they told tales of themselves, and while the stories lost much in the telling, they gained much as well, through the ages. The most interesting tale concerned a specific location in their kingdom, a location they considered the most wonderful on earth.

They referred to the former site of the singular black spire, which had been worn down through the ages and grown a thick mantle of fresher sandstone. Though it had lost much of its mass, it still towered high above the surrounding countryside, and its striking red cap, hundreds of feet thick, had crumbled and collapsed into a visually stunning array of titanic blocks and slabs. Around this impressive natural monument the Yavapai wove their curious legend. This place, they said, was an abode of the gods, where the supreme deities came down to speak with those privileged men who adored them.

The local Indians called the red tower Tobai-Tolomay-Ignata, or

CATHEDRAL ROCK

"House of the Great Ones Who Speak to Their Chosen," as one might freely translate. According to the Yavapai, the voices of their gods could be heard calling from the mighty peak, and men, the wise and the strong, could climb to the top in order to respond and converse. Many did so through the years, seeking boons from the masters of the world, or hoping to bask in the presumably healthful glow which must radiate from or reside in the vicinity of the Great Ones.

It must be said that their gods were harsh gods, and that most of the recorded pronouncements from those wonderful beings took the form of stern demands. The people believed, accepted, obeyed. The gods required that animals be driven to the site for sacrifice; this was done. They ordered that war be waged upon the neighboring tribes, and that choice captives be sent up for similar reasons; this was carried out. In time the gods insisted upon greater numbers of human sacrifices, without concern for quality, sex, or age; this too the believers fulfilled. Eventually the medicine men brought down from the mountain unanswerable demands for yet more sacrifices, and since the surrounding tribes had been decimated or driven away, the favored ones must be acquired from among the Yavapai themselves. Once again they obeyed—for all such commands were in accord with the nature of their ultimate deity, the omniscient and all-powerful Xenophor—and during the years to come the gods were honored or nourished by the lives of their stoutest worshipers.

Even within the context of the legend, one may ask what the Yavapai gained from such devotion. Their history, as it can be reconstructed, indicates that they fell upon hard times. The population of the valley dwindled. The tribes beyond shunned them, killed them when they could. Trade ceased. The great stone pueblos crumbled from neglect; there were no longer sufficient people to maintain them. Eventually came the great civilizational collapse. Warring parties from outside the valley intruded and destroyed or chased away all that remained of the once proud and terrible Yavapai. The survivors still dwell over the southern mountains in the Prescott region, and they still tell their strange stories of the old days.

When the white settlers began to arrive they knew little of the tales of the Yavapai, but they knew promising land when they saw it, and during the latter Nineteenth Century their towns began to spring up in what they called the Verde Valley. The natural beauty of the Red Rock Country intrigued them. One location, more than most, impressed: the great monument the Indians had called Tobai-Tolomay-Ignata, and which the pioneers, having learned a smattering of local tradition, chose to designate Cathedral Rock.

Visitors would pause to stare at its glory; one man elected to assume it for his homestead. A Mr. Thaddeus Morgan raised a trim wooden house on its upper slopes, right under the craggy stone cap, for his family and himself. He had all the water he needed from nearby Oak Creek, and he admired the amazing view from the site. This occurred in 1878, according to the records of what became Yavapai County. Mr. Morgan and his family, sad to relate, did not prosper in their new home. It seemed the land close by the peak was not so fertile as could be desired or expected, and other problems arose while he tried to make good on his dreams. He failed disastrously. The crops planted by Mr. Morgan grew inappropriately, if at all, producing no marketable bounty. His livestock dwindled in numbers faster than he could purchase new animals and, incidentally, the hunting was always poor in his area. His family grew reclusive, callous, strange. They spoke of hearing voices. Mr. Morgan, a stalwart Christian gentleman, became by degrees ever more pious. Then he slaughtered his wife and children, subsequently killing himself.

After that no one chose to live on Cathedral Rock. In later decades, however, the population of the region boomed, and the tourists made their way in droves to the Verde Valley and the spectacular Red Rock Country. Cathedral Rock proved a powerful draw, especially for one class of visitor, a class so taken with the site that large numbers of them came to stay, settling in the burgeoning town of Sedona.

These people, the children of the "New Age" as they styled themselves, began pouring into Sedona and the surrounding countryside some decades ago, during the Sixties, when fresh ideas were as welcome and plentiful as they were cheap and lacking in quality. After their curious fashion they deduced the existence of strange and magical properties in the Red Rock Country. Now, it soon turned out that no feature of presumed mystical import attracted them as did Cathedral Rock. Before long popular rumor maintained that a great vortex of psychic power resided at its summit, and to that spot the great pilgrimage began.

The results were interesting, although not taken seriously at first. Many true believers spoke of the sense of "Oneness" they discovered there, while others referred breathlessly to the insights gleaned from inner conversations with the spirits of the place. According to the New Agers, at Cathedral Rock the gods of old, the real rulers of the universe, talked back. They also, it seems, made suggestions. The odd sub-current of mental obedience which marks such people led them to say and do many unusual things. A statistically impressive number of them went mad, and a distressing portion of those committed freakish and unspeakable crimes. The crimes tended to center about the ancient red tower.

For years this trend was treated as an unfortunate by-product of demographics. Then the National Forest Service, in its wisdom, decided to erect a visitor center at the summit of Cathedral Rock, just under the gigantic sandstone formations. There would be on site a permanent staff of rangers who could cater to ever larger numbers of paying tourists and local pagans. That sounded like good policy, one the taxpayers would approve. The center, despite the location which made construction an immense chore, opened on schedule. The effort was praised in all the newspapers.

Then, after scarcely a month of operation, came the shocking tragedy. The center, as hoped, proved popular. People came in droves, and many—very much against the rules—wished to camp out around it. The Forest Service personnel loved their work; after a few weeks on the job, they never wanted to leave. Taken together, this group certainly seemed to be a happy bunch. That being the case, it came as rather a surprise that one dark December evening, just before closing time, the unthinkable happened.

There were no survivors. Given that sad fact, much reconstruction of the crime scene remains guesswork, but it appears that the staff instigated the deed. They killed all of the visitors present—twenty-three of them all told—gunning down most, stabbing to death the rest. Before the night was out the staff had killed themselves as well, some of them opting for rather inventive means, but before their collective suicide they did something more with the bodies of the slaughtered. They used the corpses, in various incised, excised, or mutilated forms, as part of a weird, fiery religious ritual. A big ring bonfire was built, and the human remains were strewn according to a geometric plan throughout. Strange engravings on stones, some of them actual Indian artifacts, were discovered scattered about. The five rangers were found in a circular huddle nearby, dead, naked, their skin gashed and slashed, these wounds being quite apart from how they had chosen to destroy themselves.

About the criminal investigation little need be said; the standard authorities could not fathom what had happened. They sealed off the site indefinitely. More pertinent is the unexpected sequel. The Forest

Service, in league with a prominent private Phoenix college, called in an expert of sorts to look into the matter. This man, Professor Anton Vorchek, had devoted his life to the study of weird and esoteric subjects. Despite an unenviable reputation—many of his colleagues would have nothing to do with him, considering him a pseudo-scientist of the rankest variety—he the authorities selected to investigate, to report, and to act.

His methods were peculiar in the extreme. He began by visiting the massacre site, then withdrew for weeks to immerse himself in geological journals relating to the area. Having learned all he could in that quarter, he dived headfirst into the anthropological lore of the region. From these sources he acquired, in considerably greater detail, the knowledge set forth earlier in this essay. Then he returned to Cathedral Rock, bearing with him machines and meters commonly employed by physicists.

Professor Vorchek discretely announced that he had discovered an incredible source of mysterious power emanating from deep beneath the picturesque formation. Its properties puzzled and fascinated him; it did not stream steadily, but rather pulsed and throbbed in what he described as a purposeful fashion. He went so far as to call that fashion "intelligent." For reasons that no colleague could accept, he chose to connect his findings to the prehistoric myth of Xenophor, making daring comments about "His eternal minions." He then left again, only to return one last time the following week.

On this occasion he arrived with another machine, one of his own devising. What it was his companions could not understand, nor did he ever feel obliged to clarify the business. He did assert that his device, if all went well, should "significantly dampen major fields of controlled force," whatever that might mean. He demanded all of the electrical power he required, and he got it. A thick cable was laid to the top of Cathedral Rock.

Vorchek's machine swallowed up enormous quantities of energy. It's operation darkened the entire Verde Valley, brought Sedona to a standstill, adversely affected Flagstaff and Phoenix. He ran it for countless hours, taking measurements and readings at precise intervals. Then he shut it down. The task had been completed, he said. The dangerous power had been greatly suppressed, and severely localized in its effects. It could not be destroyed—such far reaching force, a force "festering within the fabric of creation", as he put it, could never be absolutely defeated—but with proper precautions it should do no more harm for long ages.   He advised that Cathedral Rock be placed permanently off limits to all but qualified researchers.

The Forest Service thanked him, paid him an astounding sum of money, and then sent Vorchek on his way. They accepted part of his advice. They rejected any idea of reestablishing the visitor center, but they did open Cathedral Rock to tourists once more; the place was simply too big of a draw. So tourists and believers once again make their way to the top, as sightseers or pilgrims. There have been no more shocking developments. So what if the very occasional visitor cracks and goes mad? The syndrome of mental disturbance, as it relates to Cathedral Rock, may still be statistically striking—cautiously worded stories still crop up in the local papers—but it has become much easier to ignore.

One may trust this state of affairs to continue indefinitely. Given what is known and not known, ask not for more.

Jacob Bleek On the Mountain

Hoary legend and wild rumor spoke of the mysterious mountain, located in the desolate wastes far from the abode of men, the mountain where on certain nights the Old Ones descended from Their fabled houses among the celestial spheres; where They fleetingly touched upon the world natural and mundane, for reasons which must remain Their own; and where a bold and learned man might meet Them at such times and greet Them, and converse with Them and share Their secrets; and to this place did go the famed and terrible sorcerer Jacob Bleek, a man most wise, learned, and daring, to the mountain he journeyed in order to seek the wisdom of the Old Ones, gather unto himself Their secrets, and thereby increase his own fame and perhaps the terror of his name.

This Bleek did do, traveling long and far across the interminable barren and blasted lands which shield the mountain from the eyes of the casual wayfarers. And on one chilly and moonlit night Bleek arrived at his destination, and beheld the stark and lonely mountain through a thin and smoky mist, and saw it framed against boiling clouds torn by upper winds and illuminated by the gentle radiance of the full moon. He saw this, and found it good and fitting, for it looked the sort of place he craved to find. Then he scaled the mountain. It was steep, and there were no pathways or other indications that mortal feet had ever trodden those slopes, and that he found good and fitting also. The going was hard and long, the footing difficult, yet he cared not for that. Physical effort counted for little, in relation to the rewards he stood to gain.

Toward the top, where a great stone mass loomed like a citadel or cathedral of granite carved over the eons by wind and rain, Bleek beheld the twinkling of brilliant lights, like stars fallen from the sky to the craggy summit. And he knew they were not campfires, for they moved, darting and drifting about the stone citadel, shimmering and winking like fireflies. These lights cheered him and hurried his steps, for he knew they must be signs of the Old Ones, who had come to the designated place and the designated time.

79

Near the top, beneath a sheer cliff of polished granite, Jacob Bleek beheld the mouth of a cave, from which a vast blocking stone had been rolled away to the side. From within there flowed soft yellow light, as if another full moon dwelt inside; and steeling himself, Bleek bravely strode into the cave, and there, as the wizard had truly expected, he did confront the majesty of those outer powers which lord over the earth and the universe, those who are the creators and the shapers, the masters of space and time.

And Bleek gazed upon the Old Ones, and shuddered; and though he still be young, from that moment, for all the rest of his days, he took on the appearance of one prematurely aged. And Bleek spoke to the Old Ones, and They spoke to him in return, and yet no words from Their voices graced his ears, for Their ways are not the ways of men in any respect; yet he understood Them, and They made Their views known to him. And Bleek asked of Them knowledge, all the knowledge of the heavens and the earth. And this, after Their fashion, they granted, in the strange cave high on the fabulous mountain.

The Old Ones revealed to Jacob Bleek all that had ever been since the beginning of time, since the Old Ones had founded the cosmos as amusement for Themselves. He observed, as if he were there to experience it, the formation of matter and the shaping of spinning galaxies and whirling worlds. He saw with his own eyes the rise of life on a billion planets, the appearance of intelligent beings, and the establishment of mighty empires, including those on his own world. He saw these civilizations rise, flourish, and decay. He beheld worlds of peace and plenty, planets of philosophers, at the height of their power, boiled away by exploding suns or crushed by hurtling comets. He relived his own life to that moment, this time as a spectator, and learned with distaste of the forces that had controlled his destiny.

Then the Old Ones, for Their own satisfaction, showed him all that was to come, all that was ordained and must needs occur, in all the remaining eternities of the universe. And what Bleek saw amazed him, for it was merely more of the same. Empires rose and fell, wisdom throve or did not, virtue triumphed or failed utterly; and he saw all the days that would be of his own long life, in great detail, living every moment as it was already written; for the book of the future, it seemed, had been already written, exactly as had the book of the past. Nothing could change a single line of their text. Of all things, this revelation pleased him the least.

And in time Jacob Bleek departed from the cave, and descended the mountain, with the laughter of the Old Ones ringing in his ears, although he heard it not with his ears; but he knew, regardless, that They laughed. He returned to the lands of men, sick at heart at what he had learned, for although he had learned everything, he had also found that such wisdom is without value. He had espied every fact of nature, yet had perceived no order, no plan, no purpose to existence. There was only blind struggling against an unmastered fate, the ceaseless waste of endeavor, motion without meaning. Even his unique, individual life—such great goals had the mage!—had been carved in stone since creation, and no matter how he strove, his life—so extraordinary, so removed from the crude wants of vulgar mortals—would never be anything more than what the ultimate powers had shown him. Those things would be, and now he lacked even the common joys of mystery which serve to tantalize and maintain the illusion of hope in common men.

What Jacob Bleek learned from the Old Ones on the mountain frightened him, and as he wearily departed he cursed them for what They had done to him; but what terrified him the most was his realization that the Old Ones cared naught for his curses.

At the Bottom of Montezuma Well

This is almost the end of the story: a dead man was found at the bottom of Montezuma Well. The well, so-called, is a large, extraordinarily deep and unusually round cavity in the earth, located atop a low, broad mound on Federal land, where it is protected by law due to the prehistoric Indian ruins which lie within the rim of the bowl-shaped hollow and on the desolate, semi-arid terrain nearby. The site is a popular destination for sightseers visiting the wonders of Arizona's Verde Valley. The ruins are picturesque, somberly redolent of age and decay, while the scenery of the locale is grimly attractive. The tourist, as he approaches by the winding country road, sees stark hills and ridges carpeted by cacti; mainly prickly-pear and cholla; parking at the public lot, he beholds the mound of red soil and crumbling sandstone swelling from the plain by Little Beaver Creek, a perennial stream along which stretches a narrow, fertile ribbon of lush riparian habitat, the haunt of many creatures struggling to survive in that inhospitable region; then, following a short climb, he reaches the summit of the mound, gazes into the unexpected depths of the well. The land drops sharply at the rim, revealing a circle of rocky cliffs, where the majority of the age-worn stone ruins are to be found, while far below, in the center of the regular bowl, lies water, a great pond filled by natural springs trickling out of the underlying limestone. The pond supports a variety of aquatic vegetation (extremely rare in those parts) as well as the ducks and other fowl or beasts that thrive in such surroundings.

The well, as a result of the pure water, greenery, and animal presence, is always an active place, and it is common to discern signs of life and motion in all seasons. It must, therefore, be understood that what, early one morning, drew the attention of a casual tourist was something markedly beyond the normal. This gentleman, along with his wife, descending the circling trail to the edge of the pond, snapping the occasional picture, observed an enormous quantity of bubbles surging up to the surface. This development meant nothing to him, but when the couple eventually returned to the parking lot at the base of the mound, he mentioned it to the ranger on duty. This official immediately checked for himself, and concluded that something curious was happening. He took certain steps, made certain contacts, and before the morning gave way to afternoon a number of his colleagues were engaged in investigating the phenomenon, which continued with slight abatement.

Using cables, pulleys, anchors and hooks, they grappled in the aqueous depths, caught hold of an object, hauled on their lines, dragged forth the dead man. So now they knew this was a case of death. All things considered, they didn't have too much difficulty identifying the victim, for there were copious evidences at hand. They deduced from the initial examination of the corpse that they were dealing with a young man in his early twenties, medium height, brown hair and beard. They entered an unclaimed car of older make in the parking lot, perused its registration, came up with the name of Mark Lindsey. The clothes of the deceased being fairly intact, they retrieved his wallet from the left rear pants pocket which contained, sodden but still sufficiently legible, the standard documents of a citizen, referring to a Mark Lindsey, aged twenty-two, five feet eight, hair and eyes brown. So it was him. The dead man wore hiking boots with tell-tale sole patterns; such prints were spotted leading into the mud at the water's edge. Fairly according to form, this might sound, if one were seeking to explain a drowning case.

This hypothesis, unfortunately, was not an option available to the investigators. Lindsey had not died of drowning; in fact, it proved impossible at the time to even guess at what might have killed him. They knew with certitude that he had been killed—had met death by violence—for, given the condition of the body, no gentler alternative was conceivable. It was hard to say just what had happened to him, although the physical details were clear enough to those who reported them. A large chunk of the head was missing, including all of the cranium and much of the face, leaving in front only the lower jawbone sporting shreds of bloody meat and wisps of brown beard. The shirt and remnants of what must have been a backpack were rent, revealing unbelievably torn and otherwise traumatized flesh, with slashes or incisions which cut right down to the bone or into the organs. Those who dragged up the body were disgusted to note that the thick pants, of a well known outdoors brand, were ripped open, and that the soft tissues of the groin were missing. They noted something more: the clothing and portions of the flesh bore signs of carbonization, suggestive of fire or some other corrosive agency. Everything about this evidence was odd, taxing their minds and their professionalism to figure out what had destroyed this

Mark Lindsey. No creature currently dwelling in the valley could have savaged him thus, while the indications of charring or corrosion were beyond comprehension. Of course they decided that they had a homicide on their hands.

Shaken and nonplussed by the accumulated evidence they surely were, no doubt about it, and they were sorely pressed to make sense of what they were seeing, so their leader back at headquarters put in a telephone call to Professor Anton Vorchek. This personage, an academic of hazy credentials and vaguely understood accomplishments, was nevertheless rather well known as a researcher into curious mysteries, a man with a good track record when it came to confronting unorthodox cases. The current situation qualified. The head ranger for the district, also the chief law enforcement official on those Federal lands, made the call, described the situation—it would be saying too much to claim that he explained it—asked for help. Vorchek replied, "Cover my expenses, and pay me a reasonable fee for my trouble, and I will cheerfully take on this case, which sounds most entertaining."

He arrived on the scene late that afternoon, racing up from Phoenix in a roaring scarlet Ferrari driven with hectic skill by his comely assistant Theresa Delaney. Professor Vorchek was himself an impressive figure, very tall and thin, sharp-eyed and hawk-nosed, with a manicured goatee and a cultured, faintly European voice, wearing a slouch hat and tailored overcoat; yet it was Theresa who first drew attention to herself, being a dazzlingly blonde and curvaceous beauty dressed to the hilt in ostentatiously expensive and loud blouse, skirt, and high-topped boots, appearing for all the world as the image of a model torn from a fashion magazine, and perhaps a slightly disreputable one at that. The men were eager to make her acquaintance, but Vorchek gave them no opportunity, for he quickly put her to work extracting an assortment of strange gear which had been cunningly packed into the tiny trunk of her sports coupe. She, with some muted grumbling, lugged most of it up the slope herself, descending into the well to deploy it while Vorchek stayed behind to question those present.

He asked if anything out of the usual way had been found in the car of the deceased. "Just this," replied a figure of authority, reaching into the passenger side of Lindsey's vehicle and removing an object. Vorchek accepted it from him, studied it briefly. "A well-thumbed paperback copy of *Aboriginal Legends of the American Southwest*, by Jonas Ellworthy. I have read it; standard stuff, though a worthwhile introduction to the subject. Still, it is most interesting that this connection should be made so readily. Yes, I have great hopes for this business." "You know something?" queried the authority figure. Vorchek chuckled and said, "I come bearing largesse of theories. My ideas, ever fresh and original, are my own, and must remain so for the time being. I shall explore, I shall test, I shall confirm; that is the method of science. When I know, I shall report."

Theresa called down that the instruments were all set, in accord with his instructions. Vorchek hastened up and joined her on the rim, where he spent time with a surveyor's stand, taking measurements of the well's dimensions, reading off numbers to his companion. Then he descended to the shore of the pond, where stood a very different device, a small, cubical machine on legs, with tiny antennae sprouting from the corners of the cube. He twisted dials, peered at the meter. Theresa remained above, nonchalantly enjoying a cigarette break, where the officers and rangers gathered around, unnecessarily introducing themselves and, incidentally, demanding to know what her boss thought he was doing. She had little of an explanatory nature to impart, saying only that "Professor Vorchek was a brilliant man, and if anyone could get to the bottom of the mysterious affair, then he would." In time he shouted for her, and she, growing tired of the customary blandishments she was receiving, rolled her pretty blue eyes and walked down to him.

"Professor," she cried as she came alongside, "this is an incredible waste of my day, and what's more, I can't help but notice that it seems to be a waste of yours as well. What have you to do with a boring police case?" "The legal angle interests me not," Vorchek assured her; "thus far your point is taken. Too bad about Mr. Lindsey, but these things happen, although there are peculiarities connected to his demise. Notice that there are still infrequent bubbles rising to the surface in that spot. If I did not know better I would speculate as to the possibility of latent geological activity, an upwelling of heat and pressure, and leave it at that. I do suspect a resurgence of dormant forces, but it is nothing igneous that I have in mind. You see, Miss Delaney, it is the location, the location itself, which fascinates me." "I don't see why. It's hot, and dirty, and muddy, with rocks and stickers and lizards. I like the ducks, but that's about it." "Ah, but haven't I ever lectured you on the subject of Montezuma Well?" "Not that I recall," Theresa replied, with a toss of her wavy hair, "but then you've lectured—that's the right word—lectured me about so much, and most of it, I'm happy to say, goes in one ear and out the other." "A bad habit, Miss Delaney; your education suffers. Do you see the reading on the meter?" "It's detecting something." "For that answer you get a gold star," Vorchek growled. "There is a definite, heightened energy field emanating from the depths of the pond. This is all for now. Let us return home and marshal our resources."

Before they took off he spoke again with the head man on the scene, who was much annoyed, for he had been told nothing by the dapper professor, nor was it apparent to him why the curious guest was there. Vorchek courteously requested that he be allowed into the late Mark Lindsey's lodgings at the earliest possible moment, in order to examine his personal effects. The official gruffly granted the request.

The next morning Vorchek and Theresa arrived at the door of Lindsey's abode in Flagstaff, a cheap apartment in a shabby part of town into which he had recently moved from out of state, taking out a six month lease; this information stemming from the local police, who were pursuing their usual formalities. They let themselves in with a key provided by the same men in blue, who had already searched the small dwelling. The place looked like a typical college student's pad, which it pretty much was: strewn, unwashed clothing, soiled dishes stacked in the sink. "What a dump," said Theresa. There were a few books scattered about. Vorchek immediately homed in on these.

"My feelers were twitching," said he; "I knew something unorthodox lay behind this business, and I was correct. Pay heed to these volumes, for they will tell us a deal." "I don't see anything that would get a man killed," Theresa observed. "These are textbooks, I suppose, on funny subjects, mythology and such, and a lot of Indian stuff. Maybe Lindsey had a big test coming up and couldn't stand the strain. Do you think, Professor, that maybe he committed suicide by tearing his own head off?" "Do not be absurd," replied Vorchek. He then snapped into his conventional lecturing mode. "Let us take these volumes one at a time. Note, for instance, this copy of Somervale's *Secrets of the Anasazi*. A scatterbrained work, to be sure, incorporating many false premises concerning that prehistoric race of advanced cannibals, yet possessing kernels of truth which might have steered Mr. Lindsey in the desired direction. Here we have *Crystal Magic* by Michael Burns; New Age popular rubbish, that. We will locate no wisdom there. Ah, but this: *The Ancient Worship of the Unnamed*, Bedlow's staid but surprisingly revealing tract from the 1890s. That could have been a gold mine of information for the deceased, as well as a trap, if he followed its implications too far. There was only one edition, and it was not in print

87

for long—where did Mr. Lindsey get this?—I see, from his university library. Such helpful fellows they are. Oh my, now look at this, Miss Delaney; this is what you would call 'pay dirt'. Our gentleman had read *The Primordial Vortex of the Verde Valley*, the amazingly cogent treatise by Mansell Murdock. The author has little understanding of the forces he describes—he gives too much lip service, at least, to public tastes and fallacies—but his research on fundamentals is sound enough, and he packs plenty of data that could be misused by the unwary. There is one item in particular that I recall—let me see—goodness, here it is, the page already marked. What do you think of that, my dear?"

"It's a map of the valley, obviously, but not a good one. The roads aren't even drawn in."

"It is not intended as a road map. See these symbols? They denote the locations of ethereal power centers. Here are two hard by Sedona, another just inside Oak Creek Canyon, still another by Jerome, and the last—over here—the last at Montezuma Well." Vorchek slammed shut the book. "That suffices for now. I must put through a call." He picked up the telephone, dialed, and when he received a response identified himself and asked by name for the chief investigator on the Lindsey case. Shortly a conversation ensued, in which Vorchek got to his point. "Is there still any sort of underwater activity? Yes, I mean the bubbles. Very good, sir; now, this is what you should do. I would regard it as a special favor if you would send down a diver, one equipped for a long descent. I recall reading that the well has been sounded to 120 feet. At a minimum, you say—that is fine—take the probable depth into account. I want the man armed with a camera that will shoot in water and murky conditions. Got that? Please, sir, no questions at the moment. I still consider this the exploratory phase. Well, hang the expense, man; get it done, and get back to me with the results, whatever they may be." He put down the telephone. "They are all alike, these bureaucrats. What say you, Miss Delaney, to some lunch?"

Knowing Vorchek's penchant for mystery, Theresa contained herself as long as she could, but over a dish of lasagna her natural obstreperousness finally broke out. "Professor, you sit there saying nothing, with a cutesie little smile, just like you always do when you think you're on to something. You spend your time, which you're forever telling me is so valuable, looking into a killing, and then all you do is poke through a bunch of flakey books and 'ooh' and 'ah'. Now you snap your fingers and order a diver just like you ordered our meal. What gives?"

AT THE BOTTOM OF MONTEZUMA WELL

Vorchek chuckled with smug satisfaction. "You know me, Miss Delaney; among your manifold charms is that of understanding and, I am assured, appreciating my ways." Theresa snorted, but he went on without retort. "It was the occurrence of the rather odd death at Montezuma Well that intrigued me, the place itself rather than the incident. To the authorities this is a brand new case, perhaps an accidental death, perhaps a murder, a sequence of developments which may have begun yesterday or shortly before. I suspect that this is merely the most recent in a very, very old chain of events—that we have come in at the tail end of something unimaginably ancient and sinister—events involving matters far beyond the purview of the police. If I choose to do anything, it will be to write the final chapter to a long and intricate story.

"Most of that story has nothing to do with Mr. Lindsey. He, I think, was an earnest amateur who blundered into a situation which he did not understand, and therefore could not handle. The police checked into his background last night, interviewed friends and acquaintances. He was a true believer of New Age poppycock, and like so many of that type he gleaned a weak fraction of the reality underlying the legends of the Verde Valley. A little knowledge, as the saying goes, in this case killed him."

"I surrender, Professor," cried Theresa. "Knowledge of what got him killed?"

"The fact of the Vortex did him in. You, see, the oldest Indian myths of which we have record—those dating back to before the Yavapai, before the Anasazi—speak of the 'Great Vortex', the mysterious source of cosmic power which forms a gateway of the Gods on Their journeys through time and space. These Entities, say the Indians, are the original Gods, the Old Ones, the Lords of Creation and Destruction. In the elder times, they claim, a period lost to antiquity, the first aboriginal settlers came to the valley, and they discovered the Vortex, and through their wise medicine men—often referred to as priests in the anthropological literature, but in those days taken for magicians— realized that it was a point of passage for these grim and powerful Gods, through which They come and go at Their pleasure from one plane or dimension to another. The Indians formed a cult centered on the Vortex and the Old Ones, worshiping Them reverently throughout the ages, offering sacrifices of game, corn, trinkets, and... of other things as well. It was a cruel religion, which is ironically fitting, for the honored Deities were cruel Gods, demanding much, impossible to satisfy. Certainly the

Indian tales suggest that no one ever benefited to any great extent from such obeisance. Those who dwelt in the valley suffered exceedingly from all forms of novel plagues, pitiful deformities, sudden deaths and encroaching madness. In time—before the Conquistadors arrived—the valley had been virtually depopulated, the pueblos abandoned and crumbling, given over to the gila monsters and black widow spiders. The cultists receded to the margins of the valley where, it may be, some still lurk.

"So much," said Vorchek, "for the old stories. Let me bring you up to date with the knowledge of science. There very definitely is something wrong with the Verde Valley, for all of the beauty to be found there and in the surrounding territory, which makes it overly attractive to settlement today. Despite all of the marvels of modern medicine, the morbidity rate there averages 11% higher than in the rest of the state; disease rates 17% higher; rates of madness—and I am speaking of crippling, raving insanity, mind you—three times higher. What deductions do you draw from that?"

"A nice place for a vacation, but you couldn't pay me to live there," Theresa concluded.

"Humor aside, that is just about right. There is a force operating in the valley, a subtle influence with long term, corrosive effects on organic life. Animals and plants, too, suffer in their fashion; unusual mutations have been observed by biologists, strange sproutings of new species that conventional theories do not adequately explain. This force is real enough, a kind of energy emanation or field detectable through proper instrumentation. I have measured it, as have others before me. It was once hypothesized to be a form of magnetism, but Hudin's geophysical studies effectively scotched that nonsense. The emanation is not one currently required by relativity or quantum theory; it possesses qualities of otherness.

Vorchek produced a ragged, yellowed sheet of paper. "This is my own copy of a valley site map, similar to that in Murdock's book. These points are the foci of the energy disturbance. This spot here is Courthouse Butte, traditionally the center of ethereal activity, the most powerful upwelling of the Vortex. The summit is inaccessible, which is a good thing, for it is sure death to go there. The red man never did—he knew to keep his distance—while in modern times his white supercessors, those who have attempted to scale that ominous stone mass, have met with loathsome fates. There is no report of any man

90

completing the climb intact. These other locations may be considered lesser subsidiaries of power, which one may visit with caution. Montezuma Well is one. The Indians tell two stories about it: one, that they dug that huge pit themselves in a vain and disastrous attempt to reach the Gods; two, that one of their Gods burrowed up there from beneath the earth one cataclysmic night, creating the huge hole as He departed for parts unknown. It is possible to approach the well, as we have, although it can be, as Mr. Lindsey undoubtedly discovered, unwise to do so."

Theresa nodded. "I get it. So the Vortex force at Montezuma Well wiped him out. That's clear to me. It's something like gravity, only it pulls your head off."

"The Vortex itself," came the crushing reply, "would not cause that, although the consequences of meddling can be dire enough. I think, Miss Delaney, that a more concrete entity dealt so hardly with Mr. Lindsey. At this moment, I suspect, something alien to our world and universe lurks at the bottom of Montezuma Well."

The next morning Professor Vorchek contacted the authorities, to be told that the requested dive was shortly to commence. He spent an enjoyably lazy few hours poring through his notes, a pastime interrupted by the receipt of a warmly worded call informing him that something had gone seriously wrong at the well. Vorchek collected Theresa and they raced back to the site, where they found pandemonium and hostility.

This is what had happened. The diver, an expert in his line, a fellow who often lent his skills to criminal cases, had gone down, fulsomely accoutered, on the end of a line. He made his descent into the muddy, opaque soup by stages, with a strong lamp in his helmet to provide him with a few feet of vision. Eventually he and, then the light, disappeared into the depths. The line played out slowly, with many halts—there had come a very long pause, followed by another descent—then the curious bubbling had mounted in intensity, and the tough cable had jerked rapidly from side to side. After this the line spun out at an untoward pace for several yards, following which pressure abruptly ceased. Those above immediately reeled in the line, only to discover, when they hauled it to the surface, that it no longer terminated in a diver, but merely in a mess of frayed and fused steel cords. Much time was allowed, but the underwater expert never reappeared.

"This is all your fault, Vorchek!" screamed the man in charge. His men had evacuated the pit, none daring to leave the rim. "What goes on here anyway? None of this makes sense, and now I've lost a man, with nothing to show for it. Tell me, Professor Hot Shot Egghead, have you anything to give me yet? Are we ever going to get to the bottom of this?" "Events take their course," Vorchek replied haughtily. "Getting to the bottom was my idea. Fear not, for we have learned much. We have determined, as you must be aware by now, that the deadly menace lies below. With luck we can keep it there until it is banished. I shall set my plans in motion, and should be ready to dispose of this business by tomorrow." "I want it done today!" shrieked the man. "I want information. That's what you're for!" "As a being of individuality and intellect," Vorchek coolly rejoined, "I define my purpose. Confronted by a problem, I ask questions, derive answers, seek solutions. I am pleased to formally notify you that the exploratory phase is concluded. Confirmation of primary theory has been attained. I have summed up the situation completely, and know exactly what I must do. Tomorrow is the day of reckoning. Have your men here at dawn." With that he bundled Theresa into her car and they sped away from the startled and fuming group.

During the drive down to Phoenix, Theresa pestered Vorchek, distracting him from his silent thoughts. "It's a terrible thing that's happened," she observed. "I suppose," he mumbled, "and yet knowledge progresses, which is an unalloyed blessing." "I wonder if the diver would agree with that?" "Perhaps not," he said with a shrug; "however, since we should not expect to see him again, his opinion is moot. I, on the other hand, am literally crammed with ideas."

"I'm just like you," she claimed later, as they worked into the night. "I ask things, and derive something or other, and seek stuff so I can solve other stuff." "Then solve this one for me," retorted Vorchek. "I would if I could," she shot back, "but you're still holding out on me. What's down there, and what is it that you're doing about it?" They were ensconced in the back rooms of his creaky old house, located in the desert under the shadow of Castle Rock, where he maintained his private laboratory. This was an expansive room, brightly lit with the radiance of numerous dangling fluorescent lamps, more resembling a warehouse than a conventional scientist's study, for in addition to work tables, instruments, and tools, it contained great numbers of storage boxes, sealed metal cylinders, bloated packages, and an array of artifacts, animal, vegetable, and mineral, scattered throughout the available space. At the moment he was tinkering with, or actually putting together, a couple of exotic machines.

AT THE BOTTOM OF MONTEZUMA WELL

"I make ready my materials," said he, adding presently: " I have gotten to the bottom of the matter. Mark Lindsey, New Age wacko, ventured to the Vortex site at Montezuma Well with the intention of reawakening one of the Old Ones, the Gods, or a servitor of same, in what must have been his private search for enlightenment, or spiritual growth, or achieving oneness, or some such rot. As a result of his auto-didactic studies he learned enough to initiate the process. He called up, out of an unplaceable realm of being, a God, demon, or creature, and brought it to Earth at a geographical point where such transference is relatively easy. Unfortunately his consideration of the problem went only so far; he did not ponder how to control the product of his endeavors, nor how to send it away, nor—being the sort of loopy, wide-eyed fellow he must have been—did he wonder for a moment if what he called up from the extra-cosmic planes might not be altogether friendly to man, or whether it might, indeed, be rather an enemy to life and civilization as we know it. Mr. Lindsey read his own, all too human, values into a being unimaginably, unspeakably non-human, and that mistake destroyed him. The thing is still down there; we must send it back where it belongs."

"Can't we kill it?"

"I do not know that we can," Vorchek replied. "Hand me that wrench, will you?" He adjusted a bolt which bound together a tangle of electrical wires. "This alien presence, being of unnatural substance, may be immune to common weaponry. Consider that a distinct possibility. Also, He may have allies who would not take kindly to His destruction. I prefer to experiment in another direction." He grunted happily as he completed a metal armature. "I once met an elderly Indian, a shaman, as he was known, a big, important man in his way. This Tonipah proved one of my best informants when I was looking into the esoteric history of the valley. An incredibly old man he was—I have never met anyone so aged—and the way he talked mystified me. When he discoursed upon former centuries or legendary eons, he had this odd habit of speaking as if he had been there, witnessing and experiencing age-old events for himself. It was he who told me of the visiting God, a fearsome Deity the tribe called Yotakor, who was drawn to earth by way of a clever shamanistic spell, and finding Himself trapped in stone gouged out the well in His eagerness to escape or to terrorize the locals. Tonipah described it as a difficult time, a highly unpleasant episode in tribal lore, but the medicine men concocted a means of sending Yotakor away, and He never returned to walk among them again, much to their relief. That,

93

Miss Delaney, strikes me as the best avenue for success."

"These machines will do that?" cried Theresa. "They can do many things," said Vorchek. "This device here can maintain polarity, or reverse it; excite Vortex energy, or dampen it; open astral doors, or close them. If I have calculated correctly, this one will prove enormously useful tomorrow." "And what about this one?" she asked, indicating. "Ah, yes, Miss Delaney, that one; another of my specialties. That one possesses a unique 'pulling' property, you might say." "What does that mean, Professor?" "You wait and see."

At first light they presented themselves at the well parking lot, where a number of grim-faced men awaited them. Vorchek's nemesis strode forward, still wrestling with his fury. "This better be good, Professor," he snarled. "If you don't deliver, I've a mind to dynamite this filthy hole." "That would not likely serve," said Vorchek; "more likely it would exacerbate matters. In addition, your employers would frown upon such vandalism at a protected archeological site. It is against the law, I fancy." He went on, as the man sputtered, "Have your stout lads move my equipment. Take this one to the water's edge, emplace the other on the rim. Cooperation means speed, and I, for one, am ready for action." These activities were undertaken, with his constant supervision lest the manhandling damage the machines.

He stood within the well, on the paved trail which wound by the crumbling cliff dwellings, remnants of a former age. "Not just these, it seems," he mused absently. Theresa came up behind him. "Talking to yourself again?" she asked with mock concern. "Always, my dear, for I enjoy stimulating conversation." "I still see bubbles down there." "There must be more to see. I will speak with this fellow." They descended to where a ranger, accompanied by the quarrelsome authority, was standing by the strange, spidery contraption on the muddy, reed-choked shore. He addressed the chief.

"If it suits you, your man here can operate this machine himself. All he has to do is throw this switch when I call down with the word." "Where will you be?" the official demanded. "Farther up the cliff, with Miss Delaney, running the other machine. Think of it as a back-up, if you like." "Have it your way. Just get it done, and be ready to explain yourself."

"Miss Delaney," cried Vorchek, "to our station." They ran up the trail to the shelter of an Indian ruin below the rim of the pit, where his other machine—the one he had claimed could do so much—stood

94

perched behind a low limestone wall, looking like a radar dish atop an instrument panel on stilts. The rectangular panel contained a monitor screen which, when he turned it on, displayed sine waves and pulsating arcs of blue and yellow light. "All right," whispered Vorchek, as he fussed with knobs, "all systems are go. I believe we are ready. Pay attention, Miss Delaney, for unless I am totally off base, what is about to occur will greatly contribute to your education. Sir—yes, you there— throw the switch!"

The ranger did so. His machine hummed, sparks crackling from its flimsy appendages. He and the head authority jumped back, made as if to flee, but when the device did not explode they eased. It continued to hum and crackle, while a thin whining grew evident. Presently the chief scrambled up the slope to join Vorchek and his lovely companion. "So what's it doing, Professor?" he barked. "Keep your eyes peeled," came the response. "This ought to be fun."

The bubbling in the pond increased, eddies of white foam lathering the scummy brown surface. Suddenly great gouts of frothing commotion ensued. It was as if the water were boiling, such was the frenzy of the disturbance. The ranger at the machine edged away, his boots splashing in the mud. A geyser of reddish foam squirted into the air, playing like a fountain from the pond's center.

"Is this right?" shouted down the authority; he had already left the sheltered enclosure and was running up the path. "I think it is," bellowed Vorchek. "Hold on!" Then something incredible happened. A massive, amorphous humped shape broke the surface of the pond, rising up just above the level of the churning water, quivering with unearthly life. That it was something alive, or animate, there could be no doubt. Its main substance, perhaps skin, was gray, oily, vibrant with nervous impulses. Dull red trails like swollen veins snaked across it, seeming to move independently of the whole, and there was another feature, a large one, a bulge just below the broad, flattened hump, something yellow, clouded, and empty; it might have been an eye. "Will you look at that!" roared Vorchek from above. "Just look at it!" He and Theresa crouched behind their wall; someone fired a shot or two, with no discernible effect; the men above them on the rim turned and vanished from view; the ranger below stood dumfounded and aghast. The mud at his feet rippled and bubbled and popped, and wormy forms began to extrude about him. They sprouted from the mud, grayish cords like knotted ropes that twitched, writhed, waved into the air. Suddenly they darted at him very fast—he screamed, a sickening sound that caused Theresa to clap her hands over her ears—they fastened upon him, dragged him down into the mud, then somehow contrived to pull his wildly flailing form into the water, where he immediately slipped below the surface. The pond belched live steam and bright flickers of twinkling light where the man had disappeared.

"Amazing," muttered Vorchek, "absolutely amazing." Now he threw the switch on his machine. The device emitted a high-pitched squeal, and on the instant the nauseous gray blob leapt about a foot higher out of the water, its eye (or whatever that feature was) turned black and sagged into its body, after which the whole noxious mass sank back into the pond, leaving behind a furious popping of bubbles, which took a long time to subside. Vorchek twiddled dials and studied gauges for several minutes before he was finally willing to announce, "Our visitor has gone. I have sent It back from whence It was called."

Rather later, over a fine seafood dinner at one of the best Phoenix restaurants, Vorchek was saying to Theresa, "It truly has been quite a day. I gained a considerable amount of information, and perhaps a modicum of confirmation. It is fair to say that I established the basics of my theory, that an Entity foreign to our world, perhaps to our universe, had been drawn down into Montezuma Well by the foolish, if well-intentioned, Mr. Lindsey, and that, as the incident with the diver suggested, It remained, unable or unwilling to leave. The machine operated by the missing ranger was designed, of course, to attract the Being, and to bring Him into full view if at all possible. That aspect of the experiment was not entirely successful, but I received enough of a look to tell me that my informant Tonipah had related his ancient lore accurately. What we saw today may well have been Yotakor, legendary deity of the Yavapai. If such be so, I think I was only fulfilling my duty to mankind by sending Him on His way."

"That's what you were supposed to do," expostulated Theresa, "but I don't see, Professor, how the rest was necessary. You didn't have to bring Him up, did you? I, for one, could have lived without that cheery sight. Also, it ate the ranger, which isn't very nice at all."

"Oh, tut-tut, my girl; I should have known that you would raise that ancillary concern. We do not actually know that the fellow was eaten; he might have been physically translated or psychically absorbed rather than devoured. Regardless, the ranger's superior certainly made a big stink over it, the way he carried on after all was done. You would think that I had achieved nothing worthwhile, when it was I, and only I, who resolved the matter most satisfactorily. If the man had not hesitated he would have gotten clear, or at least had a fighting chance to do so, and what more do we get in this life? Think of him as a casualty to science, a martyr in the cause of knowledge. The net gain is astronomical. That being said, once the poor man had done his duty, it was time for mine, and I did it. Regretfully, the situation could not be allowed to continue. I ran the machine which opened a narrow crack in the dimensional scheme, and then thrust Yotakor, or His close relative, back into the extra-cosmic darkness, hopefully never to plague us again. It was all my doing—no one else could have done it—and that, my dear, is the end of the story, and a big deal."

Theresa thought about it for a moment, then returned to her blackened tilapia, mumbling, "Well, that's a good thing." "It is," agreed Vorchek, who paused likewise to savor a bite of grilled trout. "I have learned, and I have been paid. For what more could I ask?"

A Nature Scene

Professor Anton Vorchek and his lovely young companion Theresa Delaney picnicked in the scrubby stand of paloverde and stunted desert conifers at the foot of the big, bare ridge. "Keep duty in mind," he had sagely advised when she suggested the idea, "yet I suppose that we must eat." A warming sun beat down on them, but at this pleasant time of year afforded them little distress. He had brought her to this lonely, untrammeled spot in the Verde Valley of Arizona, ostensibly to improve her education, which he professed to find sadly lacking. Now they ate fried chicken, potato salad, and baked beans, washed down with raspberry tea, beneath the ridge upon which, far in the distance, at its highest point, stood perched a picturesque Indian ruin, a fortress-like survival from the harsh epochs of prehistory.

"Once this was a land inhabited by man," Vorchek observed between sips of tea. "This would have been a fertile landscape, teeming with farms and farmers." "I find that hard to believe," Theresa replied around a chewy mouthful of drumstick. "It's desert, and as far as I can see that's all it's ever been." "Not at all. In the days of the Anasazi and the Hohokam the valley was thickly settled. Something happened, and the people went away, and nature encroached again where man had driven her out. It was all very long ago, Miss Delaney, but it did occur that way. Do you wonder why?" "I guess I'd better, shouldn't I?"

"My dear," Vorchek responded gruffly, "of your inherent charms I could say much—one of my favorite topics, in fact—for they are legion, but they do not advance your knowledge one whit. You must pay attention, examine your surroundings, theorize. You are the student; consider this a lesson. I say that man has gone from this place, which is a mystery demanding solution, crying out for such, yet life still reigns here. Look about you, and catalogue what you see."

"I see plants and rocks." Vorchek urged her to develop the theme, so after a gastronomic pause Theresa blurted, "There are these trees, if you can call them that, and lots of little things I would call weeds back

99

home, with a few tiny flowers mixed in, blue and white and yellow; there are these drab gray rocks poking out of the ground, with some orangey-red ones scattered about, and quite a bit of orange dirt and dust; there's the ruins up there, where you can barely see them from here, and down below us something else under those cliffs across the way, that big brown patch; oh, and there's plenty of bugs flying around, too, several kinds I think, including bees, not to mention ants, which aren't flying; so there."

"Very good indeed," said Vorchek. "You sum up the basics nicely. There is actually a great deal here, thriving after its fashion. I brought you, and my equipment"—he indicated his bloated satchel case—"because there are mysteries attached to this locale, unusual features here worthy of analysis. For instance, these bees of which you speak. I have noticed them as well, have paid them close attention. I detect peculiarities. I will bet that you can, too, if you try."

Theresa stared, pondered, turned her pretty head this way and that as she tracked the flitting creatures. "Maybe they aren't bees after all," she shortly admitted. "They don't fly right, by which I mean they dart rather than cruise, and their buzzing is funny, too, more of a whine like a machine sound. Also, they aren't going after the flowers the way I'd expect bees to do; they seem more interested in this chicken, come to think of it. Get away, now!"

"They are not bees, or perhaps I should say they are not bees as we know them. They are a hitherto unknown species of carnivorous insect. Careful scrutiny of these 'ants' reveal other curious features. Instead of twin feelers, they bear one large antenna, held rigidly before them like a horn. Also—see that one, creeping up your arm?—they possess an unseemly, thoroughly improper multitude of legs."

"Yucko." Theresa brushed the thing off her creamy exposed skin. "Now, Professor, I might have overlooked that bee thing before, but I wouldn't always have missed the centipede ant. What gives? Are these oddball insects what you would call 'remarkable local adaptations?'"

"That would scarcely be an adequate answer. Biologists have passed through this valley in droves, recording species, noting strange types, losing track of them, then finding still other weird forms. You and I come to this especially out of the way section, and sure enough we find still more. The immediate solution is simple: these are mutations of a drastic and ongoing sort, occurring at a rate uncommon or, possibly, unknown elsewhere in the world."

Vorchek fell silent as he stuffed his pipe and puffed it alight. "The

100

typical evolutionary mechanisms," he said presently, "are not sufficient to explain what is happening here. Some kind of force is operating within these dreary, shunned expanses, an uncharted impulse which induces biological distortion to an incredible degree. I have been looking into the matter, collecting pertinent information. I am now convinced that whatever power rules here, it is not Darwinian." "God, then?" suggested Theresa. "If so," Vorchek observed, "then it must be an unconventional sort of god. Let us tidy our trash and move on, down to that brown patch of yours. There will surely be more to learn within its confines."

As they walked, pushing through the less dense sectors of scrub, she carrying the plastic cooler, he the satchel, Vorchek puffed on his pipe and continued to lecture. "What we approach is the great Tavasci Marsh, the only natural feature of its kind in the state. Subterranean water, bubbling up through unexplained pores and fissures in the earth—geologists assure me that the rock strata in these parts are all wrong for that—which allow moisture to seep up from below at a steady rate into this narrow, winding basin, a former bend of the Verde River. A unique environment, an enclosed ecosystem thriving in a unique place; that affords us majestic opportunities for study. To my knowledge, this watery haven has not been entered by trained researchers since the unfortunate Holbrook carried out his work in the forties." "What happened to him?" "He died of a cancerous, wasting disease, perhaps one contracted in this vicinity." "Professor! Shouldn't we clear out?" "Life is risk," Vorchek replied, as he tapped out the charred contents of his pipe against a boulder.

Viewed from its edge, the marsh appeared as a vast sea of cattails, an unbroken mass of rustling, wind-swayed stalks and germinating heads, with the skeletons of dead cottonwoods hugging the margins. Nothing resembling a trail led into it, so they beat a path with their boots and flailed belongings. The ground underfoot grew damp, then squishy and sucking with mud, until they came to a murky pool of standing, odorous liquid. Water striders skimmed its scummy surface. By the edge of the pool the cattails were crumpled, tottering and lifeless, forming a thicket of rancid decay.

"They grow heartily in the presence of a little," Vorchek pointed out, "but they can not stand too much of this water, and no other plants can tolerate even the slightest of tastes. I would not advise drinking this." "It never even occurred to me!" Theresa said warmly. "It's filthy stuff. Is there something in it, Professor, that's bad for plants?" "There is something unnatural in everything hereabouts," he replied. "I want to know what it is."

As they prowled by the side of the pool, which extended for the space of an acre or more, Theresa made a discovery which drew from her a startled squeal of dismay. It was a long dead, long rotten bird, tangled and held fast within the grip of a tightly constricted clutch of cattail leaves. So complete was the wrapping that the remains of the pathetic prisoner were hardly discernible; she had to have been looking directly at it to notice the grisly image.

"Amazing," cried Vorchek. He donned his reading glasses and leaned in for a close view. "Thank you, Miss Delaney, for calling my attention to this. I ask you to note the unusual segmented formation of these leaves, almost like fingers, and these minute, rubbery appendages intruding into the corpse. None of this is customary to cattails. Perhaps my eyes deceive (there is a first time for everything), yet I could swear that this interesting specimen of flora seized the bird in life and refused to let it go. The creature perished, obviously, and then; well..." Well, what?" "Still, to this moment, the cattail feeds." "Horrible!" "A fascinating mutation. I estimate that three genetic alterations could produce this result."

They tramped on through the marsh. Now that they knew what to look for, they spied many another hungry cattail trap clutching its desiccated prey. Small birds constituted the chief victims, although a matted clump of leaves and stalks low to the ground occasionally contained the bones, the withered flesh, and the dried fur or fragmenting scales of the lesser terrestrial animals of the region. "This place is disgusting," Theresa cried at last, as they peered into one more faux nest to find the telltale signs of untoward death. "Nature in action," Vorchek told her, adding, "though a perverted nature. I had noted the absence of avian species from an environment which should have been paradise to them. The reason is clear. As I say, there are powers at work here of which most know nothing, and I know little. It is time to correct that. Give me a hand."

Where they had crushed out a tiny gap in the cattails he set down his satchel, opened it, began extracting the contents and, with her aid, deploying them. What they put together, with much professorial instruction, was a spidery contraption, a cubical metal box atop a tripod, with a number of straight and curved antennae protruding from the box, which also bore a number of dials and switches, and a meter. Vorchek installed a large, flat battery into a back panel, then turned on the device with the flick of a switch. It hummed smoothly, the meter needle rose, wobbled, steadied upright. Then he twiddled knobs, whistling to himself as he did so. The strange instrument emitted a burping sound, after which the hum mounted in intensity, attaining an uncomfortable pitch. The needle swung sharply to the right.

"As I expected, Miss Delaney. I knew it, I absolutely did." "What does it mean, Professor?" "This is a special machine of my own devising," he informed her with smug pride in his voice, "which monitors esoteric energy frequencies." "Oh, well, I know that." "You knew nothing of the sort. I am telling you.

"It is thus so," he said in his best lecturing manner. "Physicists are fully aware of the standard universal forces which shape our world and the totality of existence—the fundamentals, you might say—such as heat, light, gravity, nuclear radiation. All of these can be measured via conventional instrumentation. There are other forces, however, not well described, often scarcely suspected, by science. These forces crop up only under unusual conditions or in specific circumstances. They do not appear to be universal, or at least have no apparent connection to the accepted, understood forces; yet they exist nevertheless within our cosmos, and the wise man, armed with masterful knowledge, keen insight, and an unbounded imagination, can deduce their presence and take steps to confirm them. I have deduced, I am now confirming. Observe my machine in operation."

"It makes noise, the needle points. I've got that. What's it pointing at?"

"Therein lies the solution to the riddle. There is an undescribed energy source radiating from that direction, either a weak source nearby, or an extremely powerful one at a farther remove. That force is the underlying principle behind this unique ecosystem. It is driving the frankly sinister biological changes which have affected this region, and I have good reason to think that it has done so for some time."

"Whatever it is," Theresa said, "it comes from that way. You're taller than I am. Can you see anything over there?"

Vorchek craned on tiptoes. "No; these pesky plants obscure everything. Heavens, what is this?" He reacted in such an uncharacteristically loud manner to the sound of something, seemingly large, crashing or floundering through the dense stalks from a point behind them, and apparently not too far away. Theresa began to expostulate, but her mentor held up a hand for silence, both of them listening as the ominous din appeared to advance ponderously toward them. "Our present situation appeals to me not," said Vorchek; "let us make for the high ground with due speed." In case she did not catch his meaning, he seized Theresa and propelled her roughly forward, then halted himself only long enough to haphazardly fold up his bizarre machine and bear it away, and within moments they were running desperately through the clutching cattails and the clinging mud.

They were both physically fit, so in no time at all, though suffering considerable anxiety, they reached safely the far shore of the swampy wilderness and climbed onto the rocky slopes beyond. From just a few feet of higher elevation they could gaze down upon the entirety of the Tavasci Marsh. The menacing sounds had receded, but from their present vantage they could detect, through the visible commotion of tall brown stalks, the track of something big creeping in circles through the area they had just vacated. As they watched a rounded, glistening, mottled back emerged briefly from the shaking leaves, then dropped down again, and shortly the indications of movement vanished beyond the more distant mass of cloaking fronds.

"I forgot my satchel," muttered Vorchek, "and my pipe has gone missing." "I dropped the cooler," said Theresa; "do you want to go back and get them?" "At the moment I have other issues on my mind," he replied. "I trust that my energy sensor did not suffer too much of a beating." He toyed with it for a time, until satisfied that it still functioned. His beautiful student waited impatiently for his attention, and when it did not come she tossed her golden hair and cried, "What was that thing, Professor?"

"Oh, I might speculate along certain lines," said he, with ill-feigned unconcern; "perhaps black bear, or elk, or a very large mule deer, maybe even a mountain lion. Sounds tend to be magnified in close terrain, and it is not necessary to assume that the creature was as enormous as it seemed to us."

"Are those animals native to this area?"

"Not especially; no, except perhaps the deer, which is the least likely of the bunch, I am afraid, to justify that ruckus. Indeed, I am hardly convinced that aural misinterpretation accounts for the phenomenon. Toward the end I caught a quick glimpse of our uninvited guest"— Theresa vociferously claimed the same—"and what little I saw did not wholly relate it to any of the possibilities I have thrown out to you. I conclude that, once again, we have confronted something beyond the norm."

"You're telling me," Theresa said vehemently. "It was another weird thing. I'll bet it wanted to eat us. Professor, I've had my fill of excitement for the day. This place is becoming dangerous to my health. If that creature had come out of the marsh after us, what would we have done, climb this cliff? We wouldn't have a chance. Let's call it a draw and get out of here. There's too much strangeness for my tastes."

"Rule Number Seven of Almighty Science," intoned Vorchek; "strangeness opens doors to truth. Identify the strange, isolate it, study it, master its secrets, and learn from it. There is no such thing as too much strangeness. I live for it. I have developed skills for ferreting it out and, so it often seems, the strange tends to seek me out as well."

"This time strangeness wasn't dropping by for a friendly chat. What are we supposed to do now?"

"Continue the never-ending research," he announced. "We make excellent progress. See, the meter still works, and still points in that direction. Let us head that way until we get a better view, and deal with whatever we find."

So onward they went, hiking under the cliffs that skirted the marsh, then clambering up the rugged ridge to the east. While engaged in this strenuous activity they had little inclination for conversation, so a long while passed before Theresa thought to ask, "Why do you think, Professor, that all these weird events have been going on for a long time?" "Serendipity, my dear, that infallible guide." "So you used, well, that?" "The dovetailing of disparate interests on my part," he translated, "which come together in a surprising fashion to illuminate truth." "I hate to suggest this," Theresa sighed, "but if you don't expound, I may miss a few minor details."

So he did. "Biologists have paid heed to what goes on out here," he said, "but their findings are constrained by the amazing variability of the changes occurring here, and their ephemeral quality. These things happen—they come, they go—it is virtually impossible to get a handle on these processes when the studies are so time-bound, merely slices of the moment in what is actually a lengthy and sweeping series of developments. In order to fully understand the patterns here, one must bring to bear a profound sense of history, which I, fortunately, possess.

"I have long examined the lore of the Indians native to this habitat, the aboriginal tales which date back centuries or more. The Yotipai in particular, who claim descent from the fabled and ferocious Anasazi, have diligently recorded (those who know little but talk much would say 'have merely concocted') and preserved an incredibly rich body of folk myth which they, naturally, consider verities. I have analyzed their legends, and among their discordant collections of heroic songs and wonder stories I have extracted certain nuggets of information which appear to impart genuine wisdom.

"According to my best informant, an elderly chief named Tonipah, who claimed, in some manner that I never quite grasped, to retain the perfect remembrance of ancient times, the Verde Valley has always been a land of strangeness and evil, from the moment the first tribal wanderers entered this precinct. Odd things happened here since the dawn of prehistory, if you will pardon the phrase, and many curious forms of worship, devoted to majestic and dangerous gods of unimaginable power, took root here. Tonipah styled himself a surviving priest of one such religion, a furtive and malignant cult which, I gather from his testimony, survives to this day in the more isolated portions of the region; like, for instance, where we tread now, perhaps. He told me, as fact, that the situation grew worse one terrible night after a great ball of fire roared out of the sky and crashed to earth in the valley, gouging the crater which is known today as Montezuma Well, popularly considered a common sinkhole. He said that this celestial object was a blazing steed which bore to the people—the devout Yotipai—a messenger of their highest god, he who is never named in any account, lest the bare mention strike down the foolish mortal who dares speak it. The messenger, a lesser being, could be named, and was called Yotakor, for some reason that made sense to the primitives. Though beneath the gods, he was still a being of awesome power and portent, and his arrival was thought to mark the beginning of a new era in the lives of the folk.

"So it proved, though the hoped for promise of the coming age turned out to be a burden rather than a boon. The known and routinely dreaded aspects of life in the valley took a dismal turn for all who dwelt there. Despite prayers, despite the demands and supplications of the holiest of wise men, the crops withered or they changed into inedible weeds, the animals went away or died or became horrors to behold, and abhorrent woes struck directly at the Indians as well. They grew sick and feeble from hitherto unknown diseases, and vile sores wracked their bodies, and their children were born dead or loathsomely deformed. Their numbers dwindled, until in time the tribal groups died out entirely or fled from the valley, no longer daring to live here, yet bound by ties of belief, so most of the pitifully few survivors came to dwell up on the Mogollon Rim overlooking their former homeland. Such are the stories of the Indians, and while one must be cautious when employing myth as a guide, I conclude that the old tales carry weight in this case. The Yotipai, as a thriving race, met an awful fate. The great pueblos were abandoned and fell into ruin. That big one we were able to observe on the ridge, a particularly impressive example, is one such. Anthropologists, to this day, formulate one hypothesis after another to explain what became of the rudiments of civilization in this part of the world. They write blandly of drought and warfare, but I think that I, by collating my several pet interests, have hit upon a surer answer."

"But what about all the white people who have moved in since?" asked Theresa. "Given what you say, we must be immune to these terrible effects. Nothing all that bad is happening to anybody now."

"These processes take time to fully reveal themselves," Vorchek replied. "We are speaking of events on a generational scale. In fact, disturbing signs have been noted since the late 19th Century, and in our own day public health officials are grown frantic with worry over certain morbid trends. Sickness rates, and those of unusual or unexplained death, are much higher in the Verde Valley than in the surrounding country, and problems of mental health have become so extreme that some researchers quietly speak of an epidemic of causeless insanity in these parts. I am afraid, my dear, that—as we may judge from the wildlife—something incredible is still definitely going on here, and man, God bless him, is not immune."

On they went, with Vorchek pausing occasionally to point out yet another oddity of the native wildlife. They came in time to a high point at the top of the ridge, from which they gained a spectacular view of the valley. From this point they could look down upon the sinuous marsh, now appearing small and distant, and the jumble of the aforementioned ruins beyond that. Farther still loomed the stark mountains denoting the southern edge of the valley, where the quaint town of Jerome perched on the steep and crumbling slopes. To the north ran a jagged line of lovely crimson at the borders of the famed Red Rock Country by Sedona. To the east, much closer to them, though still a far walk, rose another scrubby ridge, and atop that stood a single isolated structure.

"Could it be?" whispered Vorchek to himself. "Let me get my bearings. Yes, it can only be. That, certainly, is too much for a coincidence." "What are you leaving me out of now?" grumbled

Theresa. "One moment, Miss Delaney; let me try the detector." He set up his machine and operated it for a period, scribbling notes in his book.

"That is the Starrett house," he said shortly, indicating the little building on the next ridge. "I have heard of it, and of its former owner. Strange it is, how the connections fashion themselves, one link at a time, into a perfect logical chain. The energy disturbance emanates from that direction, and is mounting powerfully now. It is time we called upon Mr. Starrett." "But you said he's the former owner," cried Theresa, "so he's not there now, right?" "A figure of speech, child."

Vorchek insisted that they continue their expedition, which grew inordinately difficult, as they made their way toward the house. They scrambled down a steep, broken slope, walked gingerly for a span through a rocky dry wash, then, when the professor judged the terrain to be suitable, began huffing and puffing up the hill on the other side. It was not an especially warm day, but it started to seem that way to Theresa, who marveled aloud that her companion could undertake, and even relish, such effort. She was healthy, in the bloom of youth, yet unaccustomed to great exertions in wild places. Vorchek, though his face glistened with perspiration, appeared in his element. "As you choose to share my interests, Miss Delaney," said he, "you too shall become toughened by experience. The most engaging discoveries must be sought, where ever they may reside. They seldom arrive by first class post."

As seen from close range, the Starrett house offered bleak prospects. It was a creaky old, wooden slat structure, unpainted, with collapsing roof, sagging porch, broken windows, and a yard—if the sprawl of bumpy ground coterminous with the house could be called such—of weeds and desert shrubs. Whoever the former owner might have been, it was plain that there had not been another to replace him. "Daniel Starrett," said Vorchek, in response to the inevitable question, "a homesteader who sought to do his bit for local urbanization back in the Teens and Twenties. He brought his family to Cottonwood shortly before the Great War, purchased a slice of land through a bond sale, and erected this abode with his own hands. I suppose it was never anything more than a well-crafted shack, although he surely had fine dreams for the future. They came to this." While he spoke he deployed once more his energy sensor. When he turned it on, the meter needle swung wildly, in rapid, random jerks, from left to right and points between. "I doubt not that we have arrived," he told Theresa. "This is the source. I should

108

have guessed. The Starrett history is fascinating enough to justify speculation." He glanced at the sun. "We still have a couple of hours before we head home."

"I guess that history doesn't include our getting a bite to eat," the girl muttered. Vorchek fished in his jacket pocket, produced a candy bar. "For emergencies," he said. "Oh, thank you, Professor!" She munched happily; then, as an afterthought, dutifully asked, "So, what does Daniel Starrett have to do with all this?"

"He had extremely poor luck in his choice of property, for one. What happened is that he went insane and killed his entire family, including two little ones; or so folks said. He claimed the house, or the land upon which it was raised, was haunted. He swore (and his wife, prior to her demise, backed him up in public) that ghosts plagued the location, materializing at all hours, but mainly at night. He said they were not 'proper' ghosts, whatever that might mean, but manifestations of especial weirdness, like nothing he had heard of before. He excavated the land, searching for Indian burials that his presence might have disturbed—a cleverly populist idea, though apparently invalid—you can still see evidences of his endeavors, in those low mounds and shallow depressions ; here, and more over there. After a few years of his antics and noise his family vanished. As he told it, they were called out of their beds by night and 'taken.' His not so close neighbors had other ideas, for his increasingly wild rantings had frightened them, and they were inclined to suspect the worst of the fellow. The Yavapai County sheriff questioned him at the time, returning some days later with a warrant, but by then Mr. Starrett had vanished as well, leaving all of his personal effects behind. The authorities theorized that he fled deeper into the wilderness and perished there, perhaps by his own hand, out of remorse for his crimes. It is a neat story, yet one open to competing interpretations."

"Even I can see that," cried Theresa. "The spooky force out here drove him crazy—is that it, Professor?—which is why he did those awful things." "A superior explanation, Miss Delaney, knowing what you and I know of the locale, and yet, perhaps, not the very best. What if the late Daniel Starrett told, to the limits of his knowledge and imagination, the truth?"

While Theresa ruminated over that, and peered now anxiously at the lowering sun, Vorchek tinkered with his machine, unsealing its backing and fussing with the wiring within. Then he suggested that they tour the ruins of the house, which she was loath to do, but he insisted, so she went along, though the activity proved to no purpose. The interior was in as bad of shape as the exterior; the meager furnishings were still extant, though they could scarcely be described as intact; all in all, it could be said that the place contained material for a low grade historical museum, but no clues to mysteries. The unflappable Vorchek, chipper as ever, professed to being unperturbed. "Investigate everything first," he cautioned, "and only then, act."

He ushered his delightful assistant back into the yard, where the two of them stood before the odd device which had served him so well this day. "Now, at last," said he, "we get down to business. The unknown force radiates from this spot; that much, surely, is clear to you. Whether from the air or the earth, this is the source. Up to this point we have done nothing but detect and read, which has told us a deal, but I would do more. My machine takes in energy waves; it can also emit them. Suppose I send a carefully modulated pulse into the energy field surrounding us. What would you think of that, Miss Delaney?"

"I think you seem infuriatingly prepared for all eventualities today," she replied hotly. "This started off as what I thought was a casual outing, for 'exploratory purposes', you said. Instead, you've had a plan in mind from the first."

"I had hopes, and that being the case, I wished my favorite, and most charming, student at my side. Let us commence. I shall throw the switch; no, my dear, that shall be your honor. You do the deed, and we will observe together."

Theresa, suddenly leery of the device, hesitated for a spell to touch it, but at Vorchek's gentle insistence she approached the machine, stuck out one dainty finger, and pressed down, flipping the indicated switch. The oddly humming and whining sensor issued a fresh sound, a low, throbbing noise like that of an overtaxed engine. The needle in the meter fluttered and grew still in an upright position; the contraption was no longer receiving, but sending. The professor waited expectantly, rubbing his hands quickly and rhythmically. The girl stood by, looking around her stupidly, having no idea what was supposed to happen. It did not seem that anything was happening; she sensed a certain hush in the environment about her, but then it was a quiet place, and she listened carefully now; it seemed that a shadow fell upon the landscape, as if a cloud had obscured the sun, when there was no cloud, but then the sun had dropped in the sky, and there was much dust, and she was staring, perhaps straining too hard. One could not make too much out of these slight, almost imperceptible, effects.

Then, however, a tiny dark hole opened in the air, a little blob of blackness appearing just over Vorchek's shoulder, a speck of night that swelled and grew in a matter of seconds. Theresa cried out, and she pointed, and Vorchek turned, bidding her be quiet and observe. The black spot grew ever larger, and where it was, the normal scenery was not, meaning that it obscured all behind it. It continued to expand, blotting out all things in that direction, until it was no longer a matter of direction, for it raced on, overwhelming the vision of the earthly terrain, shutting out the light, until everything far away had vanished, and then the house disappeared, and then the professor too, swallowed in pure darkness. The dark came on, advancing like a tidal wave, and, to her shock, Theresa could not any longer see herself. The world was gone, and absolute night reigned supreme.

She had awareness of herself: she could feel the pounding of her heart, the dryness of her tongue, the unpleasant surge of her stomach. She existed, but sight had departed. She called out, she shouted Vorchek's name, and she heard her own voice, which sounded hollow, and she heard the response of his voice, demanding calm, his voice sounding far away and reedy. Then she thought no more of sounds, though she screamed shrilly, for a white shape emerged from the utter blackness. It appeared small at first, as had the black hole, and then the shape grew as that had, an appearance like unto a stealthy approach. The shape spread and grew vast, yet it was not clearly seen nor explicitly discernible; it was hazy, amorphous, shifting, more like smoke or liquid than any solid thing. It was real, however, and there was enough of a concreteness to the thing to identify it as a vital being rather than an inanimate object. One could speak of a body, and physical features of sorts, but they were unlike anything that she had ever seen before, and they were intensely, excruciatingly horrible.

She screamed again, a mindless shriek, and she heard Vorchek, from somewhere at the end of the invisible world, roaring in triumph, "I behold Him!", and she thought to run, but she was petrified by terror, and knew not where to flee, for she could see no place to go. The incomprehensible, the monstrous entity opened wide huge gauzy arms, and those arms swept at Theresa very fast, and there came a sibilant hiss from which dripped grotesque sounds like words, meaningless words of venom; and then she heard again a familiar voice, now in a tone of cold, stern command, saying, "Miss Delaney, listen to me, understand and obey. Do not panic. You have not moved in space. The machine stands before you. You know the switch. Turn it off now." She felt herself blink, though the ghastly vision did not change, save that the horror hurtled at her in a rush and its frightful vapors seemed to brush her tingling flesh. Then she reached out, and her fingers gripped the unseen device, and she fumbled with her fingers across its surface until she found a switch which she prayed she knew, and she pressed it down the other way.

The sun beamed upon her where she stood on the wretched lawn, with Vorchek's machine at her fingertips, the ugly old house tottering beyond, the professor a few short feet away, and the stark and bare landscape of the seemingly sane and recognizable earth stretching in all directions exactly as it should. Then she fell limply, and Vorchek came to her, tenderly helping her up from where she had fallen, and once he had retrieved his machine he lent his arm to her support as he bore her away from that place, on the long and tiresome journey back to civilization.

Much later, under very different conditions, Professor Anton Vorchek expounded earnestly and cheerfully to Theresa upon their strange experience. They sat in his cozy study, sipping wine after a revivifying meal. "Of course I had realized," said he, "that something strange was going on in that region, that nature had taken a peculiar turn. I had the biological reports and observations, such as they were, and there were the legends of the red man to consider, which had not been often done by others. Piecing together the facts, I tentatively concluded that an obscure cosmic force was at work there, one worthy of investigation. I devised my energy sensor accordingly, and gave it the additional function of emitting its own special energy field, thinking to make my ultimate test at the Tavasci Marsh where, for all I knew, the disturbance originated. The realization that the infamous Starrett case was uniquely bound up with my problem came late in the day, but once I had added that datum I felt myself on solid ground, and could make a better guess as to what we might be facing.

"In the Verde Valley there exists a crack in the space-time continuum, A vortex, as such curiosities have been called, where the forces operating in other dimensions or planes of being leak through into our world. It has existed there for ages, altering nature in a major and nasty way, and if my informants be right, it was enhanced centuries ago by a visitation out of that realm by a terrible being, a product of a very different system of nature, whom my old friend Tonipah called Yotakor. Mr. Starrett of dismal fame, and his unfortunate family, settled themselves, quite by chance, upon the very spot, or one of the spots, where the forces bleed into our dimension most strongly. In time he might have been driven insane—it has happened to others—but I think he reported truly as best he could. Something had come to him at intervals, something from beyond, a series of mild though frightening appearances at first, which eventually must have turned deadly as the being grew interested in the steady presence of living organisms—human organisms—at the site. The wife and children, then the man himself, were taken away into the dark voids, as had happened, according to myth, in the heyday of aboriginal culture thereabouts. This more recent evil was also perpetrated by the entity which I will style Yotakor, until such time as the evidence suggests differently. I gathered that He could come of His own will; I wondered if my unusual appliance might be powerful enough to deliberately attract this being. Well, we performed our test—you observed as did I—and I dare say you know the rest."

"I can't but think," said Theresa, "that our escape was a lucky break. There's no way, Professor, that you could calculate the danger, except that you knew menace existed, and that it could be deadly to human life. Once Yotakor came, I thought we were finished, but you stayed cool enough. You must have already analyzed the situation to the last decimal place, in order to know how to deal with the peril."

Vorchek laughed quietly. "My dear, you credit me with too much knowing, and I remained 'cool', as you say, because there was no sense in behaving otherwise. I am perfectly willing to panic or otherwise lose my head, if that serves a legitimate purpose. At the end, when all seemed lost for us, I gambled; just that, and nothing more. I had, through my generated energy pulse, dragged our visitor out of His dimension at a time, it seemed, not of His own choosing. There was a modest possibility that, if we canceled the pulse, He would go away, at least for the time being. Think of it as yet another experiment, one that happily succeeded."

"I can't believe we did it. It was a lunatic risk."

"But worth it," Vorchek pointed out. "Please, Miss Delaney, just top off my glass. It was worth it, I tell you. You have excitement in your life, and knowledge accrues, both of which are very good things. It is always my way, and I trust that it shall be yours. Think of the stories you have to tell, if anyone will listen?"

The Search For Maltheus the Wise

L ately came into my possession a manuscript composed by Jacob Bleek, the reputed sorcerer of old, recounting a fabulous dream vision which occurred to him during the course of his incredible journey over the earth in search of the ultimate wisdom of the Gods. So far as I can tell, this document constitutes a brand new find of a hitherto lost portion of that grim old wizard's works, one which has never been previously scrutinized by modern scholars. I can not be categorical, for in the last century Obermeyer and Ebsen wrote general treatises on Bleek's dreams, which it was the mage's penchant to record, but it is not clear that any recent authority makes reference to this particular episode. Further back in time, so it appears, the document was more widely extant; Alfonzo the Seer of Toledo curtly alludes to the tale in his ponderous tract *Los Ananiades*, and the Saxon Harold of Dunstan comments upon its "devout improbabilities" in what is known to historians as his *Private Journal of Mysterious Happenings*; so the tale has been known in the past. Given the vagaries of preservation concerning Bleek's literary corpus, as well as the rise and fall of interest in such arcane matters, it is, perhaps, little wonder that the text dropped out of sight for many years.

Yet it remains a tale well worth the telling. The episode appears to date from an early period of Bleek's suspiciously long life (I say this in reference to the odd claims made for his remarkable longevity by colleagues or near contemporaries), when he had journeyed into what he obscurely terms "an oriental land", a principality seated far within expansive, abundantly watered tropical forests surrounded by bare mountains and hot deserts, seeking a famed philosophical mage who styled himself by the name of Maltheus. Informed rumor reputed to this worthy—none of who's works have survived to the present—a vast body of lore relating to ancient dealings with the Gods: how such attempts had been conducted, the fates of those who made the attempts, and intriguing speculations as to how such fates might be avoided by the inquisitively wary. Within certain magical circles it was whispered that

115

Maltheus had translated the totality of the prehistoric Rhexellite tongue, that curious language said to date from a murky past era which seemed to contain so many provocative allusions to the natures of the Great Ones who hold all the universe beneath Their sway. This man Bleek earnestly desired to meet, so he ventured to the far eastern city of Elibama, where his colleague was last known to reside. In his account he describes the city in poetic form, as is always his inclination throughout his preserved writings, an unusual trait in such a morbid personality, though the form was more common to intellectual men of his day than it later became.

City of granite spires towering fair

Revel shaken palaces, thatched mud huts

Priests in chariots, peasants in the ruts

Great Maltheus here chose to build his lair.

There he received sad tidings, which were like to overthrow his plans. The folk of the streets of Elibama knew Maltheus—indeed, they took pride in him, for his renown extended to distant lands, and wherever men respected learning they hailed him justly as Maltheus the Wise—and they could point out his fine castle on the outskirts of the noblest district, but such knowledge was unlikely to serve the itinerant foreign wizard, for the man he sought was dead, by his own hand. As Bleek came to understand the matter, Maltheus, for all his wisdom, had grown into a bitter, morose old gentleman, much given to misgivings, self-scorn, self-reproach. So unhappy became the man that he began to dabble in the esoteric mysteries offered by the forbidden cult of Blug, an evil, furtive movement rightly suppressed by the pragmatic masters of the city. Maltheus had joined the cult in due course, and having fallen under its baleful influence it was only a matter of time before his black moods and inner miseries swallowed him whole, until at length, in final despair, he called down fire from the heavens one night to incinerate himself, a titanic hurricane of fierce wind and blazing fury that roared down onto his citadel, charring him to ashes, then burning even his ashes away.

News of these developments left Jacob Bleek at loose ends. He managed to force entrance into the castle, found nothing of substance, only fire-blasted wreckage. That Maltheus had possessed critical information the seeker did not doubt, but the barrier of death stood between him and his prize. Being himself a master of the black arts, Bleek boasted of some expertise at wringing secrets from the lips of corpses, be they willing or recalcitrant, but in this case there existed no sacred tomb to violate, no mummified body to covertly acquire, no putrefied brain to squeeze by magical skullduggery. There were especially risky and reprehensible means by which wandering spirits could be persuaded to speak, but such means were chancy, prone to failure. The situation did not look good for Bleek. He took lodgings in the cheapest quarter, where for three days he fumed to himself while fussing with his papers, gleaning outrageous hints as to how he might contact his deceased fellow sorcerer. On the third night he acted, holding solemn ceremony in a lonely copse screened by trees from prying eyes, where he made a magic of raising. It did not work, and comment was excited by the prior disappearance of one of Bleek's close neighbors, a poor man without family but, as it turned out, many vocal friends. Local suspicions forced Bleek to vacate his rooms in haste, leaving him at his wit's end as to where to go, or how to proceed.

He spent days trying to contact other members of the Blug cult, whom he might pump or bribe for relevant data, yet every such attempt produced grotesque results. People would scream at the mere mention of that coarse word; without exception they denied any personal knowledge of its organization or practitioners, snarling hatefully at him when he spoke respectfully of the connection between that group and the beloved Maltheus. No one would confess to membership and, being an unauthorized religion, there was no open house of worship where he could inquire. That obvious recourse led to an utter dead end.

Benevolent fortune came to his rescue. While ambling through the market places of Elibama, sniffing for clues which would aid him, asking sly questions the import of which he could deny, he chanced to be overheard by a lean, dark, hungry-looking young loafer wrapped in tattered rags of clothing bearing traces of worn and faded finery, who exhibited signs of inordinate curiosity and made to follow him into the twisting alleys winding between the crumbling mud brick walls and drab house fronts off the main square. At a blind corner Bleek rounded on the man, daring him to initiate hostilities, threatening him with unnatural retribution. The man pleaded innocence, identifying himself as Barhatta, a sunken nobleman of once important and wealthy family. He said he needed money, claimed to know a thing or two. Their conversation went something like this:

"You ask after Maltheus the Wise," said Barhatta, "as if seeking a friend, yet I know from your words that you have heard of his death. All hail that great lost one! If his friend, then you too must be a man of mystery, for Maltheus broke bread only with those mighty and learned like himself. Do you seek to follow him whither he has gone, in order to transact grave business undone?" Bleek allowed that something of the

117

sort was in his mind. "It is spoken among the priests," averred Barhatta, "that there are those who can grant such boons. I know of them, from sitting at the feet of priests in my youth, and I have a fair idea where they reside. There are possibilities for dealings between you and I." Bleek hinted that he possessed copious resources, was known for a generous benefactor among those who served him well. Barhatta grinned, nodded eagerly, then grew sober. "Surely, though, only the bravest of the holy would dare follow where Maltheus has gone. For mark you, that wise one, out of misery and madness, consigned himself of his own free will to the foul clutches of the cult of Blug, and he died still locked in the embrace of that evil Lord, and his soul has gone to dwell for all eternity, as they say, in the bosom of that monstrous Deity. If all this be true, would it not be death to your own soul to attempt to reach him?"

Bleek was irked by these references to Blug, for he knew nothing of that entity or of His followers, though he would never have confessed to such ignorance; so he adroitly questioned Barhatta, framing his queries in such fashion as to suggest all knowledge on his part, as a mere desire to test his informant. The man proved voluble, his information distressing. "Blug is the epitome of squalid evil in this world, the Lord of Decay, Lord of Filth, Lord of Hopeless Sorrow. His followers themselves designate Him by all these titles, and many more, all revealing His abysmal loathsomeness. Everything foul and rotten in this world belongs to Him, and many there are who worship Him, though they know not His name, for He attracts to Himself those who blackly despair, those who hate life and the world because they hate themselves, those who are miserable without cause or with little cause. Blug whispers to them, pours reeking slime into their ears, feeds their misery until they can no longer stand life, come to long for death.

"His most favored slaves, those who take strange joy in sorrow, know Blug, know Him for what He is, yet they find Him good. These special worshipers established the cult, which has existed since time immemorial, and they foster it to this day. They know Him, and they love Him. Can you believe that? My life has been one of unfulfilled promises and shattered dreams, yet never would I embrace the Stinking One. I could not sink that low! Those who do find happiness in bowing to Him, though not all can tolerate His hateful gaze for long. Wonderful Maltheus could not, thus he took his own life, departing forever from the ken of common men. Which reminds me, good sir, that you proclaim yourself generous, while I am a good man at heart who finds himself desperately in need."

Bleek impatiently repeated his views on that subject, at which Barhatta told him, with a confidential air, a tale of a dreadful place a day's journey to the east, perhaps somewhat more, a horrid land where common men never dared set foot, but where Maltheus had been prone to paying visits during his days of glory. "It is called the Valley of Voltakis, a very old name which means nothing in our tongue; an ill regarded place considered by the local folk to be a dangerous abode of monsters or demons that lure men to destruction by offering fantastic gifts in exchange for human souls. Such stories emanate from that valley that it freezes my blood to think of them, yet they are recounted as verities by those who know of these matters. I, of course, have no traffic with monsters, and can not tell you truly what the denizens of that land may offer, but their powers are said to be terrible and mighty. What I can do is lead you there, for I know its location, and despite the dangers I crave regular meals once again, a habit adopted in childhood, one for which I have never lost the taste."

Bleek seemed more impressed by the potential nature of the gifts than of the perils, for he made a deal on the spot with Barhatta, giving him modest coinage to refresh himself and purchase supplies for the trip, promising more gold in plenty if he would act as guide. They would commence the journey on the morrow, at the market square where they had first laid eyes on one another. Barhatta went his way whistling, leaving Bleek with the afternoon in which to further enhance his stores of vital information. He hoped much from the young nobleman, but the cunning mage was an old hand at stealthy dealings, and he would verify the man's weird account before he committed himself further.

Jacob Bleek presented himself to the shaven-headed priests of Elibama, insinuating himself into the inner sanctum of the main temple, there requesting audience. The lesser spokesmen of the city's many-armed and many-headed gods were nonplussed and incensed by his intrusion. They called for the high priest, a beefy, rotund fellow named Kandraputra who with sneer and frown threatened Bleek with swift death. The wizard offered a purse of gold to the local deities, thus shortly found himself in private and comfortable communion with that master of the temple. With such an exalted and learned host Bleek saw no need for dissembling, so stated plainly his purpose: to seek the shade of Maltheus, wherever it might currently reside, and to receive from that lost spirit the wisdom of the ages. Kandraputra had something to say pertinent to the matter, confirming the claims of Barhatta, and rather more besides.

SCIENCE AND SORCERY

"So mage seeks mage," intoned the chief of the priests, as he passed a fresh glass of wine to his guest, following their sumptuous meal. Reclining onto his cushions he said, "Sorcerers are ever a troublesome lot, nor is it often my way to favor them. Even Maltheus the Wise I disliked, though he were a noble and brilliant man, one who deserved a better end than he demanded. In your case, however, I need not conceal nor evade, for there is no chance that you will succeed at your task.

"That you are capable of contacting the dead I grant; I have heard many claims of the kind, know that such is possible in special circumstances. Maltheus himself once demonstrated his technique to me. A curious rite, one with obscure and unpleasant features, but effective it was, and enlightening. Then too, I doubt not that you may ask for a boon from the evil dwellers in the Valley of Voltakis. These be no refugees from a children's story; they exist, to be sure, lurking there inside unfathomed caverns, of strange powers, though I question the merits of any aid they may give you. They are deceitful, if tales be accurate, prone to granting what seems the heart's desire, while providing otherwise, requiring in addition a fearsome price in return for their services. Seek them and they may, if it amuses them, point you toward your destination, but however you strive, all will be for naught, for it is impossible for you, a mortal man of reasonable sanity and love of self, ever to tread the path that Maltheus has chosen. He has consigned himself to the kingdom of Blug, and there you may not go, nor—should you contrive to venture there—will you find your kindred mage amenable to persuasion. That is a realm of absolute spiritual death, a grim land where Blug reigns supreme, holding court among His chosen, where all worship with unalloyed fidelity the dark Lord of Decay. You can not offer Maltheus anything that he wants. Mark you: he has what he wants, for all eternity, and nothing will tear him away."

Bleek would know more of Blug's mystical domain. "The legends of our holy fathers," said Kandraputra, "speak of the Black Swamp, a rancid mire not found on any map, rather located beyond the rim of the cosmos, beyond the seat of the fair Gods, where Blug rules eternally from His dark throne among His people, a place to which all the misery and filth of our universe drains as into a vast cesspool. Everything there, plants, animals, and men, is unclean, unwholesome, diseased. Blug wishes it so, therefore it is. More than that living man can not say, for Blug guards well His secrets.

"How to get there is a question no healthy man can answer; perhaps the seers of Voltakis know. Those who have journeyed to the

Black Swamp never intend to return, while our sacred literature reveals nothing concerning the possibility of escape. The spirits of those sickened in mind go there readily enough, thus egress can be achieved, but regress is another matter entirely, of which you must be certain, lest you be imprisoned there forever with the souls who embrace their own torment. Can you stand to think of that, Jacob Bleek? Is this knowledge you crave so precious that you would risk damnation, or worse than damnation?"

Bleek brusquely thanked the priest for the proffered information, made his way back to his lodgings in order to prepare for his journey on the morrow. That night, very late, he made the magic of seeing, by which he hoped to catch a glimmer of the daunting land beyond time and space where Blug held perpetual sway. He saw nothing at all, an outcome which irked his mind and taxed his brain, for the method had been uniformly successful when applied to terrestrial cases, occasionally had granted him glimpses of mystic lairs where demons abode. He could not see into Blug's kingdom, nor could he contact Maltheus through (what passed for sorcerers as) conventional means. Truly his predecessor must lie now in a realm distant and forbidden beyond previous conception. Bleek thought, on the other hand, that his magical eye might reveal something of Voltakis, so he trained his roaming vision toward that place. He saw something; nothing edifying, naturally, but sufficient to convince him that the trek could prove profitable.

Come the morn, at first light Bleek met Barhatta in the deserted city square, finding the fellow ready for travel and true to his promises. He looked a new man, his hair curled and oiled, his beard trimmed, his clothing smart, his boots shiny. Barhatta brought with him three mules, one burdened with six days' provisions, the others outfitted for riding. "It is rugged country," he explained. "Horses will not do. These animals will see us through, save we require mountain goats for climbing." Without further delay they mounted their cantankerous steeds, wound their way through the sleepy lanes of Elibama, out the city gates, from there set a course along a disused eastern track. For hours they rode through dense jungle, first passing the scattered clearings of villages and farms near the city. When the clearings vanished, the green oppressiveness of the jungle swallowed the pair. Throughout the morning and into the afternoon they saw no man or habitation, only the unbroken canopy of trees with its furtive natural denizens, monkeys and birds and coiling serpents. The mules staggered up a steep rise, where from the top the travelers gazed down onto a sere plain, ringed by jagged peaks, through the center of which a winding dark gash slashed the monotonous brown landscape. Bleek knew from his visions, without the eager prompting of Barhatta, that he beheld the entrance to the Valley of Voltakis.

They made their way posthaste across the mountain-ringed plain to the mouth of the valley, where high cliffs began to loom. There, at the foot of a jumble of big boulders, they spied a curious image, much weathered, chiseled into a vertical slab of native rock which stood alone like a forgotten stele. It appeared to be a crude representation of a myriad of staring eyes enclosed within an oval, as if a larger eye encompassed the rest. Having discerned this foreboding feature in his visions, the sight pleased Bleek, though his companion, who had heard of it, visibly shuddered. They peered into the gloomy interior of the valley, one view of which could inspire caution in the bravest man. Barhatta dismounted from his mule, advised with studied casualness that they make camp. Bleek insisted that they proceed.

Barhatta laughed harshly and replied, "No farther will I go. I have fulfilled the conditions of our agreement: to lead you safely and truly to the shunned valley. Here it is, as promised, and you may go forward as your heart desires and as foolishness dictates. As for me, I have other things to do." Bleek testily informed his guide that a serious misunderstanding had arisen between them; that he had hired Barhatta, truly paid him well, in order to be conducted into the presence of the valley's mysterious occupants. This task the young nobleman would complete, or draw forth the ire of his master. "Better alive and unfaithful," stated Barhatta, "than fidelious and dead. I return to the good world immediately." Bleek nodded, saying that he saw sense in that position; leaned forward on his mount, cast a handful of bluish powder at Barhatta's mule, muttered curious words. The mule shriveled, sagging under its saddle, withered into something small and ugly that crept out from beneath the mass of leather. It was a toad, which hopped away among the rocks and quickly disappeared. Bleek noted that, like mule, man is but an animal, and what became of one, could be visited upon the other. Barhatta quailed, made as if to speak, said nothing. The wizard announced coolly that his guide would henceforth march before on foot—as a good servant should—and that no further delays would be tolerated. The cowed man meekly obeyed.

They entered the valley, which Bleek poetically describes after his common inclination, as follows:

Drear and dark and barren of healthy life

THE SEARCH FOR MALTHEUS THE WISE

Black stone walls gouged by a poisonous stream
Blood-curdling horrors in grim caverns teem
A hateful domain, yet with wonders rife.

They trekked into that fastness of hot stones and sun-scorched weeds, through the valley—which seems to have been more of a narrow, winding gorge—meeting no living thing save scorpions and spiders and their creeping prey, until the approach of evening made the setting of camp necessary. Bleek grudgingly acquiesced, though he took no chances, and after their simple dinner of traveler's rations he prudently bound Barhatta hand and foot lest he slip away or make mischief in the night. The poor fellow remonstrated, but he might have been talking to the wind, for all that his pleas availed him.

Next day they went on, ever to the east, riding or trudging onerously along the banks of a weedy, discolored creek, within the walls of a sheer canyon of pure basalt. At times they observed dark openings into the solid rock, but after a modicum of scouting the mage would goad his mules and his man onward. Bleek kept his eyes to the right, knowing from his magical vision what to look for, plagued by the thought of missing it. Presently he spied a cave mouth in the wall, low down towards the bottom by the rancid stream, an opening flanked by curious, olden symbols chiseled long ago into the rock. These symbols, which his esoteric arts had warned him to seek (to avoid, as Barhatta averred), were not new to him; he recognized them as ancient letters of the primeval Rhexellite language denoting the presence of forbidden mysteries, and which he had been assured, in this case, would lead him directly to the ominous denizens of the valley. Those beings were supposed to haunt the cave so marked, to be approached only under cover of darkest night.

Jacob Bleek timed his subterranean expedition accordingly. He waited until the sun disappeared behind the close, steep walls of the chasm, when every trace of aerial illumination had faded away, and a chill, clammy breeze swept the gorge, then lighted a torch and clambered into the fearsome chamber, driving Barhatta before him. The sorceric author admits to a certain trepidation, while boasting of greater determination.

Who dwells within these chambers stark and cold?
Those whom mild and tender eyes dare not see
Yet these feeble fears shall not deter me
Where great truths beckon that I must behold.

There was something to learn inside, and he lived to learn, so he would enter.

Within the entrance the basalt gave way to softer bedrock, malleable stone long worked by the gnawing elements. They crept along a low passage which twisted and turned and sloped slightly downward but, for the longest time, showed no signs of ending. Spears of dripping limestone dangled from the roof, daggers of rock rose from the floor. Barhatta could scarcely walk, so great was the mantle of fear that befell him in that Stygian tunnel deep inside the cheerless bowels of the earth, until at one point he staggered, half in a faint, crying out to his Gods to save him. "What have I done," he mumbled pathetically, "that I am sent to my doom, far from the sun and the sky? Is there no justice for a poor man? I ask merely to live, nothing more." Then he hurled himself at Bleek, tried to lay hands on him, but the wizard coldly and methodically slapped him down. Barhatta sobbed brokenly, but he henceforth mechanically obeyed the order to march.

Bleek lost track of how far they plumbed the depths of that nighted realm, but eventually they reached a juncture at which the pressing walls fell away and they found themselves within a broad stone room of surprisingly regular circularity. The floor was bare, the walls blank and smooth, the high ceiling lost in darkness. At the back of the chamber Bleek noted, as he stepped forward into the void, an entrance to another tunnel, while around this, standing forth from the rock, an arch of yellow metal glistened in the flickering light of his torch. Repellent designs of antique style were chased into its gleaming surface. Oblong benches of basalt flanked the arch, occupied by strange, seated, cloaked figures resembling crude statues. Another, similar figure, wrapped in a long robe, stood within the arch. That figure suddenly moved, its robe flapping open, and Barhatta screamed; not due to any inherent menace in the motion but rather, perhaps, because such a nightmarish form had moved at all.

It was not a man, although it possessed superficial aspects of humanity. One might write, as did Bleek, of a head, and arms and legs attached to a trunk, but there the illusion of kinship ceased. Pale it was, like a cave worm, fearfully thin and wiry, with very long limbs bent at multiple joints. It stood upright like a man, yet when it advanced from the yellow arch it seemed to scuttle as might a crab or spider. There was nothing manlike in that locomotion. Its hairless head was little more than a distorted, lopsided skull over which the skin was tightly drawn, with holes for ears, noseless nostrils, a small red mouth filled with many tiny, pointed teeth. The small, dark round eyes gleamed from deep sockets and greenly reflected light as would the eyes of animals, yet there was cunning in those beady orbs, a steadfast, malign intelligence. They regarded Bleek evilly, and as the wizard gazed back at them a third, previously invisible eye unsealed above the other two in that grotesque skull, a moist red eye which possessed even more mocking intellect and malevolence than the others. The figures on the benches rose and stood to attention, a row of dreadful, silent, skull-headed horrors.

Jacob Bleek knew not what was expected of him, so he planted his torch in the loose detritus of the floor and crouched down before the things, averting his gaze from those foul monstrosities while he muttered to himself an olden spell which was said (and to which he could testify) to further an audience with certain types of unorthodox entities. As he chanted under his breath he heard a satisfied sigh emanate from the apparitions. Their mouths worked hideously, drooling saliva. The central being advanced, shambling horribly, while Barhatta wailed and crouched down to the floor in terror to prostrate himself. Bleek rose to his feet. The thing made straight for him, halted, thrust its ghastly three-eyed visage forward into his, nose to no nose, glaring intently. That frightful little mouth twitched and gaped spasmodically over those needle-like teeth, and from those thin lips issued a harsh, sibilant voice which spoke in a long dead human language, yet one that Bleek knew well from his arcane studies: the tongue of the fabled Rhexellites, those pioneers in magic and weird secrets of a lost, age-shrouded era ignored or forgotten by history. No human being had spoken such dialect for millennia, yet this demon—or whatever manner of being it was—attempted to make itself understood in that tongue.

"Jacob Bleek," rasped the voice, "what would you have of us? This place is our outpost on your world, where we dwell content without the company of your kind. We seek nothing of you, yet perchance you seek something of us? Has mere curiosity driven you here? We think not, but if so, your fate shall be hard. Have you come for knowledge? We know many things, much of this earth, more of... elsewhere. Think hard upon your desires, Jacob Bleek, ponder them intently so that we may know them as do you." The sorcerer obeyed, without a word, marshaling his thoughts, focusing them upon one crystalline idea. The monstrous spokesman smiled—a terrible thing to see, for that mouth was never designed for smiling, and there was nothing of kindness in that cruel, twitching spasm—and said, "Very good, O wizard. A strange request, one unlike any we have heard before, yet it amuses us. A healthy, sane man, a man with prideful spirit, one who would stride his world and other worlds like a giant; this man seeks the dire prison kingdom of Great Blug, would journey there of his own will. And yet this is no jest, not even of cosmic proportions, but a matter of utmost gravity. You search for the miserable soul of Maltheus the Wise, though he has passed into that darkness where he can not be sought. That is impossible, of course; however, we can, of course, arrange it.

The dread speaker smiled again and croaked, "Knowledge can be shared; knowledge can be yours; the precise location of Maltheus in that forbidden land beyond sight and sanity is known to us. We can send you there to him. What is that? You ask also for the ability to return to your world at a time of your choosing? You demand much, you insist on complications. Still, we may be flexible, if you satisfy us. Give us what we crave, and all that we have to offer is yours. Treasure means nothing to us, while your life would still our hunger for but a brief moment. On the other hand, your spirit is rich and meaty, and we have use for such delicacies. Feed us your soul, and you shall surely possess aught else."

Bleek politely, yet sternly, averred that as he had his uses of his own for his soul, he did not consider it suitable coin for negotiation. The horrid spokesman grinned crookedly (or at least the fleshless mouth stretched and flexed in a weird approximation of such) and sneered, "We can destroy you on the instant, if you do not appease us." Bleek replied evenly that they could kill him if they chose, but that he desired a lesser trade, one that would grant him a boon in return for a price he could afford, one that would leave his mind and soul intact. The demon mused silently for a period, blinked its red eye and asked, "What price will you pay?" Then Jacob Bleek did a terrible thing, one that should have shattered the conscience of any man, be he ever so greedy, yet which troubled him not at all. Without hesitation he offered to the creatures of Voltakis the soul of Barhatta.

Throughout the discussion that man had moaned and whined on the stone floor, ignored by all present. Now he howled and cringed, made as if to roll or crawl away. "A human of noble birth," mused the demonic being, "with a fair mind, and much life within him. He is not the best possible morsel, but he will do. We accept him." The other cloaked forms, who had stood idle all this while, now lunged forward, surrounding the shrieking Barhatta. Said the spokesman, "Agree now, Bleek, on your honor, on your soul, thus sealing the bargain." Bleek agreed, and the awful beings clustered about Barhatta seized him with their claw-like hands. He screamed once more, begged for mercy, stupidly implored the wizard to save him, then was gone, along with his tormentors, they dragging him kicking and mindlessly praying into the lightless corridor beyond the golden arch. Shortly the horrible sound of his pleading voice dwindled, faded into black silence.

"It is done," said the remaining monster. "Now you receive your due, unless second thoughts assail you." Bleek sternly informed his host that he was ready. "Excellent," cried the three-eyed thing. "We commence. I grant you a vision. You shall sleep, and in your slumber you shall dream, and in that dream you shall see marvels. No paltry illusion will this be, but a voyage of your soul from this place to that other." The speaker folded its skinny, segmented arms, motioning curiously with its bony fingers, and at that moment Bleek fell into a swoon. Blackness like death engulfed him—the world stopped for him—mind and matter seemed to cease.

Jacob Bleek awoke, and even before he unsealed his eyes ran his hands across his body. He felt the sturdy fabric of his traveling cloak, felt the yielding substance of his living flesh. He lay curled and prone on a soft surface, a nauseous odor assaulting his nostrils. He sat up, blinked and stared. The cave of Voltakis had disappeared, and he found himself elsewhere, although the initial sensation of sight told him little. He sat in the midst of a dark, boundless, undulating plain, a dreary expanse broken only by clumps of vaguely perceived bushes or other growths. The earth beneath him was damp, soggy, a thin mud that reeked of unmentionable foulness. A trace of the gluey paste clung to his cheek, which he hurriedly wiped with a rag. Over all reigned a kind of dim twilight, a weak sepia illumination radiating from no apparent source. The sky above him appeared merely a gloomy dome, without sun or clouds or stars.

He pulled himself up from the nasty mud. In every direction the vista was the same:

Empty, morbid land beyond sun and moon
A deathly stillness, quiet unbroken
Where nary a word is heard or spoken
Nor wind to carry a desolate tune.

The abject lack of sound or motion disquieted him most. He felt an impulse to shout at the landscape, to hear his own voice, to bathe in the friendly echoes, yet dread clogged his throat, so that a triumph of will was necessary before his tongue gave utterance. When it did his voice sounded thin and reedy, and no echoes came back to him.

In the absence of landmarks he saw no sense in puzzling out a

127

course, so he chose a direction at random, commenced walking. He tramped through the mud for ages, or so it seemed. Measurement of time was well nigh impossible, but he suffered a sensation as of long, weary hours or days, with patches of wild shrubbery advancing and receding as he trudged, always with a near identical view before him. The plants did not wholly resemble any he had known before, consisting of multitudinous thin branches thrusting up from the polluted, foul smelling soil, bearing small, fleshy leaves that irritated his skin when he touched them. Neither in they nor in any other feature of the plain did he observe variation of color, there being naught but bland, numbing sameness.

Came a time, however, when he spied a darkening of the terrain before him, and as he made for that he realized that the undergrowth grew more densely ahead, and higher. Now he struggled through a thick forest of spreading bushes and stunted, sagging trees. The latter looked unhealthy, glistening with dark sap and dangling streamers of parasitic growth. His high boots sank deeper into the slushy black mud. On the other side of a slippery mound he beheld a noisome rivulet of murky fluid trickling between crumbling banks of oozing mud. Bleek pondered all that he saw, deduced with grim pleasure that he had penetrated far into the shunned region that fearful men called the Black Swamp.

As he made his way into the heart of that land he began to observe other attributes of the place, aspects which caused even his iron soul to recoil. The growths seemed to clutch at him with an unholy animation, sending forth feebly creeping tendrils to snare his limbs. He now glimpsed evidence of faunal as well as floral life (though he doubted whether anything truly lived there, in the earthly sense), and what he saw repelled him exceedingly. Where he set foot, there minute creatures like insects or arachnids scuttled quickly from view or swiftly burrowed into the thick mud. Shapes the size of rodents, only fatter and more awkward in their movements, wriggled away beneath the shrubs or took cover in the ubiquitous patches of darker gloom within the undergrowth. Once something rather larger started from his path, and his fleeting glimpse suggested to his brain a parody of a human form, although a second thought assured him of that being impossible, for what he recalled resembled nothing like a man. Certainly he saw many dead things lying half concealed in the clinging mire, all far gone in decay and unrecognizable. The hideous stench of the place, borne to his nostrils on miasmic vapors, mounted in intensity, attaining a degree of cloying ghastliness that staggered him. It was all he could do to control himself and avoid retching.

Bleek emerged from a dense thicket of subtly waving fronds and vines onto the edge of a very large clearing, a treeless expanse filled with steaming liquid. The gooey ground dropped down a few feet to the edge of the troubled, bubbling fluid. The dark pond or lagoon stretched before him into the murky shadows and mists of the horizon, however far that might be, but he detected a rising of the land in the center like a wide, flat island. Toward this he made his way, slogging forward without thought or consideration for his actions. He proceeded in that direction because he must, because it seemed the only possibility. He splashed into the warm, filthy water, which proved shallow, never reaching his knees—though it seeped into his boots, the feel of the stuff against his skin and between his toes making him ill—and sloshed his way across, endeavoring to ignore the putrid items which came to his attention. Objects of various sizes drifted on the oily surface scum or bobbed up from below, apparently bodies of organisms in varying states of decay. Some of them might have been human bodies, though it was hard to be sure, so bloated and corroded were they. He had naturally assumed that all of these objects were long dead, but he had cause to reconsider his views when one shape flung forth a skeletal arm, with shreds of rotting flesh adhering, to grab at his thigh. He thrust away the weak stumps of fingers, and the thing sank out of sight. Paying now more heed to his immediate surroundings, Bleek realized that several of the gangrenous shapes bore horrid vestiges of humanity and a faint, reprehensible imitation of life. At one point he noted that a number of unspeakably deformed, diseased human faces were swimming about him, the remnants of their features barely awash, those with intact eyes solemnly watching him. At other times manlike caricatures would heave themselves up from the underlying ooze, thrash wildly or flounder hopelessly before sinking back, their rotted throats gurgling on the sewage of the lagoon.

Sound had not previously constituted a notable aspect of the Black Swamp, but now a startling species of noise antagonized his hearing. Bleek heard a low, hoarse chanting and singsong ululation wafting down the minimal slope of the island. He wearily struggled up through the sodden muck, as he did so detected motion in the gloom, and a hint of something large and dark looming beyond. At closer range the moving forms resolved themselves into swaying, writhing, staggering shapes approximating the human. There were people there, passable specimens of the human family, male and female, with reasonably intact bodies and powers of locomotion. They danced, after a fashion, and sang, in a manner of speaking, in a wide ragged circle about the great black central mass. Jacob Bleek knew them for what they were.

New acolytes of Blug, freshly favored
Gathered in a madly delighted ring
Praise to their Lord their cracked voices sing
Joyous offerings of the souls Blug savored.
One step from life, not quite degenerate
Distraught faces one might still recognize
But raptured, a holy glow in glazed eyes
Prancing with glee at their abysmal fate.

These odd carolers were, indeed, much more entire, more properly connected physically, than their brethren in the water, even possessing rudiments of clothing, lingering relics of their former state. Bleek thought he might find Maltheus among them if he could bring himself to enter their swirling ranks. He could, because it was necessary, so he did, wandering throughout and around among the crazed throng, gazing earnestly into their faces, speaking to them, moving on. They sang mainly of the greatness of Blug, somewhat of their own worthlessness; never did they reply to Bleek's queries, nor acknowledge his presence. Eventually he grew tired of them, passed beyond their circle of despairing happiness, advanced warily toward the center of the island, where loomed that giant dark lump.

As he approached an obscuring mist seemed to dissipate, granting him at last a plain view of the source and focus of the reveling. There squatted great Blug on his low, rough, featureless throne of damp, lichenous granite; Blug, the God of Decay and Insane Misery, Lord of Filth and Squalor, a vast hill of heaving, quavering intelligence and unhallowed craving and bottomless hunger. Nastily black was that faceless, shapeless, pulsating mound of monstrosity, with patches and striated veins of unhealthy gray, and oily and formless, with folds of Its liverish flesh hanging down over Its eternal pedestal of crumbling stone. From that pile of incarnate disgust radiated a stench so extreme in its vileness that the visitor felt faint with sickness and loathing.

The incredible sight stupefied, stunned Jacob Bleek. Not for the first time the dreadful thought scalded his mind that Blug might reach out to destroy or captivate him, punishing the arrogant mortal for this unbidden intrusion into His domain. Bleek did not think it likely—all testimonials indicated that this Lord held dominance over only those who willingly embraced Him, a desire which Bleek, for all his faults, could not comprehend nor ever accept—but the creeping fear could not help but insinuate itself into his mind and nag at his determination. Evil wonders seemed possible in the domain of Blug. Bleek frantically reminded himself that the demons of Voltakis had promised him safe return.

More worshipers, a lesser inner ring, crouched or lay sprawled at the foot of Blug's throne, where His bulk lapped over the stone. They appeared more wholesome still than their dancing fellows, as if they had just recently stepped out of life. Fair forms they were, many of them, though soiled with detestable mud and filthy drippings of trickling juice from the sluggishly heaving dark bulk above them. All of them were engaged in some curious activity which Bleek could not readily identify. He gradually closed for a better look, halted in his tracks when he grasped the enormity of what he saw.

From the lower fringes of Blug's great corpus protruded an array of moist whitish masses like hellishly thick, swollen worms. These protuberances emerged, growing out of the underlying flesh, inflating in width and hanging limply into space, slowly pulsating and emitting frequent streams of oily liquor from their tips. This occurred as he watched, but most of these grotesque swellings were already occupied and being put to use by the chosen. Huddled against the base of the throne or reclining in the mud, these worshipers—the specially favored?—pressed their splayed hands against the stone for support and took those organs into their mouths, their jaws stretched widely and tightly, and from their rapid facial motions and other signs it was evident that they were gulping down the syrupy product of their God. The noxious nectar squirted past their lips, dribbling onto their chins, but they seemed to be endeavoring to quaff every last drop, as if they imbibed wine of rare and ancient vintage.

Specially favored or specially blighted, Bleek could not bear to see this vomitous act of degradation, yet he stayed, for he must, and—as destiny had written, he supposed—there he found the eternal shade of Maltheus the Wise. He knew the man so soon as he saw him, though they had never met in life. The magic of Voltakis worked truly, leading him unerringly to his goal. There lay Maltheus, once noble of bearing and demeanor, sucking greedily at a slimy teat, and when Bleek called out his name the pitiful soul squirmed and endeavored to shy away, without releasing its oral grip. Bleek remembered the warning of Kandraputra, that he had nothing to offer the damned man in return for his secrets, and he knew this to be so, but though he could not offer, he possessed

131

the ability to take away, or to threaten thus. Bleek stooped down, gently began to wean Maltheus from his hateful connection to Blug. Maltheus thrashed, struggling spasmodically, lost his grip, wailed like a disappointed infant. His human tormentor dragged him from the base of the throne, wrestled him upright and held him fast in a sitting posture in the mud.

"Please," gasped the spirit of Maltheus, in a cultured voice that had once commanded respect and awe from his peers and from multitudes, "please do not do this to me. You know not what you do. He beckons, He calls, He provides, and I must drink. Release me, I beg of you." Bleek beheld the high, noble brow and strong, long-bearded features of this ethereal human debris, and the sight shook his composure, without softening the hardness of his resolve. He patiently explained the purpose of his mission, ignoring the grotesque pleas of his victim, repeating over and over his need for the secrets of the Gods, making clear that he desired only those secrets, that he swore, once satisfied, to release the dead mage back to his degrading lusts. Finally Maltheus went limp, the feeble fight gone from him, saying, "I know of you, Jacob Bleek. Our fellows told tales in former days. I know you will never rest until you work your will. So be it. The totality of my life's worthless labors resides safely and securely in the terrestrial plane, in a concealed chamber beneath the keep of my castle, a room cunningly hidden from prying eyes. Dig there, in the floor of the feigned lowest level, and you shall find all that you desire, the meaningless leavings of my misspent life.

"For know you, Jacob Bleek, that the entirety of my earthly existence was composed of folly and foolishness, a miserable, hopeless quest for that which can not be attained! I sought those secrets before you, grasping for the power and the glory of the Gods, only to learn that I reached too high, that my aspirations were without value to They whom I sought. Those Great Ones care nothing for us, seeing us as playthings or insects, holding us in Their grasp and toying with or crushing us as Their amusement dictates. I realized this—came to know my true position in the grand scheme of the universe—could not bear the revelation. I longed for a new God, one who would accept me as I am and deal with me justly... and I found Him.

"I implore you, before it is too late, to accept Him into your heart." Bleek released the wreckage of Maltheus the Wise. The fervent acolyte of Blug rolled and crept and slithered on his belly back to the throne of his Master, there frantically reattaching himself, slobbering and choking happily as he gagged on a slimy teat that swelled and extended to meet him. Bleek turned away in a revulsion of empathic horror, and then the lurid nightmare landscape about him darkened and faded. That last view of the Black Swamp, the insanely delirious worshipers, the soiled throne and the vile dark Lord lingered in his mind while blackness shrouded him. Then he stood bathed in the red glow of dawn, standing in the mouth of the demon-haunted cave in the Valley of Voltakis, with his camp below him and the two tethered mules glumly grazing in a dry thicket of brittle weeds. He had been returned as promised, once the search was concluded and his goal accomplished, and the deed had been done, so far as he could tell, in the passage of a single night. Mysterious and powerful were the dwellers in the land of Voltakis.

Jacob Bleek journeyed back to civilization, an easy ride (packing as he did food and drink for two, which cheered him much), back to the city of Elibama where, one night not long after arrival, he led a tough, well paid gang into the deserted castle of lost Maltheus, tore up the floor of the deepest level of the keep, and Bleek descended alone into a hitherto unsuspected chamber, where he found the documents he sought, the magical secrets of the dead sorcerer, a veritable library of cosmic knowledge locked away in numerous iron-bound trunks. The task of retrieval was not so simple as it sounds; Maltheus, out of spite or forgetfulness, had failed to mention that he had emplaced unusual mystic safeguards, murderous defenses which his colleague had to overcome before the intellectual treasure could be seized. Bleek triumphed, however—he was practiced in besting such guardians—and he bore away his prizes, which subsequently revealed much to him of a nature useful to his grand quest. Embedded within those notes he did recover the sacred mysteries of the eon-dead Rhexellites. More remained to be learned, a deal more, but Bleek had gained, and he was pleased, grateful to his fellow magician. Through the coming years he pondered often the lore of Maltheus of Wise, the arcane fruits of a life steeped in wisdom and experimentation. He refused, on the other hand, ever to dwell on the fate of Maltheus, or the last words of that man to him. He writes:

> Naught I derive from this discarded life
> But a poor tale of madness, best untold
> That heart is stilled, that soul congealed and cold
> Which gave way before cares and horrors rife.

Such thoughts were not meet or wholesome for a great wizard like Jacob Bleek, who dreamed of accosting the mighty Gods of the universe, in order to wrench Their secrets from Them.

Vorchek's Vacation

"This is more like it," said Theresa to her companion as they arrived. "Peace and quiet, fresh air, beautiful scenery. We need a break from the common routine." She parked her car, an expensive red coupe, in the little lot under the great, old trees, got out to stretch. Her companion extricated himself from the small, tight vehicle. "Do you think so?" said he to his comely assistant; he being Professor Anton Vorchek, noted scientist and researcher into unusual and often lurid scientific questions. "By now, Miss Delaney, I would have thought that you realized there is very little of the common about my activities. This outing of ours, in fact, might be considered rather ordinary by some, for we are doing that which many others are wont to do, when they can." So it seemed, for they had journeyed to the delightful Oak Creek Canyon, the jewel of Arizona, in order to spend a few days at an isolated retreat, the Creekside Resort, a collection of well-apportioned cabins nestled on a wooded bluff overlooking the lovely stream. Below splashed the ever gushing waters; above loomed the awesome red cliffs, towering spectacularly for a thousand feet. It was Vorchek himself who, quite uncharacteristically, had suggested their getaway, hinting that it should prove a welcome interlude from the strange matters with which they often dealt, and which, occasionally, Theresa was known to find oppressive. Now, however, he seemed oddly amused by her attitude.

"All I mean to say," replied the girl, "is that I welcome an opportunity to put aside mysteries and horrors for a change, and indulge in some pleasant fun. Don't fuss with me, now—surely you agree—this vacation was your idea. I don't suppose there's something you haven't told me?" Vorchek grinned, then stated in his perfectly modulated, slightly accented voice, "There is much about much, always, my dear, that I have not yet told you. Stick with me, and eventually you will know all. In the meantime, let us bear upon present matters necessary and sundry. Check us in, if you please, while I gather the bags." She did so, and he did so, and shortly they were ensconced in Cabin Six—Palo Verde, it was named—a fine, stylishly rustic set of rooms with all of the required amenities and, most importantly, none that were not. The arrangements generally satisfied Theresa, although she did notice certain conspicuous lacks. "There's no TV," she pointed out with genuine wonder, "cell phones don't work, and the only regular phone is in the office." "As we desire," noted Vorchek. "Without distraction, we may more readily concentrate upon our mission." "What mission?" came the cry. "This is the first I've heard about any mission. What are you up to now, Professor?" "All I meant," he said smoothly, "all I could possibly refer to in this case, is our chosen task of enjoying ourselves. I, for one, intend to enjoy myself hugely. Look at all that beauty, right outside the window: the cool trees, the pretty little path, a pair of happy rabbits playing leapfrog."

Theresa accepted his answer. She informed him that she was hungry. It being too late for breakfast, which the resort provided, and far too early for dinner, which also constituted part of the package known as the "American Plan", the genial Vorchek suggested that they drive into Sedona for lunch, sight-seeing along the way. His companion eagerly accepted the advice. Soon they were heading south on the fine highway, stopping occasionally to enjoy pretty overlooks of the creek or majestic vistas of the impressive canyon walls. "Absolutely nothing we have to do," Theresa mused at one especially scenic locale," for day after day, as we please. It seems too good to be true." "Doesn't it?" replied the professor. They entered the ornate tourist center of Sedona, at the southern end of the canyon, where they treated themselves to messy but scrumptious cheese steak sandwiches from a walk-in sidewalk stand. That welcome task out of the way, Vorchek further suggested a visit to the local historical museum, which its brochures claimed to provide interesting attractions. Theresa agreed dutifully, although she was seldom as keen on such places as he.

The Sedona Museum of Pioneer History, as it was formally styled, actually consisted of a large park containing numerous old buildings and artifacts of former days, along with a visitor center which doubled as a research library. Vorchek, being who he was, immediately made for the latter, notebook in hand, which Theresa had not realized until now he had brought with him. "I may wish to take a few notes," explained the professor. "There are items of interest in local lore. I should not be long. Amuse yourself with the sights." So she did, as best she might, after he identified himself to the attendant and disappeared into the musty, bookish rear chamber. Theresa spent the better part of an hour wandering about the buildings: here a stone cabin, once the home of a founding resident, there a barn containing horse buggies and farm implements, beyond that a tin shed cluttered with a dead notable's rock collection. She saw these things, and other things, until eventually she thought she had seen quite enough of such for one day, or indeed a lifetime, so wandered back to the main building, to see if Vorchek had, for once, gotten his fill of research.

He had not—he never did—but he proved gracious about it. "I trust, my dear, that I have not kept you waiting. One can learn so much in places like this. Information gets tucked away among books and documents, lost to the great world, unless one knows where to poke for it. Why, just now I have been reading fresh details about the very spot where we are staying. There are items of history which have been left out of the advertisements for the Creekside Resort. They actually go back quite a ways." He had no interest in the other offerings of the museum (the girl surmised that only the book collection had lured him there), so they departed quickly.

Returning to the cabin, they decided to "seriously unwind", as Theresa put it; make no further plans, go nowhere in particular, just relax, and do only that which felt pleasant to them. For her that meant sprawling herself on the big, soft sofa with a mass of tourist flyers and guide books for company. Vorchek vanished into the bedroom, from where he presently emerged, having changed out of his fine suit into durable, if still natty, hiking clothes. He, ever bubbling with energy, now hefted his backpack and recommended a walk about the expansive property, all of which was supposed to be charming. She agreed, with the slightest of frowns, for she abhorred haste—her brilliant mentor always contrived to seem busy and rushed, regardless of circumstances—but she pulled herself up, changed into her own version of outdoors gear, which appeared as expensive and fashionable as her regular attire, and joined him.

Their tour of the grounds bore no resemblance to a genuine hike, being no more than a mild stroll among the cabins and into the surrounding greenery, but for all that they found much of natural beauty to enjoy. Birds sang among the numerous paths which wound among the trees on the bluff, and one trail dipped down into the bottom land of the stream, to which they shortly made their way. Oak Creek ran fairly wide and deep at this point, with high stone banks forming shelves of red rock, like a giant's staircase, which made access to the water easy. It was a lovely spot. White rapids splashed and gurgled above and below the quiet pool, which seemed to invite swimming. "We must try it sometime," said Vorchek. "Even here it becomes noticeably warm in the direct sunlight." From the bank they gained remarkable views of the red cliffs towering into the sky on both sides of the canyon. Theresa, who had come prepared for this, began to snap pictures with her camera. Vorchek, who had also come prepared, extracted from his bag a complicated device which he began to erect on a surface of level stone.

"Oh, professor, now what are you doing?" "Surely you are aware, my dear, of my intense interest in the art of surveying." "No, I'm not— I've never heard any such thing—nor did I have any idea that you brought gadgets with you." "I always travel with gadgets," he replied cheerfully. This particular one consisted of a small telescope, with several dials and meters, on a tall tripod. "I am verifying our exact location in space. My readings provided specific coordinates for this property, relative to certain outstanding landmarks. I wish to verify them. See that one formation, which vaguely resembles a ship? Now look up there, at that prominent spire. I am calculating angles and distances." "If you must," Theresa sighed.

Vorchek concluded his arcane business, apparently satisfied with the results, then abruptly announced that they had viewed everything of merit for the time being, and should return to the cabin to prepare for dinner. Theresa was not one to argue with that, so they leisurely wound their way back to the tiny outpost of civilization, where she amused herself for a spell with her glossy brochures, while he indulged in papers and books of a more formidable cast. Afterward, having changed clothing again (for both agreed on one thing, the necessity for proper attire at all times) they walked to the communal dining room, a fair sized hall with huge redwood beams in the ceiling and deep shag rugs on the floor. There they met the few other guests, and indulged in a glorious home-cooked repast of pot roast, creamed corn, green beans, mashed potatoes with plenty of butter, chased with apple pie and dollops of whipped cream.

The owners and managers of the resort were a youngish couple by the name of Evans, who also cooked and served the meal with their own hands. During the feast they formally introduced themselves to such guests as had not yet dined there, making several rounds to ensure that all present, who were paying well for the privilege, enjoyed their stay. Many a glowing comment they heard. The ebullient Vorchek struck up a conversation with them, plying them with smiles and questions. "How long had they owned the cabin complex? How did they come to acquire it? Did they do a handsome business? Did they get many repeat visitors?" Such questions he asked, seeming innocuous enough to Theresa, but as the gentle interrogation continued she detected a tense undercurrent, a mounting abruptness to the answers, a tightening of returned smiles. When the professor asked, in what should have been an artlessly casual manner, "Is it true that you got this place for a song?" his companion thought that their host and hostess responded with real testiness; certainly they made a sudden and successful, if awkward, attempt at breaking off the discussion. They went about their rounds, glowering now, leaving Theresa puzzled, while the professor, without a care in the world, ate with gusto, chirping about irrelevancies.

Later, back in the cabin, where they had retired for the night, she asked him about what she insisted on calling "the incident". He was calmly dismissive of her concern, but also told her of a few facts which had come to his attention. "I have researched the history of this location," he said. "I did so before we came, among the public records, and since our arrival at the museum. I appreciate knowing something about where I am staying. The earliest, haziest portion of the story goes way back. There are reports that Indians used to meet in this vicinity in the olden days, by the creek under the big red spire. The medicine men would meet there, using the rock shelves like benches, to hold their ceremonies. After they vacated the territory the land fell empty until 1905, when a fellow by the name of Snelling opened the first resort here, which he called the Oak Creek Inn. It did not last long—apparently tourism had not yet caught on in the area—but it is prime real estate, and very pretty country for travelers, so a man called Hodgson took it over for a little while; and then came Morton, who renamed it the Oak Creek Ranch, and Phillips, and a string of others, including Baseheart (who gave it its present name in the sixties), leading up to our present Evanses. Portifoy, the previous owner, went bust after only a few years, and our current hosts were able to pick up the property solely by assuming his debts. Here they are, doing their best I am sure, and yet at peak season the numbers of guests are few, while I have gleaned certain information indicating a steady erosion of financial resources. I would think they could clean up with such fine and expensive accommodations, and yet it seems that they suffer. What do you think, Miss Delaney? Perhaps sound heads for business do not gravitate to the Creekside Resort."

"I suppose," she replied, "sound heads avoid it like the plague. I don't get it. It has everything I want. Everything is just right here. It should be a gold mine for them. Maybe the kinds of people attracted to running such establishments aren't the cleverest when it comes to counting their pennies. I wouldn't know." There was much truth in that statement: Theresa, independently wealthy by inheritance, had never stooped to counting pennies. She rather pitied those who must.

"So," continued Vorchek, "out of idle curiosity I asked my questions, in all innocence, only to find that, just perhaps, they were not wholeheartedly appreciated. These things happen. Think nothing of it; to bed for us, I say, for we have a big day planned tomorrow, if we intend to take that hike up the canyon."

They slept. In the morning they woke early, long before the sun peeped over the top of the canyon. Professor Vorchek rose first, active and chipper, making sufficient noise with his toilet to ensure that no one within earshot could long remain abed. Theresa got up, frowzy and grumbling to herself. Vorchek hailed her when he became aware of her awakening. "I deem that a recuperative rest," said he. "I had not realized how much I needed a vacation. I feel years younger, and I am old enough to fret about such things." He carefully combed his short, neatly trimmed beard. "Last night dreams came to me, quiet, engaging dreams which entertained me at the time, though now, sadly, they slip away. I am sure there was something soothing about them, perhaps even a sense of importance to them. Is it not funny how a dream—even an unremembered one—may strike a person?" "Yes, professor, very funny." Theresa padded into the quaint and cozy bathroom in her pink bunny slippers, sighed, wearily proceeded to wash her face. "What is the matter, my dear?" asked Vorchek. "Do the comforts, the relative silence of nature, not suit you?" "I'm sure they did," she responded unhappily, "but I had dreams too, big enough to wake me a time or two, and they weren't all that cheery, so I had trouble getting back to sleep. I guess it's just one of those things."

The solicitous Vorchek chatted and flattered and wheedled the girl into a good humor, and when she was ready whisked her off to the resort's superb breakfast. They ate ham and eggs, and red-eye gravy, and biscuits with butter and jelly (the latter made from apples grown in an old, historic orchard on the canyon floor right down the road), drank quantities of fresh orange juice. They enjoyed it hugely, although their hosts seemed reserved and had little to say to them this morning.

VORCHEK'S VACATION

"Thrill me, Miss Delaney," urged Vorchek. "Tell me about your dreams."

"There isn't much to tell," she began, after a pause for another bite of succulent ham. "It wasn't really separate dreams, but one long one, which stopped when I woke, and then picked up again after I fell back to sleep. I was in a dark place, but there were lights nearby, flickering lights that cast a reddish glow. There were other people around me, in a kind of circle; strange people, all men, definitely not anybody I knew, although I couldn't see them well. They were talking, all of them, in low voices. I could hear their words fairly well, yet I couldn't understand them. Then the scene got darker—this happened more than once, and it was always this that woke me—it got darker, but the lights were still there. It was as if something big and black entered the circle of strange men and approached me. I felt briefly terrified, for there was something there, and I looked right at it, but I couldn't see it. I never did see it, because I didn't keep asleep." She stopped, to scrape up the last bits from her plate. "That's it; that's all there was. It doesn't sound much in the telling, but I didn't relish the experience at the time. So, Mr. Genius, what would the psychologist say about that?"

"There are many possible explanations," he drawled, "most of them humdrum and mundane. Let me check them off: what you ate last night did not agree with you; the unaccustomed darkness and peacefulness of the locale temporarily disturbed you; a nagging thought from regular life intruded and assumed odd forms; something you read got under your skin and emerged within your subconscious. Any one of these could be the answer. Do any of them seem likely to you?"

"Not really." "Very good," said Vorchek, who actually appeared pleased by what he heard. "In that case, given the dwindling range of allowable explanations, perhaps we should assume that the disquieting vision is entirely meaningless, representing nothing, connecting to nothing, a not uncommon condition of dreams. What else could it be? I hope that you are in fine form for our hike to Thomas Point."

The professor referred to a popular trail which ascended the eastern wall of the canyon, some miles north of their lodgings, promising to offer grand vistas of the magnificent terrain. Theresa assured him that she was in good fettle, and much looking forward to the day's expedition. That being so, they did not tarry, but returned to the cabin to gather their gear, and in no time had driven up the road to the trail-head.

The trail, a narrow path carpeted with dry pine needles, zigzagged unrelentingly upward along a brutal series of switch-backs. Theresa had occasion to think, and even found a moment to complain, that the professor had underestimated the difficulty of the climb. "The ascent is somewhat steep," he admitted as he marched along stolidly, "and the trail rather rugged, to be sure, but you must grant that the shade is welcome." So she did (in a gasp), for their route wound up through a pretty evergreen forest which, for a time, held the ever warming sun at bay. That changed, however, when they emerged onto the higher slopes, an open, scrubby region which spared them not the direct rays. The girl thought the hike lasted forever, but in a little over an hour they had reached the summit on the rim, atop a great, flat formation of limestone, forming a platform from which they could gaze down into the scenic splendors of the canyon. Theresa admired the view; Vorchek involved himself with his latest enthusiasm.

"Professor," cried his companion, after she had gulped a live-saving mouthful of water, "are you surveying again?" "Merely amusing myself," he explained, adjusting his instrument on the tripod, "by establishing our precise position. It is wonderful, I say, how much can be known, so easily. Observe, if you will, how readily one may identify yesterday's landmarks from here. There the ship, there the spire, and down there— look, by the riparian belt of the creek—our resort, clearly visible, and the red rock ledges at stream's edge. All may be seen from this spot, and possibly from no other. That may have been important, in ancient times, to the aboriginal inhabitants of the canyon." "Why so?" "Oh, did I not tell you?" Vorchek chortled, sitting down by her on the rocks and puffing his pipe alight. "This remarkably level mass on which we presently sit was favored by the Indians, utilized in yet another aspect of their spiritual ceremonies. When conclaves were held by night on the creek-side ledges—the very ones, by the way, which we explored yesterday—a separate party would make for this place in order to kindle great bonfires, visible from far below in the darkness, where strange rites would be performed in unison. It makes for an intriguing anthropological subject, one that has not been properly analyzed by students of native lore. To be fair, the Indians are not loquacious on the topic. I possess special informants, however, who have told me much."

"You're up to something," Theresa asserted baldly. "I know you are. This is just like you. What's it all about?" Vorchek grinned and tipped back his big hat, shook his head vaguely. "What can it be about? Such suspicions, Miss Delaney, are unwarranted. We came here to revel in nature's glory, as others have done so before us, throughout the ages. The old ones took such matters seriously, and I am always keen to know of the folkways and beliefs which descend to us from the past. Unique rituals were performed in these places—that much I have gleaned—and I would know more of them. I sincerely hope that my questing attitude will inspire within you a kindred interest rather than ire." "If that's all it is," she replied wearily, "then quest all you please. I'm just not looking for adventure."

"Indulge yourself," he said sagely, "in the adventure of rocks and trees, clean air and clean water. There can be no harm, only good." So it seemed. They tarried long at that high place, basking in the scenery and the warming sun. Then they wandered along the rim, Theresa noting with joy every new vista, Vorchek halting occasionally to take fresh measurements. Early in the afternoon they descended, an easy hike to the canyon floor, returning to their cabin after lunch in Sedona. Simple, relaxing amusements followed until dinner, when Theresa observed that their hosts were still "snooty". The professor averred that she was mistaken, for there could be no adequate cause. After that meal, with evening gathering darkly, he suggested another stroll in the lovely creek bottom.

There lingered some natural light by which to see, and Vorchek had brought his flashlight as reinforcement. The smooth, wide ledges of stone at the water's edge particularly interested him, and he spent a considerable time walking those surfaces, and peering into the murky hollows beneath them. Tucked here and there into rock crannies he spied traces of crude drawings which he identified as Indian petroglyphs. "Hundreds of years old, at least," he stated. "I have read of them, so I knew they must be somewhere about. Little remains, I see, although it appears that this star-burst symbol predominates. Look here, and there. It is significant." "We can see them better by daylight," Theresa opined. Night had fallen heavily now, with only the twinkles of stars overhead and the dim cabin lights filtering through the trees above the bank to supplement Vorchek's flash. "We could," he agreed, "but the atmosphere would be wrong. Some sites are best viewed in darkness. We see this as it is meant to be seen, as it has always been seen since the ages of prehistory." He stooped, produced a piece of chalk, drew a circle around a faint, deeply ingrained stain, as if from an old campfire, on the ledge. Theresa asked why he had done that. "I mark the spot for future reference," he replied. "We will return in the morning, after a sound rest."

Rest proved a selective concept that night. Vorchek, after scribbling some notes, hit the bed and sank instantly into slumber, dropping into unconsciousness with a smile. Theresa struggled with sleep, tiredness her only ally, for her mind continued to work long after she implored that it desist. She had questions to ask of the professor, questions which she had not ventured, for she feared the answers. By this time she guessed that he had something on his mind—yet another weird line of investigation, presumably, of the sort that always fascinated him—although so far it seemed innocuous enough, whatever it was. Surely their getaway was more than a vacation to him; he had plans, at least for purposes of research, which would be revealed in due course, probably to focus upon an unpleasant subject. The professor was a wonderful fellow, she thought, and she could not imagine life without him (it would certainly be dull by comparison), but his penchant for thrusting himself deep into creepy mysteries—and dragging her with him—had led in the past to difficult and dangerous situations, the very sort that she had been promised they were escaping from. Maybe his current enthusiasm was a little thing, a quaint historical footnote, a minor loose end which would be cleared up and forgotten. That would be nice. There need be no complications to entice him and scare her.

Theresa dozed, scarcely knowing that she did, and she dreamed. It was a curious experience for a dream, because she vaguely sensed that she ought to be dreaming, yet effort was required to convince herself that she was doing so. The setting very much resembled her vision of the previous night, although she saw more detail now. She found herself in a place of illuminated darkness: blackest night, yet with a flickering fire burning before her, and countless bright stars above. Strange looking, scantily clad men crouched about the fire, and around her, so it appeared, in a circle. This time the situation seemed more clear to her. She recognized the location, or thought she did; surely it was the largest rock ledge in the creek bed below the resort. From her current position she could see other ledges rising up the bank, ledges which also bore solemn watchers, barely visible at their farther remove from the flames. The waters of Oak Creek must be flowing beneath her, but she could not see them, for when she tried to turn for a look, she realized that she suffered from constraint. In fact, she was bound hand and foot with crude cords. Knowing this, she felt, as for the first time, the coarseness of her bonds, and the hard, uncomfortable stone beneath her body, which lay at full length on the ledge. Her bare feet pointed toward the fire, the heat of which irritated her toes. It occurred to her then that she was naked, a captive of the spooky men.

They began to chant, in a language which meant nothing to her—a harsh, guttural speech—and without any ostensible physical cause the fire flared, burning brightly and intensely, dark gray smoke billowing upward. Curiously, at that very moment of greater light the scene darkened dramatically. She observed less, as darkness spread. Then she realized that there was more to that darkness than an absence of light; a form, a substance of blackness, intruded upon the scene, encroaching upon and obscuring the illumination. A shape—a nightmare outline all in black— rose up before her beyond the fire, plunged through it suddenly and reached toward her. At that she screamed and awoke.

Perhaps she, instead, awoke and screamed, or maybe there were two screams, one of illusion and one of reality; regardless, Vorchek bolted instantly awake and then was holding her, attempting to calm her and stifle her sobs. "What is happening to me, Professor?" cried Theresa, and he demanded, "Tell me all."

Dawn broke. They skipped the provided breakfast, for there was much to discuss, matters which need not be aired publicly, and they made a casual meal, when the time came, from various snacks which they had brought with them. Vorchek, with an air of harried sheepishness, felt called upon to explain himself, for as it transpired there was a great deal that he had not told the girl, and a goodly amount of it seemed pertinent to her progressive dream affliction.

"There is no point," he admitted, "in reticence at this juncture. As I suspected, you have become thoroughly involved. Before we ever embarked upon this trip, I had deduced that esoteric forces were at work on this spot. My research has indicated psychic survivals here, emanating from the distant past, a period of such fabulous antiquity that the record of those days has quite vanished from conventional, acceptable history. I have gathered historical data concerning odd and unpleasant happenings here; hauntings, if you will, which I presume are responsible for the recurrent and otherwise unlikely difficulties which have for so long annoyed the owners of the property and defeated their hopes of commercial success. Weirdness reigns here. Most people feel it, even if nothing truly terrible happens to them, and while they are eager to come, they are often as eager to leave, and they do not return. Enterprises like the Creekside Resort thrive on repeat business, but this outfit seldom gets it. You begin to realize why.

"Armed with this preliminary knowledge—confirmed by what I

145

gathered the other day at the museum—I undertook a different line of study, which I counted on bearing fruit. I examined, with an open mind, the native legends concerning the locale, in so doing mined a lode of precious and provocative lore. There are stories; well, there are many stories, but here is the one which I think most applicable to your concerns. In ancient times, so long ago that even folk memory forgets the chronology of the era, there existed on the plains to the south, in the vicinity of modern Sedona, the seat of a mighty civilization, one which vanished eons before archeology allows for the rise of a high culture—in this region, or perhaps any other—and which has left virtually no solid trace of itself. In that supposedly impossible past a great city was erected there by people who, if myth tells truly, were the ancestors of the aboriginal tribes whom we still study, and whose primitive leavings scientists still sift from the earth. That city (which even in story has forever lost its name) was a grand place, a burgeoning metropolis of limestone towers and red rock palaces. Its inhabitants were cultured and wise, keenly aware of aspects of existence which have been forgotten in our times, but which the red men who descended from them remember in a hazy, barbaric fashion."

"Fascinating, Professor," interjected Theresa, "but nothing you're describing has anything to do with my dreams."

"But it does, my dear. I come to the linkage." Vorchek paused in contemplation, puffing on his pipe. "Native tales claim that the olden civilization ceased to be one fateful night long ago in the mists of antiquity, when the wise men and seers of the great city attempted to communicate with the ultimate gods of the universe, whom they worshiped and adored. Instead, they called down upon themselves fearful forces of absolute evil, which fell upon the city from the sky, obliterating it. The civilization died, along with most of its denizens, the handful of survivors plummeting to a savage condition of life. Medicine men of the Yotipai tribe, the people who dwelt here when the white man arrived, speak to this day of the 'Age of Misery' when the folk lived like animals, and knew no gods. In a later epoch they recovered somewhat, reestablishing a mode of piety, although one of which their forbears would not have approved. The Yotipai, you see, worshiped—perhaps out of fear—the great dark powers that had slaughtered their kin in the remote era of the city.

"My plan of action, as I conceived it, was a simple one: I wished to identify and precisely locate the exact seat of the surviving influence,

146

through my arts open that doorway into time just a crack, sufficiently to peer into those vanished years and glimpse what I could of those halcyon days of the fabled city. Now you appreciate my sudden fondness for surveying. I did identify the source of disturbance—those red ledges by the creek, which formed a ceremonial site until sometime in the last century—and I, unbeknownst to you, performed certain arcane calculations, equations of a type designed to make use of that psychic remnant and open that door. This I did, and, as you are aware, I too have dreamed. I saw the city in its glory, but imperfectly, as through fog. What I saw, however, was stimulating enough to lead me on and increase my desire to see more, and better."

Vorchek scowled. "I never intended or expected my scheme to impact you in any way. Knowing your moods, I saw no reason to acquaint you with my plan. 'Let the girl have her fun', I told myself. So much, it seems, for good intentions. There were untoward consequences. I reconstruct the situation thus: as I cracked the space-time continuum, ever so slightly, reaching back into that distant age, something leaked through from the other side. A less remote, less powerful (though still rather alarming) influence reached forward into the present, a shade from the gloomy period of evil darkness worship, and that influence, I regret to say, seems to be attracted to you. One can imagine the sorts of ceremonies performed on those ledges. There would be callings to the Dark Ones, and offerings would be made as well. Considering the attention that you have received, and the tales you have to tell, there is little doubt in my mind as to the nature of those offerings. Anthropologists of this territory have a deal to say, in an offhand fashion, about relics of human sacrifice."

"That's horrible!" cried Theresa. She lit a cigarette and blew smoke. "It fits, though. Those could have been Indians I saw, and I knew they were up to no good. They intended to kill me." "They were only visions," the professor pointed out. "They could not really hurt you." "So you say. It all seemed pretty real to me. Also, there was more: that dark thing at the last, like a shadow, but solid. It was heading my way."

"Yes, there is that." Vorchek drummed his fingers nervously on the arm of his chair. "I am certain that no harm could befall you physically; virtually certain, that is. There is the matter of the spirit to consider, however. Were that to be captured, there would be little of worth left of you. I can not allow such a risk, even if it be minimal. The effect of this place upon you is baleful, possibly destructive. You must go."

147

"Me? Professor, what about you?"

"My work is not yet complete. I wish to harness the energies accurately enough to gain a peek at the demise of the city. Another session is required. I remain. Apparently there is no danger to me. I will finish the job, then write my notes at leisure when the trip is over. You, on the other hand, must go. I shall bundle you off immediately."

Vorchek was adamant. Despite her protestations, Theresa found herself packed and pushed out the door within the hour. She would take the car, she was informed, and return for him the next morning. The girl sourly acquiesced, but refused to go any farther than Sedona, where she would arrange to spend the night. Vorchek agreed, deeming the distance from the source of the psychic disturbance to be adequate. After all, he observed, thousands of people lived there, day in and day out, without experiencing weird difficulties. So she left, presently to check herself into an equally expensive and especially ornate resort in town, and there, and in the surrounding neighborhood, she managed to amuse herself, although her mind often strayed to her companion and his doings. She wondered about his activities, wishing to take part and help him, as was their long custom. She would have called him that evening but, of course, Vorchek had no telephone at his disposal. She consoled herself by thinking that he would reveal all in the morning, and that she could aid him later with the preparation of his report.

Events did not develop so simply, however. Theresa stayed up late that night, trying to guess what the professor was doing at any given moment. The answer, as always, was that there was no telling with him. She situated herself in a big, well stuffed recliner, flipping through a travel magazine, attempting to distract herself, until something happened. She nodded off, is what happened, but that was not obvious to her at the time, as is ever the way. In the mists of drowsiness she felt a presence, or presences, as if someone or something far away were searching through darkness; searching for her, she thought, probing through the black fog of unnatural night. Whatever it was cast about, first this way, then that way, always a little bit closer, then seemed to home in suddenly, with great determination. There came a burst of light, a painful green flash, and then she was aware of new surroundings.

Theresa lay on stone, tightly bound, with the bonfire blazing at her feet and the reddish ledges rising up beyond. Around her chanted and danced the coppery men with their feathers and their face paint, all in frenetic motion. The ceremony was wilder and noisier this time, as if her captors really meant business now. They cried out in their unplaceable language, calling to something that lurked beyond the flames and the darkness, something that dwelt infinitely far away, perhaps, yet which heard and would respond if it chose. Theresa screamed—her scream vibrated strangely in her ears, as if it were the voice of another—for she knew what was coming, what would happen next. Despite the bright blaze the darkness encroached, pressing nearer to her, and a black shape seemed to detach itself from the gloom, a shadow of substance that moved as if alive, as if drawn by an irresistible craving; a craving only for her. It advanced, and the men howled triumphantly, and the thing loomed over her, and she saw at last its face. She screamed again, and the sound of her extremis rose to a pitiful shriek of hopeless terror.

Then the other figure intervened. Another dark form lunged into view, but this was the wholly human shape of a tall, lean man dressed in a long loose jacket that billowed about him as he confronted the thing. Arms outstretched, the man thundered unknown words in a magnificently familiar voice, cast into the air from his right hand a dusty powder that sparkled redly by the light of the fire. The scintillating motes swirled, fastening themselves upon the massive, moving shadow, and when they did so the black image made a sound which was not proper for human ears to hear. The shadow receded, or dwindled, or in some fashion reduced, in scarcely the blink of an eye, until it was gone. The Indians, taken aback by the incredible intrusion, had held back, but now made as if to come at their unwanted visitor. He seized a burning branch which lay half within the fire, brandishing it before him, shouting in a tongue which surely resembled that of the attackers. They recoiled as if stunned, began slipping away into the darkness, glancing hatefully over their shoulders as they disappeared into the night. When they had departed the man, none other than Professor Anton Vorchek, knelt to Theresa and gathered her into his arms.

The girl came to herself in surroundings which she recognized as that same cabin at the Creekside Resort, from which she had been driven out the previous morning. Vorchek hovered about with hot tea and ministrations and a curious tale, one remarkable for what it contained, as well as for what it lacked. He had, that night, indulged in his final experiment. At midnight he had repaired to the ancient ceremonial site, laying out his esoteric materials on the stone ledges above the creek and, via certain verbal formulations of antique repute, had opened wider, under conditions of full consciousness, that which he described as a doorway into prehistory. He had seen again the glorious city of the forgotten days, and had beheld, momentarily, the events of the fateful night on which it met doom. The wise men of that age, he said, must have been both brilliant and brave to attempt such a feat, to call down to themselves those mysterious dwellers from the outer spheres, whose natures and intentions could only be assumed until it was far too late. That cunning experiment had gone horribly wrong, and the Dark Ones had swarmed from the sky or appeared suddenly out of nothingness. The folk began to shout, the city began to burn... and at that point, with his interest and curiosity equally aflame, he had sensed a counter-force coursing through the dimensional crack, repelling him, driving him back, obscuring all images. Darkness enveloped him, and he briefly imagined himself under psychic assault, until he realized that the intense power flowed past him, toward an indefinite destination in the present. All sense of immediacy left him then, though he possessed vague memories of mental anguish and unspecified tribulations, but when full awareness returned he was back on the big ledge, crouching over the naked, unconscious form of Theresa Delaney. Of how she had come to be there he knew nothing, although he guessed at dreadful developments, and in short order he conveyed her to the cabin where he wrapped her in a blanket, tending to her until she was ready to speak, and to enlighten.

This she did, while her unwitting savior marveled at her story. "Sedona was not nearly far enough," said he, "for once having fastened upon you, the force was capable of reaching through distance of space as well as time. I must bear that in mind in future. The influence at the city site has entirely faded, but the medicine men of the Yotipai and their forebears kept it alive and powerful here throughout the eternities. Fascinating, that the secondary source should harbor such grave danger—including, as it turns out, a physical peril—when people live happily above the scene of the root cause. Oh, my dear, I will have to investigate this. I say to you that much more remains to be learned. This region is a mine of supernatural ore, begging to be excavated. I shall delve again, but alone next time."

"But Professor," wailed Theresa, "how far is far enough? The dark force snatched me from miles away and brought me here. If you hadn't charged in when you did, that would have been the end of me." "True, but perhaps no longer relevant." "So you say."

"I do," Vorchek replied with emphasis. "It still amazes me that I was capable of intervening, for we resided within somewhat different planes at that point, yet I managed the crossing at a subconscious level; and a beautiful transition, too. Regardless—though we must not tempt fate—I think you safe now. That powder I employed to banish your tormentor must have been the essence prepared for me long ago, by a local gentleman, for just such circumstances. Tonipah was his name, a mighty shaman of the old school, who knew a thing or two about protection from intangible menaces. We may have seen the last of the Dark One, or it may have lost its taste for you. I am impressed that its unholy desire for you attained such heights. You, too, may possess properties worthy of analysis. That will wait, however. For the time being, you require peace and quiet. The Creekside Resort, I fear, will not serve. I must call for a taxi if we are to retrieve your car."

"The sooner we clear out," said Theresa, "the better. We still need a break from mysteries and nastiness. Let's take another vacation, but this time, I'll pick the place."

An Eastern Tale

Jacob Bleek, the chronicler of old, collector and compiler of many a strange and frightful story for posterity, relates a legend said to be ancient when he wrote it down, of a young man who lived in the wonderful oriental city of Elibama in the dimly remembered heyday of that jungle shrouded metropolis. Naught remains there now save picturesque ruins, overgrown with a silent mantle of creeping green, but when Bleek composed Elibama was still a fair city with some claims to glory, and there are extant reports, of a dubious nature, that Bleek actually visited the locale early in his career, which may explain how he became acquainted with the story. Who told it to him he deigns not reveal, but it is known that the priests of the city's many gods were wise, powerful, and learned in olden lore, so perhaps they passed it on to the inquisitive traveler. Regardless, there dwelt in Elibama this young man, by the name of Bombas, a poor man since birth who did not relish poverty or its accompanying travails, rather dreaming of wealth and all the pleasures it could bestow.

In those days, of course, a poor man likely remained poor until he died. That was the nature of the world then, just about everywhere, certainly in Elibama. Bleek poetically describes the ways of that fine city when it rose like a great jewel out of the surrounding tropical forests:

Lordly prince with avarice staggering
Rapacious soldiers cruel and swaggering
Clever priests lusting ever after alms
Peasants in squalor fobbed with gruel and psalms.

It was not a good time to be Bombas. Poor he was—existing in a wretched mud hut, surviving hand to mouth on the pathetic fruits of his little garden—and ill contented to be so, for while he lacked all else he possessed imagination, could conceive of a better state for himself. Indeed, a survey of his milieu suggested alternative states of being, for there were those within the range of his gaze (prince, soldiers, priests, for example) who lived grandly by his standards, and he had the daily image of the fairer aspects of Elibama ever before him. Such a beautiful city it

153

was, with its marble palaces and temple towers, its gigantic statues of the gods chiseled from indestructible granite, its lofty walls and ornately carven gates. Much treasure poured into a principality strategically situated on lucrative trade routes. Elibama offered so much, and could be a joyous place to live, if a man could hope for more opportunity than that of huddling in a hut beneath the lowering city walls.

There was little, of ethical sort, that Bombas could do to enhance his station in life. One must be born to the title of prince; warriors were selected from the noble families; the priesthood demanded rarefied education which Bombas lacked. He might resort to thievery, as others did, but the penalties were atrocious; or he might flee to other lands, but he knew little of the world beyond the jungle, nor whether foreign realms differed in significant particulars from his own. He spent his tedious, aimless days, therefore, wracking his brain seeking unusual avenues of prosperity.

A desperate and dismal thought did occur to him. The priests spoke much, and with great disfavor, of a horrid, desolate land far to the east, a dreadful place known as the Valley of Voltakis, where dwelt evil monsters. These fearsome entities, said the priests, lived for the sole purpose of amusing themselves by entrapping foolish mortals, luring them to their doom by making false promises, offering much but delivering little. Those nasty beings, so preached the acolytes of the Gods, fed on human souls, and would resort to foul trickery in order to satisfy their vicious spiritual hungers. The folk of Elibama were strenuously warned against ever journeying to Voltakis or trafficking with its denizens. Among the peasants, however, different tales were told. Rumors circulated that the curious creatures of Voltakis were magicians of a kind who wrought miracles for those who dared beg favors of them. There was no limit to their power—the priests, by comparison, appeared as charlatans—and the man who could satisfy them could ask any boon he pleased, and have it for the asking.

Bombas appreciated that variant of the tale, which struck him as being more in line with the way the world ought to work, if there be any justice at all in the universe. With his aspirations and dealings in Elibama destined to fail, why not strike out into the blue, journey to the fabled valley, meet these wise beings and dicker with them? He had nothing to lose, he assured himself, yet all his fantasies to gain.

His friend Motra demurred when told of the scheme. Bombas did have this very good friend (an aspect of his life to which he paid less heed than he might), an excellent fellow wholly dedicated to him since

154

childhood, who wished him happiness and long life, but who thought poorly of courting mysterious dangers. "Seek not the Valley of Voltakis," warned Motra, "for the ways of its occupants are not our ways, nor those of any man. The priests who care for our souls have spoken, tell us that those demons weave snares for the feet of the unwary. The risk is great, nor can such monsters ever produce true happiness. Shun them, live your life as best you can, be content. There is much of goodness in Elibama." "Well do I know," warmly replied Bombas, "that much goodness exists, for I see it in the hands and purses of others every day of my lowly life. I would have some of that in my hand. If the demons can produce miracles, then I will ask them for a treasure fit for a prince; surely a little request by their standards, for I might demand they make me emperor, or grant me wings for flying, or rearrange the stars to spell my name. You see, Motra, I am reasonable, nor will not ask for too much, lest the Gods envy me. I shall go." Motra could not convince him otherwise. In fact, Bombas begged his devoted friend to accompany him on the frightful trek. Motra suffered an agony of misgivings, but he was a faithful friend of the bosom, so he allowed persuasion and flattery to triumph in the end. They would go together. "At least I may watch out for you," declared faithful Motra.

They departed early one morning before dawn, stealing out through the city gates to the east, with a single mule between them to carry their supplies. Passing beyond the belt of farmland that encircled the city, they plunged into the vastness of the jungle, a region of towering, canopied trees and murky swamps, tenanted only in the infrequent clearings, crossed only by a few tracks and aimless footpaths. They pursued as best they might an eastward course, eventually finding themselves on a particularly reprehensible trail, seldom trodden by human feet, which did point them ever to the east. Colorful birds flitted in the creepers overhead, beasts lurked fleetingly glimpsed in the undergrowth, while gloom reigned eternally within the shadowed forest. For days they marched.

Came they to a rise, and when they crested the ridge they peered from behind the trees down into the Valley of Voltakis. They were sure of the place, for they gazed into a land quite unlike their own, where the jungle which had shrouded them all of their lives gave way to a barren, bowl-shaped plain, largely devoid of flora, surrounded by jagged, rocky peaks. Through the center of the plain ran a small stream which trickled off of the mountains, collecting in a narrow channel before disappearing into a distant gorge. They descended the ridge onto the plain, following the miserable, brackish gray watercourse which drained unerringly to the east. All that day it took them to reach the point at which black walls of basalt rose above the stream, were they stopped short.

Carven on a great vertical slab of blackness at the mouth of the gorge were strange olden words which they could not read, and a curious graven image which they could describe, but not identify. Chiseled into the volcanic stone they beheld a picture of a gigantic eye, one with a myriad of tiny eyes scratched within, thousands of them. "This be not good," said Motra. "This be a land of terrible magic, where many eyes will watch us, though we see them not. Bombas, my dear friend, let us return." "This is a land of marvels," cried Bombas, "so replete with glorious wonders that a million eyes would not suffice to see them all. Let us persist. We go forward." Jacob Bleek, that hoary old mystic, claiming to know a thing or two of such matters, interjects his own views within his rendition of the tale.

> Gaze not overlong on the million eyes
> That great Xenophor from the dark unseals
> 'Tis a vision of fate the wanderer feels
> Glowering amusedly from cosmic skies.

Bleek suggests that the pair had entered a domain where other gods, unknown to common men, reigned supreme, provides further elements of the story to indicate as much.

The shadows grew long, so while Motra could not win his beloved friend to the side of safety, he did successfully argue for a nightly halt. There they made camp and fed themselves from their meager stores and afterward, well into the evening, brooding Motra attempted to sway eager Bombas from his hazardous course. The latter was adamant, so at first light they proceeded into the chasm, which narrowed and rose about them until soon they trekked by the rancid, discolored stream between soaring walls of dense blackness which shut out all but traces of sunlight which filtered dimly from far above them. In that canyon they observed naught living but thorny weeds, scorpions, spiders, and green-glistening beetles.

What, precisely, did they seek? Bombas did not know, believing only that they should accost somewhere in that awful place the dwellers thereof. He expected to stumble upon a fairy town or a grand castle where wise ones were like to live. He did not foresee quite what he found: a dark, ominous opening in the sheer wall to his right, atop a heap of precariously jumbled boulders; the entrance into a foreboding cave, the mouth flanked by starkly pale pillars of granite, crude steles into

156

which were carved more unguessable writings and more weird pictures, some of the latter of a cast most terrifying. Motra, certainly, took this view, for he said, "Are those you wish to meet within the cave beyond the pillars? If so, it is death to approach them. Those are drawings of souls in torment, souls of foolish men beset by monsters. The priests speak sincerely. Bombas, friend of my boyhood and my heart, do not sell your most precious possession to evil ones in exchange for baubles. Never will you find your happiness in this horrible land, only death or that which is worse than death. Let us go at once, and before the blue sky fades into night let us put miles between us and this cave."

Snarled Bombas, "Silence, Motra. Defy not my will nor sap my strength. The magic workers of Voltakis reside within that cave. So be it; what is it to me that they choose earth and stones for their roof, that they hide themselves in burrows? Did you expect an easy path to their door? They cater only to the brave, I tell you, and that is I. We shall light torches and enter their kingdom. Surely my goal be not far."

They climbed the dangerous rocks to the crumbly ledge where the cave mouth loomed. With wooden staffs and pitch they fastened torches, ignited them, stepped gingerly into a black gloom which swallowed them whole. They advanced along a gently descending, ever narrowing passage. Such darkness enveloped them that the remembered night of the terrestrial surface seemed like bright, cloudless noon. Their feeble illumination sputtered and flickered, offering only that bare radiance necessary to set one step before the other with faint hope of safety. Their heads occasionally scraped painfully the hard ceiling; at times the walls pressed against them, so that they must squeeze through with special care. The tunnel wound down, down for a frightening period, and there were confusing twistings and branchings which gave rise to fears of becoming lost in the black fastness. Then, when they could scarcely more endure the ordeal, the walls fell away, and they entered a lofty chamber of unknown extent.

The ceiling was lost in darkness far above, the opposite side of the chamber vanishing in murky mystery, but there was something to see nevertheless. Five figures stood before them at the limit of visibility, gaunt, pale, robed forms that might have been men. Here Jacob Bleek remarks:

Adventurers to the Voltakis caves
Terror must face in mocking human form
Beings wise and canny beyond the norm
Who may deign to grant what the seeker craves.

157

Bleek goes on to describe the underground dwellers of Voltakis, and certain features of their subterranean world which do not appear in the tale, which makes one wonder how much of his information is purely hearsay; he almost seems to write from personal knowledge. Regardless, as he relates the story the central figure stepped forth at this point into the wavering light, and the thing was most certainly not a man. It walked with a curious motion, as if moving on legs with too many joints, and when it waved its inappropriately long arms above its head they seemed to bend improperly at too many places. That head was nightmarish: hardly more than a skull, and a malformed skull at that, with dead, hairless, blue-white skin stretched tautly over the misshapen bones. Ears and nose there were none, only holes, and two deep holes of sunken sockets from which tiny bright eyes peered maliciously. The mouth was small, pursed, and when it opened to speak there gleamed numerous needle-like teeth.

"Brave traveler," hissed the awful creature to Bombas, with a note of sarcasm or secret amusement in its voice, "you have come far from the land of men to seek the wise ones of Voltakis. You have arrived. That you desire something of us is plain, for it is ever so. We take no interest in you or your kind; we are content here, dwelling joyfully in our perpetual night, yet you will confront us in our realm. Our powers are great, our possibilities limitless. What do you want, and why should we give it to you?"

"I am a poor man," cried Bombas, "who would be rich, who hungers for the princely wealth that brings all fame and happiness. I come to you, mighty magicians of Voltakis, for only you may grant to me that which I need as I crave air and food. Work your spells, say your words, mix your potions, and give to me what I desire: the treasure of a prince." "Readily spoken," mused the grotesque thing of the inner world, "but why so readily granted? We may act if it pleases us to do so, yet for our efforts there must surely be recompense. It is right and just that he who offers nothing, receives nothing in return. What do you offer?" "I said I am a poor man," replied Bombas. "I come to you as I am, with virtually all of my earthly possessions on my body." "Poor in material worth," said the monstrosity, "but rich in spirit. We of Voltakis are not statues of marble. We thrill to our own species of lusts and hungers, which you can satisfy. Give us your soul, and you shall have aught else."

"That he shall not do," thundered Motra, who leaped forward

before his companion and thrust an accusatory finger at their horrid host. "Bombas is my true friend, and I journeyed with him to this place of evil solely to protect him from the snares of cunning monsters. I defy you and your foul trickery. On my life, I say you shall not have his soul."

Intoned the demon in its reptilian parody of speech, "What say you, Bombas?" And Bombas, without hesitation, stepped from behind his defender, replied simply, "I will have wealth, and I shall pay. You may take the soul of this Motra."

"So be it," snapped the creature of Voltakis; "It is done!" At those words the other four figures, until now silent, motionless, and wreathed in gloom, lunged forward and seized the startled Motra. He screamed and dropped his torch, and struggled, and cried out to Bombas, who did nothing as the beings fastened upon his faithful friend to hustle him away into the impenetrable darkness beyond the range of the remaining torch. His shrieks lingered a while, then faded and died. Motra was gone.

"Offer and acceptance," whispered the hideous spokesman. "The deal be made. In exchange for a mere soul of common man, you, Bombas, receive in return the veritable wealth of a prince. To that you are agreed? Rest, then, content. Already the treasure of a prince—gold, jewels, priceless ornaments of silver—awaits you complete in your hut back in Elibama. Go there at once, without delay, and you shall learn for yourself that I speak truly. That is all." And the thing turned away and followed its grisly fellows into the darkness.

So Bombas made his way back to civilization with elation (though without Motra), tingling with anticipation at the thought of the treasure awaiting him. Not without difficulty he escaped from the dreadful cave, entertaining himself through those grim miles with visions of the fabulous palace he would have erected to his glory. He recovered the mule, laboriously followed the poisonous stream in the black canyon to the desert plain betwixt the stark peaks, dreamed of the coterie of submissive dancing girls who would offer their charms for his delight. He bade farewell to the shunned domain of Voltakis and plunged back into the oppressive jungle, where the mule sickened and died from snake bite, but Bombas went on, and came the morn when he spied the lovely, beckoning towers of Elibama, fair city where he had been pauper, now would be as prince. He hastened, as weariness would allow, through the gates to his pathetic hut, raced inside to behold what should be there if the monster magician of Voltakis had not lied. Bombas shrieked his joy. The fiend had spoken truth: the dirt floor of the mud and thatch hovel lay buried beneath a thick carpet of glistening coins, gold ingots, silver necklaces, anklets, armlets studded with jewels, heaps of gems that twinkled like stars. Indeed, Bombas possessed now the treasure of a prince! He flung himself into the midst of all that splendor, wallowed and swam in it.

Then the brutish soldiers burst in, arresting Bombas on the spot, confiscating his new found wealth, forthwith hauling man and goods to the palace for questioning. Said interrogation did not last long; the furious prince and master of Elibama cared not how Bombas had committed the crime, the exact details of which remained forever a mystery to the authorities; it sufficed them to know that someone, in the wee hours of darkest night, had spirited the prince's treasure from his well-guarded storehouse (collusion being suspected, those guards paid with their lives) and removed it to the peasant's hut. Asked to explain, Bombas gabbled such a story that the prince and his councilors laughed heartily out of genuine humor before they decreed his fate. Said fate involved imprisonment in the foulest dungeon beneath the palace, prolonged torture and a miserable end, which need not be further elaborated.

Although he was not an altogether good fellow, one may spare some pity for poor Bombas, who thought to traffic for gain with strange powers beyond his ken. The lords of Voltakis employed some manner of subterfuge against him, though he received exactly what he requested: the treasure of a prince. In retrospect, one may argue that Bombas should have established that said prince was in no position to demand it back. The moral of the story is weak, if age old. Jacob Bleek sums up the matter succinctly.

> If beggars would fare with demons nicely
> Attaining all that makes their hearts flutter
> Calculate well before tongue does utter
> Be sure of what's asked, and ask precisely.

Under the Natural Bridge

The quaint little Arizona town of Payson is surrounded on all sides by a wild and rugged country, a land of rolling hills, stark cliffs, and steep ridges, where well-watered valleys and narrow ravines plunge precipitately into gloomy depths. Over much of this difficult, untraveled terrain lies a thick, dense cloak of murky pine forest, a largely unbroken expanse of old growth which has, for some reason, never attracted the heavy hand of destructive civilization in the past, and has proven remarkably unamenable to development to this day. It is a pretty land in its own harsh, forbidding way; there are those fantastic variations of elevation and geological form which picturesquely catch the eye, and there are colors, too—the somber green of the vast woods, the many slight shadings from brown to orange in the soil of the higher exposed summits, and the stratified hues of gray and white and red and pink and black found among the boulders and facing the cliffs of granite, limestone, and frozen lava—which draw the attention while they, curiously, seem to repel the visitor; for few ever go there, and fewer still ever stay. Payson has its season of tourists, those who long for a quietly pleasant interlude from the wearing aspects of regular life, but the people come there, pause for a period, and leave, without ever choosing to venture into the oppressive remoteness which presses upon that human outpost.

The wildest and most inaccessible territory lies to the north-west, where the rocky, clustered hills turn aside to reveal a fairly level plain of sere grasses and low scrub, which stretches off to the south for some miles, with the peaks rising higher on all sides, before terminating at the slope of a narrow mountain valley which drops into depths unseen. There is a road, of sorts, which shoots across the plain straight like an arrow, a terrible road laid down long ago, scarcely fit for any kind of motor transport, but perhaps once thought suitable for horse-drawn conveyance. The route dates back further still in time, for it marks the course of an old Indian trail. Man did live there in the shunned country long ago, before the white man came, and once upon a time in considerably greater numbers, as is attested by the crumbling prehistoric ruins which mar the skylines of the flat volcanic mesas and which have left rubble-strewn mounds scattered about the forsaken plain.

The so-called road dives steeply down from the plain into the constricted valley, twisting and turning and winding along the hazardous slope from one switch-back to another, and during this descent the quality of the driving surface is not to be happily described. One may ask how a native goat could dare that soft, eroding path, but it has been done, for in a former era the Indians made their way down to the bottom, and in a rather later age a rancher made the valley his abode, spending many years in a determined yet, ultimately, unsuccessful attempt to eke out a living while hoping to earn his fortune.

This he failed to do, for reasons obscure, although the valley bottom is a fecund realm of great broad-leafed trees and tawny meadows, moistened and vivified by the perennial waters of Pine Creek, which trickles down always from hidden springs in the hills and has, through the course of sweeping geological ages, carved the valley which bears its name. The Pine Creek Valley is, objectively speaking (if one may speak objectively of such matters), a beautiful place, a teeming haunt of wildlife and, ostensibly, a suitable habitat for man. There is something more of interest down there, also a product of the relentless actions of the flowing waters, although this unusual feature is not immediately discernible. One may stroll across the meadow, where the tall grasses sway in the wind and underground water bubbles up in green-fringed ponds, until the even surface terminates at the upper rim of a mighty cliff which plunges sheer to Pine Creek far below among the rocks. The winding stream appears to emerge from the base of the cliff. If one backtracks a bit, and turns to the right a little, one soon arrives at the top of another cliff which looks down upon a narrow ravine, through which the creek courses until it disappears beneath one's feet. What is this? The creek has vanished under a mountain of limestone. In truth the probing, corrosive tongues of spraying foam and swirling eddies have eaten into the rock over millions of years, nibbling at the stone via infinite gradations until the channel has chewed its way right through the enormous mass, cutting a tunnel under the earth. This marvelous formation is known as Tonto Natural Bridge.

The natural bridge may be justly deemed one of the wonders of the world. There are others of its kind, and better known, to which the tourists flock in awe at the lovely power of nature, but there are none so large and magnificent as Tonto. Hundreds of feet rises the bridge of native rock from the small stream that fashioned it, hundreds of feet runs the vast tunnel below the massive arch. So broad is the bridge that the casual visitor may walk across it without ever knowing that it is there. Descending to its base requires an arduous descent along a minimal path down the southern cliff face (or a much longer, and in some ways equally difficult hike along the rocky, overgrown banks of the creek to the north face), but this can be done, and the reward for the effort is ample. Artesian waters from the upper meadow splash down in a tall, cooling waterfall over the enormous opening in the cliff, a great gap which resembles the mouth of a gigantic cavern. So deep is the tunnel that the far end can not, at first, be seen. One must enter the eternal gloom of the tunnel, and fabricate a perilous trail among the huge boulders which have crashed down from the jagged ceiling, wading through cold pools of the still churning creek, before daylight may be spied ahead, and one confirms that this is not a fabled entrance into the inner bowels of the planet. Tonto Natural Bridge is a grand place, a fitting destination for the lover of natural beauty, but not many go there. The entire region constitutes a world of mystery, sensed rather than cogitated, one that tends to repel, so few there are who embark upon the trek, even when they are aware of the proximity of such a vista.

Yet, on this warm morning, three made the trip. They came by jeep, passing along the disreputable high clearance dirt road to the edge of the valley, and then commencing the agonizing, teeth-gritting descent of the steep slope. They accomplished this task in a welter of orangish dust, and when they had completed that lengthy, bone-jarring drive they ground to a halt on the fringes of the quiescent meadow in the shadow of the tottering, long abandoned ranch house. The three exited the jeep, pausing to beat the dust from their wind-soiled garments. The trio presented a disparate sight. The obvious leader of the group was the tall, thin, bespectacled gentleman with the oilcloth hat, neatly clipped iron-gray beard and smart attire of leather jacket, tie, and pressed long pants into which his walking boots snugly fitted: Professor Anton Vorchek, lecturer on sundry matters, lifelong student of the strange and explorer of mysteries. He was dressed properly for the day, yet had dressed well, as was his wont. His beautiful assistant joined him, the delightful Theresa Delaney, a young, bright-eyed blonde who seemed overdressed for the occasion in what might have passed for an expensive designer's vision of a stereotypical safari outfit: a small, bowled velvet hat, tan, form-fitting blouse, short, open jacket trimmed with fur, a heavy tan skirt and high, fashionable boots. She prided herself on always looking her best, with only necessary concessions to functionality. On the far side of the jeep, now rooting through his backpack, crouched the third member of the party, a young fellow who seemed out of place among such company, with a lean face sprouting two day's growth of stubble and wild hair tucked under a baseball cap turned backwards: Jason Crawford, a graduate student of the professor. His clothing, though suitable for the place, stood in marked contrast to that of his companions, while being quite typical of his type. He wore two layers of ragged shirt, the outer layer boasting some sort of irrelevant citation or advertisement, wrinkled denim shorts and clunky, big soled shoes without socks. He was comfortable, and he gave no other thought to the matter.

The natty professor surveyed the scene, taking in the soft golds and greens of the pleasing meadow, the ancient trees beyond, the surrounding hills and ridges farther away, paying special attention to the ruins of the historic house before him. The structure was a hopeless wreck, with sagging wooden walls, vacant windows, broken door, and collapsed roof, with the tall limestone chimney alone remaining intact. "As I had previously gathered," said he, speaking in a well modulated, slightly accented voice, "the old habitation is useless for our purposes. If we stay, we camp; and we do stay, until our business be complete. Miss Delaney, consult the checklist again. Verify that we have everything, and then you and Mr. Crawford sort the gear. I shall explore the rim of the ravine—" he indicated the tree line beyond the meadow—"and the cliffs, which should be to our left down the valley, there seek the best avenue of descent."

Theresa, in her official role of private secretary the organizer for the team, shrugged and went about her business while the professor departed. Jason joined her, eager to lend a hand to the lovely girl, which she politely discouraged, although not sufficiently to stop him. He launched into covert conversation so soon as their third member was out of earshot. "What is Vorchek like in real life?" asked the graduate student. "You would know; you work for him." "We associate," replied the girl. "I help him in his work, among other things. What's there to know? He's a professor interested in weird stuff. You know that much—it's why you're here, I suppose—and if you've listened in class you also know he's accustomed to getting results. The professor is a great one for new knowledge. Sometimes I think it's all he lives for." "Well, it must be boring following him around doing the dirty work for him." "I don't describe what I do in that light, and its seldom boring; no, never that." Jason leaned closer and grinned. "So what do you do in your off time?" he asked. "Mind my own business," she snapped.

Professor Vorchek returned. "Proceeding down the cliff," he announced, "is as good a way as any, and shorter. There is a path that will serve, if vertigo be not a concern. Excellent, my dear: everything we need in bundles of three. I shall carry the scientific equipment—Miss Delaney, you can surely handle the foodstuffs and drink—while you, Mr. Crawford, will port the camping gear. I trust that it be not too large a load for you." Vorchek collected his materials and set off for the southern end of the meadow, traveling easily. Theresa scooted after him, wobbling a bit from the weight of two modest coolers. Jason staggered in the rear, mumbling quietly to himself, carrying by far the biggest burden.

"We have entered a region," lectured Vorchek as he marched, "where strange things are said to happen, of which strange tales have been told. The earliest recorded Indian legends refer to powerful forces lurking down here, and such stories have been generated into the historic period. In our time we have acquired some scientific evidence which may connect, in some fashion, to these claims. Soon, my friends, we will know much more. We approach the heart of mystery, and we make up an expedition uniquely suited to uncovering that mystery. Myself, with my specialized background in science and ancient lore; Miss Delaney, ever the most charming and gracious of assistants—" she chuckled good-naturedly at that—"and, of course, Mr. Crawford, my student, who is sure to prove useful, as only graduates can, and as a result of his eager endeavors here will undoubtedly earn his cherished 'A'. Useful chaps, graduate students, and never more so than at present." Jason, breathing somewhat heavily by now, did not chuckle, nor make reply of any kind, save to roll his eyes when no one was watching.

Quail called their startled cries and flew out of the tall grass by a little bubbling pond. As the three hikers went on they came across more water emerging from the springs, which coalesced into rivulets and sluggishly flowed down the almost imperceptible slope to the south. They came to the edge of the cliff, really an alarming drop, though it afforded them a fine view of the lower valley, a green, overgrown place which might more properly be labeled a narrow canyon. Vorchek peered over where the little streams trickled into the void. "Down there we go," said he. "See the path zigzagging to our left? It may not look much, but will surely suffice. The Indians made use of this path in lost ages, while

165

later Harbury drove cattle down this during spells of drought." "Who's Harbury?" wheezed Jason, who had dumped his load. Theresa cried, "Didn't you pay attention to anything? Harbury is the rancher who used to live here." "Quite right, my dear. Wallace Harbury was the name of the man who staked this claim, the fellow who named the natural bridge as well. In case it is not obvious to you, we are standing on top of it now." "It isn't obvious," she replied. "Professor, it's a pretty enough spot, I suppose, but it's awfully tough getting to the place, and I wonder if it was worthwhile trying to run a business here. Did Mr. Harbury finally give up?"

"Follow me in single file," cautioned Vorchek, and with that he stepped down from the rim and began the long descent of the problematic trail. "Abundance of water," he observed shortly, "is ever a great attraction in Arizona, where ever it may be found. In Harbury's case, there may have been another draw, if local folk history be accurate. My sources, certainly, inform me that those who came before him had another reason. Regardless, he did not 'give up'. He labored here for years prior to his unfortunate demise." "Oh, he died," muttered Jason. Said Theresa, "Demising people usually do. What exactly happened to him?" "He took his own life, some time after the disappearance of his family." On that unpleasant note they trudged onward for a time in silence.

As they plumbed the lower gorge they gained a better view of the wonders to their right. At the bottom they saw a jumble of great, mossy boulders, into which the spray of the thin waterfall spattered like constantly driving rain. The narrow, stony trail—which Theresa described as "horrid"—veered to the left, affording them sufficient vantage to reveal a suggestion of indentation in the lower cliff face. As they wound down, and still further down, the indentation lay exposed for what it was: a massive cavity in the naked rock, the roof of which soon loomed above their heads, long before they reached the bottom. Presently they attained the lowest level, where the path petered out, and there, at last, they gazed upon the vast opening beneath Tonto Natural Bridge in all of its glory. Gigantic and dark was that tunnel, surmounted by the huge and massive arch oppressively hanging above. Vorchek smiled, nodding to himself. Theresa gasped in awe, saying, "It looks like the entrance into another world." Jason allowed that he desired to carve his initials in the stone for posterity. "I can not sanction defacement," the professor said crushingly. "We establish camp here by the creek, on that dry, open patch below the rocks. Mr. Crawford, I delegate the task to you. Come, Miss Delaney; you and I have instruments to erect."

Jason mumbled to himself yet again, while his companions cheerfully set about tinkering with the various odd contraptions that the professor had borne with him. By sheer chance, perhaps, they contrived to finish their duties about the time that Jason completed his. Three pup tents had popped up on the level terrain by the banks of Pine Creek, along with a bundle of cooking gear and other sundries. Vorchek's devices stood just outside the mouth of the tunnel, three unusual, spidery contraptions of polished metal and gleaming glass. "Already we are well situated," he chortled. "Miss Delaney, we approach the fabled 'Hour of Delectable Lunch'. If you would do us the honors, there are mortal needs to be satisfied. What have you provided for us today?" "Once I have it all together," replied Theresa, "it will be beef stew cooked in the pot, simmered in a wine base, with small red potatoes, tea and fresh biscuits fried in butter in a real cast iron skillet." "That skillet is incredibly heavy," Jason noted.

With the fire laid, culinary arts were practiced, and lunch was served, and it was everything that the mistress chef had promised. Professor Vorchek discoursed while he ate. "You both should know by now," he drawled between bites, "a deal concerning the matters which bring us here, yet I have not, until now, tied together for your benefit the logical links of evidence. This I shall do. We have arrived at a very peculiar place, one of the strangest in the world, if the tradition of accumulated lore be our guide. Why now, you do know, though not all of the ancillary background. Six months ago Eddison, of the physics department, detected unusual energy readings, a form of radiation which he deemed unclassifiable, or at least previously unclassified. He consulted the records and, searching through old files, discovered two earlier, similar instances of energy outbursts, one dating to the Forties, the other back to the Twenties. He localized the disturbance in northern Arizona, establishing a meter in Payson, among other cities, and was able to narrow down the source to this immediate region. He consulted with our geological staff, who were unable to propose any natural sort of magnetic, electrical, or other type of particle emission to account for the phenomenon. At that point I was drawn into the investigation, rather against the wishes of Eddison—he does not care overly much for me, I am afraid—who argued that the case was beyond my provenience.

"Granted, my areas of specialization are anthropology and other matters related to the remote past, but I am quite aware of developments in his field, and tend to make better use of them at that when it comes to exploring arcane puzzles. It happens that I already knew items of interest involving this region of which he knew nothing, nor cared to know, which I immediately connected to his findings.

"What I know is the lore of prehistory, as it has been handed down to us, and the facts of history, as recorded by those who experienced them. I begin, as always, with the former, for origins are ever located in misty antiquity. According to the oldest documented myths of the Yotipai—who inherited much from those who came before them—the specific site of Tonto Natural Bridge has always been a sacred place, much honored and feared by the primitive inhabitants of ancient times. I am reminded of the comment you made, Miss Delaney, upon your first clear view of the formation. The red man truly believed that the tunnel was a primordial entrance or gateway into another world. They were not avowedly fantasizing, nor did they mean it in any conventional, physical sense. They thought that the huge chamber opening before us was the geographical connection in our world with an opening into another, into a shadow land where the principles of life and existence are not as they are here. That mystical realm was the abode of the Gods, into which no man might safely enter, but of which chosen wise ones—the 'medicine men' or 'shamans'—might dream or cunningly speculate.

"Such is the standard tale. I learned more, several years ago (this was before your time, Miss Delaney), from an immensely aged Indian gentlemen named Tonipah, who claimed to be one of the last surviving priests of the aboriginal cult which dominated this land before the white man swept in, and who professed to remember all that had been handed down from those olden days. He intrigued me very much, and not only because he proved a gold mine of information. He had a curious way of speaking, a habit, if you will—one which he occasionally attempted to restrain or conceal—which led him to relate his accounts as if he had actually lived the circumstances he described, and was therefore recalling from direct memory rather than from older informants of his own. At times he was so convincing, so artlessly sincere, that it spooked me to listen to him. Listen I did, however, as no one else had ever bothered to do, and in the course of our association I recorded hundreds of hours of absolutely fascinating material."

"You better watch out, Professor," Jason broke in. "Some of these old guys will spin any story if they can get something in return. Did

Tonipah cadge anything off of you?"

"I'm all too aware," Vorchek retorted, "of the human propensity for devising rewarding fictions. Many myths are nothing more, and in our own times people are fooled, via the influence of television and other forms of mass media, into believing all sorts of odd and fantastic claims which have no evidential merit. Indeed, virtually all popular beliefs of our age fall into that worthless category. Tonipah, however, provided an enormous mass of facts and data which I could analyze. In those cases—lamentably few, to be sure—when I was able to check his accounts, I always, in the end, verified them. That being so, I placed great faith in the esoteric lore he possessed."

"So what did he tell you," asked Theresa, "about the natural bridge?"

"Ah, yes; this is where I hit the jackpot, as they say. What I received from Tonipah was, to all appearances, an insider's view of the archaic magical ceremonies once performed here, and the supposed responses derived from those rites. Now, let me frame the issue a little more neatly. According to the Yotipai, as my prime source has it, it was not possible to approach the Gods directly. In most times and places the connection could not be made at all. At the rare foci of cosmic energies—as the site of this bridge was understood to be—where the power of the Godly plane occasionally leaked through, the attempt could be made, but with no assurance of success, and there were extreme dangers involved. I would go so far as to say that the mere attempt was perilous, and the unlikely event of success, almost necessarily fatal. The Gods, it would seem, cherished Their privacy. However, at the geographical foci other, lesser beings were known to appear at intervals, entities of great power themselves, with whom the wise men could have dealings. These creatures were conceived to be—let me employ the word 'middlemen'—those who could be approached with a reasonable chance of physical or spiritual survival, and from whom one might glean genuine wisdom, perhaps wisdom of a sort that emanated, in a roundabout fashion, from the Gods Themselves. These creatures (I call them that, incidentally, because they are never described in pleasant or wholesome terms) were honored as the 'Messengers of the Old Ones' or the 'Walkers of the Dreaming Road' or some such fanciful designation. It was these who were seen to appear in the tunnel by night, these who were favored by ritual, these who granted peculiar requests.

"The highest priests knew when the Messengers came, for the best of the wise men could sense the opening of the celestial portal and feel when those beings passed into our domain. When this happened they would make ready, and under cover of darkness the priests, their youthful acolytes, and one other would enter the tunnel in the depths of night. They would light bonfires atop the giant boulders within, fomenting great blazes which illuminated the roof far above them. This first step of ritual served to reveal the Messengers who, if truly present, would be seen hanging from the ceiling like monstrous bats. Such was the nature of those things, as Tonipah explained it to me. With the presence confirmed, the main body of the ceremonies began, a festival of rude music, singing and dancing, and the drawing of strange diagrams on the dirt floor or in the mud of the creek within the tunnel. These abstract images were crucial to the rite, for some held that they constituted the actual communication with the entities, all else being naught but window dressing. They had to be presented in a precise, accurate fashion, or no results would accrue. What do I mean by diagrams? Let me tell you this much. I pressed Tonipah, and he let slip that he knew well the ancient images through which mortal men conversed with those whom we would style fiends. Naturally I pressed him further, and he eventually condescended to drawn them for me. He drew them quickly, easily, as if from long practice."

"He could draw anything," Jason pointed out. "What's in a picture?"

"You would not say that," Vorchek replied testily at this interruption, "if you had seen them. They were not pictures, in the main, but rather complex diagrams incorporating, among other things, unusual geometrical forms. There was little or nothing representational about them, yet they supposedly conveyed meaning to those others. Contemporary geometry affords few parallels. I have seen similar carvings and painted materials at the Palatki site in the Red Rock Country beyond Sedona, and I am familiar with the ruins of an especially ancient Egyptian tomb, its occupant unknown to history, where the walls are decorated with like motifs. No, young man, these diagrams were important, impressing me as much or more than anything else I learned from Tonipah. He later admitted that he earnestly regretted showing them to me, insisting that I return them to him, or he would break off our interviews. I let him have his way." The professor grinned. "I had made copies, of course."

"How does one communicate with a geometrical diagram?" asked Theresa.

170

UNDER THE NATURAL BRIDGE

"There are ways, my dear, although I can only speculate in this specific case. How does one communicate with any symbols? Geometry encodes information as does any other design. The earliest human scripts were geometrical in form—I have always found that interesting, for it opens up entertaining possibilities about the past—while a combination of curves and angles can impart data as well or better than any other method. One may deduce that the Messengers 'spoke' in such arcane terms, and the wise men among the Yotipai, or their forebears, had deduced the same from lengthy trial and error. At any rate, that is how it was done and, I have been told, it worked.

"Now we come," continued Vorchek, "to the final, dreadful aspect of the ceremony. Remember how I said that one other was brought to the nighttime rite? There were the priests, whose presence was necessary, for they knew what had to be done; there were the acolytes, who needed to be taught the hoary secrets of their elders; and there was the other, routinely a young fellow of no special standing or importance, who was brought to the appointed time and place under false pretenses. He would be told or promised anything, whatever it took to get him there, for he was the designated sacrifice, an offering to the Messengers, who had a craving or desire for such gifts, it would seem."

"I don't see why those creatures would be interested," said Theresa. She lit a cigarette and leaned back lazily on a convenient rock. "Unless they eat us, that is."

"Perhaps they do, although I doubt it. One serving of humanity could not go far among a group of such entities. As the Indians understood the process, they were offering a gift of the soul rather than the body. The latter would count for nothing 'over there,' while the former, apparently, possessed properties of value. In effect, the priests had negotiated a trading system with their dread visitors: a soul in exchange for what the Messengers were willing to provide."

"But what was that?" Theresa persisted. "What's the point of it all?"

"Knowledge," replied Vorchek, "a glimpse behind the veil, a peek into the forbidden realm of the Gods. The wisest of the wise were granted visions of the world beyond ours, a chance to gaze upon genuine images of that otherwise inaccessible and dangerous land. Tonipah assured me that his people thought that the only true knowledge ever bestowed upon man, for it was a view through a window into reality as it really is, the reality underlying the thin, superficial world which is all that

171

we commonly accept."

"I get it," blurted Jason. "It's, like, a way to achieve oneness with the universe, to see the big reality and become part of it."

"It is not 'like' that," said Vorchek, "nothing like it, I am afraid. The kind of universe which has been traditionally painted by ancient lore is not one we could ever wholly embrace, nor would it be likely to embrace us, save for our destruction. Do not take seriously, Mr. Crawford, the pleasing rantings of the bead fondlers and crystal peddlers. The mysteries I explore are much grimmer than they could ever face."

The meal was long over, the refuse cold, the embers of the fire turning to ash. Vorchek poured his final cup of tea over the fire to douse the smoldering remnants, then returned to his instruments, which fully occupied him for a spell. Theresa and Jason remained behind to clean up the camp site, where the suddenly observed scuttling of a scorpion taxed her nerves. Presently the young man sidled close to her and whispered, "You'd better watch out, honey. I think the professor has it in for you." She shot back, "He doesn't, nothing of the kind. What makes you say such a stupid thing?" "It finally occurs to me," observed the youth, "that Vorchek isn't just angling for a cheap grant. He really takes all this stuff seriously." "Of course Professor Vorchek does; he has devoted his entire career—his life—to investigating weirdness that nobody else can explain." "Yeah, I figured that out, and I know what the other professors, not just Eddison, say about him. Well, look at it this way: he's the priest—scientists are the priests of our times, aren't they?—and I'm the acolyte, his student, here to learn—here to waste my time on nonsense, more like—and you? What are you here for; just to cook the stew? Unless you serve a purpose you're not telling—is that how it works between you two?—unless it's that, then he's lured you here under false pretenses. You know what that means, don't you?" "I don't have the slightest idea," Theresa said haughtily, "nor interest in what you're saying." "It means," Jason replied, with a triumphant grin, "that he's going to feed you to the Messengers!"

Theresa escaped from him shortly to join the professor, who had been happily oblivious to their conversation, by the instruments at the mouth of the tunnel. He busied himself recording readings from meters and wiping off droplets of spray which the wind tended to blow over from the waterfall. She asked him, "You wouldn't feed me to the monsters, would you?" He turned to her, removed his glasses. "My child, what are you talking about?" "Nothing, really; but you are an odd

172

one—I've always known that—and there isn't much you wouldn't do for science. I have a funny feeling about this business, that's all. Are there actually such things as Messengers?" "I think so. I postulate that they are more able to intrude upon our plane when the cosmic barriers weaken which, I think, is what allows the mysterious energies to leak through. That process, as detected by Eddison, is still ongoing. Look at those dials." "Yes, very nice. So you intend to make contact tonight?" "You are a treasure, Miss Delaney. That is precisely my plan. Think of what I may see." "But what can you offer them?" Vorchek chuckled, pausing to light his pipe and puff it ablaze. "That is of no concern to you. Certain childish aspects of myth I dismiss."

Jason joined them, approaching hesitantly, acting guiltily. "Hey, I didn't mean anything by it. I was only having fun." At Vorchek's request he explained himself. "See, that's all it was. Can't a guy have a good time while on a major scientific enterprise? I'm just, like, amusing myself."

Vorchek smiled, exhaling smoke. "You are like that, are you? Very good; excellent, in fact. There is no reason why we should not amuse ourselves. I, for one, am very much amused." Theresa broke in with some warm words bearing upon the subject of misplaced humor, but the professor admonished her. "Miss Delaney, that will do. Let us have no more of that. We are all friends here: you and I of long standing, while this gentleman is a more recent acquaintance, but he is not to be slighted on that account. A kind heart, my dear, is a great asset, and that you possess, as I know better than anyone. I expect you, therefore, to make allowances for the individualistic foibles of others. Mr. Crawford here, as I vaguely recall him telling me, has no family—is it not so, sir?—and has only arrived in town this semester—I have that right as well?—thus even without close friends to cheer him. Let us fill that lack. Meanwhile, sir, let me be the first to tell you how good it is that you have chosen to join us on this important mission. You are everything I desire in a graduate student—you are the archetype—I go so far as to say, that if you did not exist, it would be necessary to invent you. Yet you do exist, you are here, and I have great plans for you. Let that suffice."

It did. Jason was extraordinarily pleased with himself after that, though Theresa continued to grouse a bit, but Professor Vorchek possessed time-honed skills for jollying her. Soon she was engaged in the useful task of keeping track of the meter readings from Vorchek's strange machines, while he took a break to consult his notes. Jason proposed to explore the gloomy expanse under the bridge, but this was forbidden, "lest the forces be disturbed." The young man glumly acquiesced. Shadows lengthened, the birds quieted as the afternoon advanced. As the sun disappeared behind the western ridge Vorchek closed his notebook and observed, "The air grows warm and oppressive. Our duties will require late hours tonight. I need a nap, which I recommend to all. We want to be fresh for the great times."

"Suits me," said Jason, who had been wandering aimlessly about the narrow valley poking at rocks and plants, and disturbing the wildlife. "I'm bored stiff." Theresa was game as well, opining that the solitude and the escalating heat made her drowsy. She made sandwiches for all, as it was close to another meal time, although no one was especially hungry yet, having eaten heartily earlier; and with that out of the way, the trio crawled into their little tents. Theresa's and Vorchek's accommodations were so arranged that they could see each other.

As they lay there peacefully, she wondered aloud, "What is it about the primitive mind that lends itself to weird rituals and nastiness like human sacrifices?" The professor, always quick with an answer, took the bait readily enough. "That trait," he explained, turning over atop his sleeping bag so that he could face her properly, "is not a function of primitiveness. It is, instead, a feature of minds drawn to the arcane and the uncanny, fueled by a craving to understand that which seems impossible to understand. Savages are wont to display it because they know less about their world—at least, that is the commonly held view—but that inner need arises at all levels of culture, including the most highly civilized. I, myself, am driven to learn, and there are those professional carpers who consider my methods queer. More to your point, I suppose, is the case of Wallace Harbury. If folklore tells truly, then he would have much to say on that issue." "What does he have to do with it, Professor?" "If the stories of his life be halfway accurate, then he took the Indian tales seriously indeed, and sought himself to put their knowledge to use." "You mean like they did?"

"I mean exactly that," replied Vorchek. "According to the standard account, as recorded in diaries of his time, Harbury had dealings with the devil, which led his neighbors to shun him, contributing more to the foul reputation of this place than any amount of half forgotten aboriginal legends ever could. His contemporaries thought that he murdered his entire family, sacrificing them one by one in the course of black rites, as offerings to great Satan himself, who presumably provided something by way of recompense, as is customary in such tales. In the end, so the folk

174

believed, he repented and, in despair over his crimes, did away with himself. I have studied the documents, interviewed the oldest folk of Payson and its confines, and have arrived at a more clear-cut and stimulating version of history.

"Harbury was a rancher, nothing more, when he came here with his wife and two sons, but he was a well read man, plus a fellow of mystical bent. He got wind of the Indian tales concerning the bridge, cajoled or bribed the surviving natives (there were quite a few more of them about in those days), gained knowledge of their secrets. The fascination seized him—I feel like I know that man—the mystique, the awesomeness, of the olden ways and what they could reveal gripped him, therefore he set out to recreate the Indian ceremonies for his own benefit. He duplicated the "Speaking Pictures", as the Yotipai called them, began to perform anew the sacred rites under the natural bridge. There is evidence that those rites never entirely faded away, or that they were covertly revived at various periods, so it may be that Harbury contrived to observe them, thereby mastering their formulations. He gained nothing, however, at first, because he lacked an essential ingredient. The time came when, out of his zeal and frenzy, he added that ingredient.

"It is fairly clear to me that he employed his family as offerings to the Messengers, sacrificing them in order to achieve those insights or visions which those formidable entities were willing, for a price, to bestow. He may have sent others as well to their doom—there are tales to that effect—I am not certain of those details, but during a span of some years he carried on this outré practice, and there are hints that he was, for a long while, mightily pleased with the return on his investment. In some fashion his educational heyday came to an end. There are reports, still extant, that in the latter days he seemed a haunted man, that he went about looking over his shoulder jumping at shadows. I have read that he once professed, after a hard bout of drinking, to have gone too far, to have opened one door too many, to have let through something that plagued him abominably. Whatever that may mean, it is a matter of record that soon thereafter he saw fit to kill himself. He... cut his own throat."

"But, Professor," Theresa exclaimed, "that doesn't sound like anything to get mixed up in. What if something happens to you?" "I appreciate the concern, Miss Delaney. Be sure that I know my limits, and my scheme involves no more than pushing a single door ajar, the merest crack through which I may peek." "Still, all of these stories involve

175

human sacrifice. There doesn't appear to be any other way." Vorchek replied pensively, "I utilize the bountiful techniques of modern science. Do not fret yourself with foolish worries. Rest, my dear."

Professor Vorchek did, most agreeably; Jason snoozed, as can any graduate student when opportunity allows; Theresa may have done, although she acknowledged afterward none of the benefits of refreshment. When Vorchek stirred again it was completely dark, and the hills, bluffs, and ridges above the valley framed a multitude of bright, gleaming stars. He directed his dazzling flashlight into the other tents and had his companions fumbling and rising within moments. "It is still early," said he. "Though it may be superstitious silliness on my part (I think not), I intend to wait until the stroke of midnight before initiating the ceremony. Surely, if we receive guests this night, they should have made their appearance by then; and then too, it is traditional, what? There is much to do in the meantime. I shall verify, for the thousandth time, that I know the procedures by heart. Mr. Crawford, when the great moment comes, I will expect you to have all the materials to hand, in the proper order, so that I may put them to use with full effectiveness. Miss Delaney, by now, I presume, you know how to operate the machines and read their meters as well as I. Is there any doubt in your mind about that?"

"None whatsoever. I could run them in my sleep."

"I beg you, my dear, not to experiment along those lines. So, very good. Here is the program for our evening's entertainment. At precisely eleven-thirty Mr. Crawford and I will enter the tunnel, there to confirm the presence of the Messengers. If they are not, then all of my arrangements prove futile. If we find ourselves among strange company, we will set to and begin at the designated time. While all this transpires, you, Miss Delaney, will operate the machines, keeping track of every twitch of those needles. I tolerate no lacunae in my records."

Theresa exploded. "You mean you're leaving me behind? Professor, I won't stand for it!"

Vorchek sighed, shook his head, motioned to Jason. "Sir, be so kind as to rekindle the fire. We require light for our preparations." Jason nodded and got to it, laughing to himself as he did so. The professor put his arm around the girl and gently steered her toward the machines at the tunnel entrance. Presently he whispered to her, "Dear Theresa, by now you should know that I do everything with purpose, according to strictly formulated plans. I have told you so often enough. On the scene, at the time of contact, my needs will be absurdly simple. All I will require from a companion is the ability to hand me diagrams and text at the proper intervals while not interfering with my attempts at communication. Of course you could do that, but so can any warm body, and I presume that Mr. Crawford qualifies. On the other hand, the sustained, unbroken functioning of these devices is absolutely critical. This squat meter tracks the cosmic energy flow; you can be sure that I will wish to study that afterward. The tall, spindly one gauges the degree of spatial breakdown and temporal warping; does not that sound interesting? This sensor with the convoluted armatures records the distance and direction of any dimensional opening, while firing electronic impulses through the opening and measuring their effects, if any; useful stuff, that. All of this is important to me, and someone with a little knowledge—a little something on the ball—must remain here to supervise them. Whom, Miss Delaney, would you recommend? It must be you. Rest assured that, if anything noteworthy happens on my end, you will hear all about it."

"It still sounds like a raw deal to me," Theresa pouted. "You don't usually exclude me. What if you get into trouble?" "Then I shall have the satisfaction of knowing that you are out of trouble," replied Vorchek. "That will indeed be a weight off of my mind. Anyway, put that out of yours. I have few fears for myself, as long as I get right the incantations. So, all clear, all understood, and back to work."

The evening crept on wearily for the younger folk, but the professor seemed annoyingly serene as he studied his materials, humming to himself. Occasionally he cast a glance at the black tunnel mouth, and once he appeared to pause, as if listening for something, or as if he had heard something. Jason once more suggested peeking into the interior, but the team leader again stayed him, and there was pregnant silence, save for the increasingly loud noises of furtive creatures in the nearby undergrowth. Then Vorchek rose abruptly, shut his notebook, drew the gold watch from his pocket, snapped it open, announced, "It is time. Mr. Crawford, take these papers, and for the love of God do not disorganize them. Miss Delaney, assume your station." The three of them approached the tunnel entrance. Vorchek added, as a quiet aside to Theresa, "If the tunnel is empty, we shall return shortly. Otherwise, we will be some time. Do not be surprised, nor react, to anything you may hear, no matter how curious it may sound. I will be chanting an ancient ritual, a barbaric Indian spell, which may sound harsh and uncouth to your delicate and exquisitely shaped ears. You will hear singing—there may be shouting—loud tones, I imagine. As you value your life, young lady, do not intervene."

Jason, who had overheard the last, began to crack a joke, but the professor cut him off brusquely. "Come," he barked (though in a hushed voice), adjusting his hat and flicking on his flashlight, and without another word Professor Anton Vorchek and the graduate student Jason Crawford strode forward into the darkness beneath Tonto Natural Bridge, the bright beam lancing a path before them. The light caught the spray from the drizzling waterfall, reflecting back a myriad of glistening stars. They walked on, ducking under the raining wetness, came upon massive boulders just within the edge of the cliff. They passed out of sight around the huge stones into the interior, and Theresa saw them no more. Soon even the flickering of the flashlight was swallowed up in that black immensity.

Theresa waited, as patiently as she was ever prone to do. She occupied herself for a period, making a great fuss of regularly checking her instruments, none of which did anything that she had not seen before. She sat down on a big rock, smoking absently, swinging her pretty legs, in darkness save for the weak illumination of the dying campfire. Twice she discerned brief stabs of light far back inside the nighted chamber, which she took to be the professor's flashlight. Then, shortly thereafter, she detected a vague, reddish radiance emanating from far within, a distant, feeble, lambent glow, which suggested to her the laying of a fire somewhere inside. That caught her attention, for considerable time had now passed, yet her companions had not returned, and it now appeared that they had no immediate plans to do so. She thought about what that must signify—given everything the professor had said—and she shuddered silently.

Then she heard a voice, a far away voice, low and indistinct, nevertheless identifiable as that of Professor Vorchek. She could not make out the words, but there was that in the tone of the voice which hinted of chanting. He was performing the dark ritual of the olden years, the fabled spell of communication with those others, formulated by the Indians of that country centuries or eons ago. The chanting rose in volume, died away, began again, continuing this pattern for a while, until something like singing, still from the same voice, commenced. The professor sang an ancient lay, one which its aboriginal originators, so he had explained, claimed was integral to the rite. The singing—a crazy, monotonous, awesome sound, redolent of barbarity—mounted in intensity, grew faster, frantic, then ceased, terminating in the loud cries of a single, unfamiliar word, repeated over and again, a strange, three syllable word which was somehow like none she had ever heard. The mere enunciation of that word caused her skin to crawl. She started seven times as it was spoken seven times.

She practically jumped out of her hide when she heard the response. Came a voice in answer—surely that was not Jason's flat, television-trained voice—an ugly, scratchy, venomous series of intonations which seemed to shape themselves into a semblance of the spooky chant. Then other, repulsively similar voices chimed in, and she knew that a multitude were gathered within the cavity under the natural bridge, and they were communicating after their fashion, responding in kind. The professor's voice joined the others, and a ghastly, unearthly harmony swung back and forth in noxious unison, rising, falling. Now there could be no pretense: contact had been made, the Messengers were present, and... open to discussion? Theresa quailed at the thought. On nights in years long forgotten by most—perhaps best forgotten—those unhallowed beings had granted great insights to a chosen few, yet had demanded a fearsome price for their favors. Knowing that much, she was at a loss to imagine what price Professor Vorchek was in a position to pay, in exchange for the pure knowledge that he craved.

The horrible singing and chanting died down, stopped without warning. A dreadful moment of harsh silence ensued. She strained to see, observing nothing other than the dim reflection of flickering firelight upon the nearer stone surfaces. No, wait, there was something, unless vision deceived; she glimpsed something, briefly, only for a second, out of the corner of her eye, a phantom image of movement which appeared high up above toward the ceiling, where she had not been looking; a ghost of movement, detected at the same moment that her quick hearing detected a new sound, as of heavy, thick fluttering, the sound of large, widespread surfaces beating against air. That unusual, soul-chilling sound was immediately followed by a calling out in still another voice, one she had not yet heard until this point. It was like a shout—no, more a scream—a recognizably human voice crying out, without intelligible words, from the darkness. There was no doubt in her mind that it was Jason's voice. She wondered what role his strange cry played in the ceremony.

Then Theresa was plagued by what felt to her the worst of fates: to sit and wait, harking to an interminable, horrifically protracted silence. She heard nothing more from within the tunnel, as if its occupants, including those familiar to her, had suddenly departed, leaving her alone in the terrible dark of the wretched valley before the tunnel, with wild animals, unseen but sensed, as her only company. She no longer actually heard the beasts of the night, which had grown strangely quiet, nor did she hear much else other than the ever present tinkling of Pine Creek. The light from the campfire winked out, and in time the traces of feebly glowing redness from inside the tunnel faded away as well. She had illumination of a sort, however, from the radiant dials of the professor's machines, which he had left in her care, and which throughout most of her solitary ordeal had done nothing to interest her. At the precise moment, though, of that dreadful cry, the electric meters of the three sensors had begun to act, or react, in a profoundly noticeable manner. The needles became agitated, swung sharply to the right and remained there, quivering on the edge of the dials, even appearing to run off the scales. This convinced her, as did nothing else, that events were still unfolding, that she waited not in vain.

She lingered nervously in the wracking quiet, hugging her jacket tightly about her slim body (for it had turned unpleasantly cool), glancing at the glowing meters or peering into the tunnel, daring herself to enter, but checking herself always, remembering her instructions. The professor never fooled around with his commands, could be artlessly unkind when met with disobedience. She tarried for an hour, perhaps more, before she noticed that the instruments no longer registered. The unknown energy flow, which had originally sparked the professor's interest and brought them all to this spot, had ceased. Now she again heard noises from within the tunnel which riveted her attention. Someone (or something!) was fumbling about inside there, stumbling and scrabbling across stones in the darkness. She heard the sound as from far away, but it approached; surely it came her way. She tensed, wishing for more light than the stars and the radiant meters provided. She thought to rush back to camp and rekindle the fire, but she could not, nervousness rooting her to place. Then she made out definite footsteps splashing in shallow water, and immediately subsequent to that the shadowy but recognizable form of Professor Vorchek appeared, lurching forward through the little stream that ran out of the tunnel mouth. Theresa ran forward to hug him happily, began to exclaim her joy at his return, but he cut her short, demanding hoarsely, "Light, for God's sake, we must have light. I lost everything: my notebook, my flashlight. I have a tale to tell, which you must transcribe while the memories remain fresh. Be my secretary before you are otherwise; my hand shakes, and I can not write."

She led him carefully through the dark to the camp site, sat him down, gave him water (which he quaffed in great gulps, though he would not eat), stoked a crackling blaze. Only then did she realize his pitiable state. His hat was missing, his jacket and the knees of his pants filthy with mud and grime, while his clothing in general stank with a bizarre, entirely unappealing odor. His face appeared wan, tired, aged. She started to ask him questions, the hundred questions competing for supremacy, but again he stopped her, crying, "Pen and paper, my dear. Write, attend, and all relevant questions will be answered. Yes, I am fine. Are you comfortable? Good, then I commence my tale, and I beg you to miss nothing.

"The beginning you know. Mr. Crawford and I entered the chasm at the appointed time, and we proceeded by the light of the flash into the interior, at a point from which no trace of the outer world could be observed. We halted on a wide, level sandbar by the creek, a spot surrounded on three sides by gigantic stones which, I admit, gave us a certain sense of security. From that point I directed the flashlight beam onto the craggy ceiling far above us. There, sure enough, were our visitors, just as the legends and reports said they would be: the Messengers, the lesser yet still powerful beings that serve the mysterious Gods of the universe. They were clustered up there, clinging impossibly to those slick, slanted or vertical surfaces, hanging easily like huge bats. They were not bats, however, nor relatives of any life terrestrial. They had wise, cunning faces, grotesque faces, with eyes that gleamed intelligently in the electric light. Why do they come here? Why do they break through the dimensions at this place? Is there a weakness here in the cosmic fabric which serves their purposes? Do they pass through in order to contact man, as our stories suggest, or do they have reasons of their own which concern us not? How is one to know? They exist—they are fact—yet they are mysteries, utterly strange and beyond us.

"I tell you certain ideas that raced through my mind, but be assured that I wasted no time on idle musings. I came with a firm plan, was determined to see it through. I asked Mr. Crawford to prepare a fire from the materials he carried. There was other natural refuse on the scene which we added to the blaze. Now we could see better still, so I need not employ the flashlight. I had misgivings about the use of electrical appliances, which is why I did not bring a pocket tape recorder. Why the concern? I knew that those who practiced the rites before me had done without such convenience, and I harbored a nagging doubt—

181

which I was, quite naturally, unwilling to test at the time—as to how a conflict of energies, even on a low level, might influence or disturb events. The fire lighted, I could see well enough to work. I could also see the Messengers somewhat more clearly. That was an unnecessary vision. I could have lived without it, and as for Mr. Crawford, I feared that he contemplated bolting. I had to take him by the shoulders and shake him roughly, before he would respond coherently to my commands.

"Now I told him to hand me the first diagram. With that as a guide I drew the ancient symbols on the damp earth near the fire, where eyes overhead could see them plainly. I took the next sheet, and the next, gouging the images in dirt, or painting them in mud on the stones with my finger. So simple, yet so effective! When I had appropriately decorated our surroundings with those curious images—so many of them meaningless to me, while others looked for all the world like symbols of esoteric geometry and curious mathematical forms—I asked Mr. Crawford for the remaining sheets, the pages of crucial text.

"I began the recitation. I suppose that you, Miss Delaney, heard something of this phase, and I can only guess at your feelings as you listened to those queer syllables formulated in the dim and dark epochs of antiquity. I employed the Yotipai chant as taught me by Tonipah, but there are other variants, from other obscure parts of the globe, which might have worked as well. Again, I had no desire to experiment with corollary possibilities before I derived results. I chanted, I sang, I slapped my knees in imitation of the beat of the tom-tom, I stamped my feet, I clapped my hands, anything to allow me to generate the proper cadence. Mr. Crawford had nothing to do with this phase, once he had passed me the writings. He crouched beneath a boulder, his head down, seeming stunned by what transpired around him.

"And then those others joined me in the ritual! I hope you did not hear their voices. They were inhuman, uncanny, aurally obscene. The Messengers, too, chanted and sang, as they must have done in the old days, when there were men more willing to listen, and as they squeaked and croaked out the traditional elements of the ceremony they grew restive, clawing at their dizzy perches and rustling their great, leathery wings. I continued with the rite, turning one page when I reached bottom and reading from the top of the next, until I had gone through all of my materials and, so far as I knew, concluded the ritual. I knew not whether I had succeeded, nor exactly what was to come.

"I found out. The Messengers spoke to me, in perfect English, at least so perfect as their vocal apparatus would allow them to imitate our tongue. I understood every word, but it sounded quite eerie. Surely the Indians felt the same when they heard monsters—is that a fair term?—speaking their language. The Messengers talked to me, and under my very respectful questioning they explained what they had to offer me. It was more than I could have dreamed. I eagerly made known to them my desire for the wonders they could bestow—I confess, I begged them to grant me that knowledge—and then they indicated that they desired something in return, according to the primordial custom. So I negotiated with them—I will not bore you with the details—but only then, when I had assured them that I could and would meet their price, was the deal made, and the Messengers spread wide their membranous wings to descended upon me.

"Here begins the truly wondrous part of my account. You are taking this all down, my dear? The Messengers formed a circle about me, enfolded me within the compass of their wings. Suddenly I could see nothing; wrapped in pitch darkness, no ray of light met my eye. They did not block the light, I aver; rather, I was instantaneously elsewhere, where there was no light. I had been transported. I felt no ground beneath my feet. My senses functioned fully, I tell you; I remained entirely aware of myself, the racing of my heart, the rasp of my breath, the heavy uselessness of my limbs. I was there, but I was temporarily in nowhere.

"Then the blankness, the nothingness, fell away from me. Still in darkness, but there was something almost natural about it by comparison. I knew that dreadful companions accompanied me, though I saw them not; in fact, I never saw those things again, but almost until the end I felt their guiding presence, and there were moments—oh, I remember these as poorly as I do dreams!—moments when I heard those sibilant, whispering voices, imparting to me arcane information as I progressed. I may have deduced certain items of knowledge, yet I believe they told me much. I run ahead of myself. I entered into this new, more natural darkness, like the blackness of outer space, only with no stars or planets in sight. I seemed to hang suspended in a void. Then I spied, at the limits of vision, faint, misty islands of radiance, at the farthest possible remove. They looked familiar to me, in a way, and I strained and stared, struggling to make sense of what I saw. It came to me, finally—perhaps they put the suggestion to me—that I gazed down upon the entirety of our universe, that I beheld distant motes of light which were surely galaxies, only I beheld them from a point outside; literally, I hung outside, looking in, seeing the totality of the known and understandable cosmos from a vantage other than natural; from a supernatural plane.

"Even as I reasoned or was prompted to this conclusion, the far universe dwindled away from my sight, as if I were rushing at enormous relativistic or hyper-relativistic speeds in another direction, toward what I could not guess, for there was nothing obviously elsewhere. Eventually the universe—our universe, with the earth and the stars, you and everything else—shrank to a fuzzy, glowing pinpoint, which then winked out. I once more floated in unnatural darkness, but this phase lasted no longer than my first exposure to the void.

"Without any warning or preparation, I found myself in another realm of vision, one largely disconnected from the appearances of the sane world we know. I fell into a place, a real place, yet one where the conventional laws of nature do not apply. Here there were no stars or planets as we understand them, but instead, burning, outrageously dazzling masses of mist or haze, and strangely planar surfaces which seemed to stretch unto infinity. The former served to illuminate this fresh cosmos, and at first glance I likened them to the glowing gas clouds of our heavens, such as the Orion Nebula. They did not, however, behave according to rule. This fiery haze would drift aimlessly and amorphously, then suddenly rush through the sky—at least so fast as I traveled, which seemed now at an extreme rate—to coalesce into strange suggestions of form. The clouds, if you will, would contract and fold and create the illusion or the reality of geometrical shapes, many resembling those I had drawn upon the mud and the rocks. These masses or objects were lively, active substances, and—maybe a squeaking voice told me this—their behavior was not entirely random. A kind of intelligence operated there. I do not know if a voice told me of the latter surfaces, the vast planes, for a short scrutiny surely revealed that they were worlds of a sort, surfaces which appeared two dimensional—I could actually see through them—yet spreading endlessly into that odd universe along their length and breadth. They were most peculiar. They angled every which way in space, moving and shifting chaotically. Hopelessly dazed by all this, I felt an attack of honest to goodness vertigo while watching them in action. They cut through one another, through the glowing masses, without incident, without any appearance of material substances coming into collision.

"And they were worlds, I tell you. As I zoomed past them (and through them!) I saw features upon the surfaces, what might have been mountains and valleys and winding courses of red fire that might have passed for rivers, and I saw—it all went by so fast—I think I saw cities, gleaming citadels of light, with other artificial handiwork of intelligence. I saw nothing of the denizens, but seemed to know something of them. I think those voices grew busy again, for I have ideas upon the subject, ideas which I must analyze and ponder before I tell of them. There were entities there, and they were wise, and eternal, and formidable; you can bank on that!

"I dived straight into the gaping mouth of what appeared to me an extinct or dormant volcano, so high that it rose from its flimsy base like a tower, and then the void enclosed me again. I emerged from that once more, realizing quickly that circumstances had altered again, for suddenly I knew that I was alone. My apparently informative companions had deserted me, and—as it happens—that was the last of my dealings with them.

"I hurtled through a vast darkness, toward a glowing, greenish mass which glimmered and seethed before me at a great distance, as I learned, for at first it appeared minute, yet rapidly expanded to fill all of that otherwise empty sky. It was as if I had entered a new universe, one which contained only a single object, though one of titanic size. I felt a force strongly pulling me, an implacable force like gravity, although I do not believe that is what it was. I swiftly approached, and as I did so, sensed a Presence. At first I peered intently, thinking the thing a planet or similar object, upon which I should discern features. Then I knew— there was no one left to tell me this—that the stupendous mass was the Presence. I fell into Being.

"Entering the mass, I felt nothing at first as its substance swallowed me. Then I felt the actions of Intelligence all about me, a universe of Intelligence; I had entered Ultimate Intelligence! I breathed It, sensed Its touch as It pressed upon my flesh. I knew that I had arrived at my destination. This was the Source of all knowledge that I had so long sought. Here, somehow, all answers could be found. With my comparatively minute mind I reached out to achieve that final contact, and I did—to the slightest degree—press mentally against an Awareness, was touched in the soul by extraordinary Mind. That Mind contained nothing resembling the human; it was not a kind of mind, but Mind personified, total Intellect. And then, my girl, I drew back. Miss Delaney, I faltered, I felt fear, for that Mind—if human standards and values mean aught in this wide world—churned and bubbled and roiled with corruption, black and foul beyond comprehension, beyond any words that I am capable of dictating to you now. I felt that I had attained my goal, reaching the core of existence, only to find a vast, filthy repository of everything that is spiritually toxic and destructive. I sensed another element within that Mind as well—a weirdly unlimited creative power, a font of magnificently boundless energies—but nothing, at the time, that could counterbalance the horror and nausea which caused me to recoil. I knew that the Intelligence was aware, for within that green mass I sensed a million eyes upon me, eyes that saw me, saw into me, saw through me, eyes that saw all, backed by Mind that knew all. It is a terrible conclusion, yet one that seems inescapable: I had come into the presence of an Entity who was omniscient and omnipotent—He who may bestow all—yet monstrously, unbearably evil. Utter knowledge dangled like ripe fruit, mine for the plucking—I had but to ask—yet I could not. I dare not! What price would He demand of me?

"I rejected the silent offer, which must have been a wise decision, for I suspect that I would not have entirely survived—as the body and mind I am now—had I taken that last step. At that moment I thought of Wallace Harbury, wondered if he had come to this point, wondered what he had decided. I thundered in my brain a despairing 'No!' and on the instant the void wrapped about me, and in another instant—as if no time had passed, no distance traveled—I was stumbling blindly and stupidly about the floor of the tunnel under the natural bridge.

"That is all," Professor Vorchek said with a sigh, after a long silence. "I live, I have learned. Knowledge has come my way, and I have accepted some—intellectual baubles—while I have spurned much more, the gold, the deadly gold. There are many possibilities before me. I must contemplate them."

"But, Professor," cried Theresa, throwing aside her notebook and pen and leaping to her feet, there in the remote and gloomy valley before the looming tunnel of ancient stone, "I still don't understand. Where is Jason? What has become of him?"

"Oh, yes, Mr. Crawford." Vorchek paused moodily, then shrugged. "He did not accompany me on my odyssey. Mr. Crawford... well, he met with something of an accident."

Late Night Movies

I recall nothing inherently unusual about the night I had my brush with the unknown. I may have felt overcome by a peculiar lassitude, or a sense of quiet unease may have crept upon me during the hours preceding the events in question. Perhaps my subconscious whispered of strange forces in motion, in the air or in mysterious realms beyond. It is difficult to say at this point in time, for my memories are colored by what happened. At the time, surely, I did not expect anything untoward. I had come off a hard week at work, with a couple of days off before me. I remember I did not eat much for dinner, seemed at loose ends afterward, as if all of what passed for variety in my life repelled me. Slumber would not come. I know that I wished to be alone. Are these indications, portents sufficient to set the scene? I do not think so. I have had other nights that began like that one, aimless nights which led to nothing. This one was different; apparently I am not required to understand why.

When faced with little to do, or a desire to do little, television constitutes a safe haven. I do not have much use for the box myself, but I enjoy movies, the older the better. It is so easy for me to withdraw from everyday cares into the world of past images, to revel in the sights and sounds of stories which often appear, blessedly, to possess no connection to the harsh tedium of the real life I have to live. That could be the way to the answer, but I still do not think so, for that must always have been the lure of popular entertainment, whatever the era. Perhaps that form of escape matters to me more; perhaps that greater need opens doors into the mind or soul which lead into unseen rooms.

I had plenty of good favorites and classics on disc, but I had watched them all enough times that their titles, just at the moment, induced boredom. I wanted to see something different, not the old reliables on hand. Anything might serve, so long as it were passable. I flipped through the television pages to find out what was showing on the movie channels. Most of them, catering to the basest tastes, offered what one would expect: contemporary films containing considerable

187

quantities of noise, moral squalor, and other disturbing manifestations of vulgar crudity, calculated to induce disgust rather than merriment. That was not for me at any time, especially not at this moment. I sought pleasurable relaxation. I leafed to the listings for the channel which ran the movies of days gone by.

Now this was more like it. They were showing movies through the night, all of them at least fifty or sixty years old, none of them the all time greats, but still fraught with possibilities. First on the menu was *Three Came to Dinner*, 1940, described as a romantic comedy, starring Walter Evans and Geraldine Lane. Both were lightweight actors, normally used in supporting roles, which suggested that this was a minor or "B" picture. The movie had already begun, but it sounded worth a try, so I gathered unto myself the immediate necessaries—a big bowl of popcorn and a bottle of soda pop—turned on the set, selected the channel and settled back on the sofa.

As it turned out, there wasn't much to that one. *Three Came to Dinner* had all the hallmarks of a film which had been cranked out by a small studio seeking a fast buck. It suffered from forced and dated humor, stereotypical characters, clumsy direction, an obvious plot. Which girl would end up with the hero? Naturally, the good girl, lacking in sex appeal, won out. I had this one figured within minutes. Often, when I catch the tail end of a show, I will not rest until I finally see the first part. In this case, that was not likely to be of future concern.

Sleep continued to prove elusive, or I was determined to watch something rewarding. At any rate, I stayed up for the next show. This happened to be *Murder By Night*, a mystery or crime thriller from 1932. It starred a much more impressive cast: Carl Lamont, Laura Wentworth, and William Bowers, Sr., in those days billed as only "William Bowers"; his actor son came much later. There was a certain staginess about the production, a sign of the times, due to the need for the actors to cluster around the hidden boom microphones, but otherwise this was a quality film. The story was simple and entertaining: a group of varied individuals are called to an old, spooky house in order to hear read the will of a recently deceased, wealthy eccentric. One of them, a rather obnoxious, arrogant fellow, receives most of the fortune, for no reason anyone else can understand. Then he is found with a knife in his back; the telephone connection is out, the cars have been tampered with and won't start, and the nearest human habitation is miles away through a gloomy forest. Further unpleasantness ensues. The movie was good fun, with something resembling a twist ending.

It was while I watched this one that the strangeness began, or that I first noticed it. There was one actor, whom I could not identify at the time, who tended to bring himself to my attention. For one thing, I thought I had seen him in the previous film, as a bit player. If so, he looked about the same from one picture to the next. In this one, he portrayed a key red herring, a businessman named Jones who seemed to be concealing a sinister secret, but which was eventually revealed to be only a love affair with another supporting character. The other thing about him I noticed was that he appeared to be trying to catch my eye.

Of course that is not done in standard movies, and it took me quite a while to realize what he was doing. I'd seen those supposedly clever asides, often comic, in which a player mugs to the audience. This was not like that. In the beginning I just felt that he stood out more than I would expect of a second or third banana. Then came a moment which made the matter plain. The hero and heroine were talking to one another, with "Jones" standing nearby, and after a furtive glance at them he raised his eyes to the screen and motioned tellingly with his hand, almost a wave. I thought he attempted to speak to the camera, but then Carl Lamont suddenly addressed him, "Jones" grimaced, as if caught in an illicit act, and rejoined the scene.

This, or something like it, occurred numerous times throughout the film. My original explanation, unbelievably faulty direction, did not hold up for long. The instances were so clear cut, increasingly bold. Whenever he was not called upon to take part in events, it did seem that he tried to talk to me. I should say, talk to the audience; at the time I did not take personally his curious behavior. It did distract me enough that I lost track of developments and failed to work out a solution to the mystery until the answer was revealed at the end. I pride myself on solving these stories long before that stage.

Murder By Night concluded, leaving me wondering how I had failed to hear about this one. A movie in which an actor had cavorted so openly, even to the detriment of the story, should not have gone unnoticed by film buffs. That is the kind of picayune knowledge they love to show off. I filed away the information, which might serve as an entertaining conversation piece the next time I was among the right crowd.

This was shaping up as a night without sleep. I felt weary, a little more out of sorts by this time, plagued by a sensation of dismal anxiety—it may have been a harder day than I realized—regardless, I determined to keep going until I dropped. In earlier years I loved doing that. Now the late night hours hung heavy, but I could still fill them as in days of yore. Having finished the popcorn, I made myself a sandwich and replenished my drink. Then I resumed station to await the next movie on the list.

The title pleased me immensely: *Rendezvous In Zanzibar*, which promised old-fashioned exotic adventure. Made in 1929, this was a late silent German production, directed by Johann Thanger, a man noted for his wild, larger than life presentations. Although I hadn't heard of this film before—which surprised me, for I thought I knew all of his—I was aware that his work marked the last gasp of the Expressionistic style of film-making which dominated German cinema during the Twenties, a style symbolized by exaggerated acting and lurid themes. Thanger's work tended toward the grandiose; this show ought to be a treat for the eyes. As the credits rolled the glorious, original Wagnerian orchestral score kicked in, music composed (as a title card informed me) especially for the film's premiere by the renowned Berchtold Hoeppner, and re-recorded for this restored television version.

Rendezvous In Zanzibar starred Paul Reicher and Theresa Heim, two of the greats. I knew him as the titular hero of Thanger's epic medieval fantasy, *Krondar the Magnificent*, while she would be forever famous as the alluring jungle heroine of *The Dark Continent*, a film also written, though unfortunately not directed, by Thanger. These two actors in the same movie! It almost defied belief that I had missed out on this one until now.

The picture also starred Calvin Hartmann. The sight of that name on the credits made me sit up and take notice. I had seen that name on the credits of the previous films, at the end of *Three Came to Dinner*, and at both ends of *Murder By Night*. The name meant nothing to me, so I had not given it any thought, but now it came back to me, and suggested a startling possibility. Only one actor seemed to have carried over from one film to another: "Jones," the red herring who had sought my attention. Could it be he, also appearing in this movie? I made a point to keep a sharp eye out for him.

I noted with glee that this version retained the original color tinting of certain scenes: dark blue for outdoors at night; warm yellow for evening interiors; purple for the throne room of the Sultan; fearsome red for the dreadful dungeon. This was a lavish, stylish production, one which represented the best the cinema of that age had to offer.

The story clarified itself soon enough. Although not presented as a period piece, it possessed plot trappings which might indicate the late

Nineteenth Century. Clothing was contemporary, but situations were not. Zanzibar came across as a quaint, Middle Eastern style kingdom, replete with walled cities patrolled by sword-wielding soldiers, high minarets packed with conniving viziers and soothsayers. Into the mix were thrown elements of African color: the Sultan and his entourage rode elephants, and he kept lions locked in his underground torture chamber, and black panthers roamed his pleasure gardens, where they ate uninvited guests. The Sultan Guzbad, played by Hans Guderian, was a bad fellow, the tyrannical villain of the piece, who, as the movie begins, executes his more popular younger brother, who had traveled to England in order to acquire a proper education, and came back with newfangled ideas about liberty and tolerance and decency, and how to implement them, and therefore had to go. The lovely Miss Heim portrayed the Princess Irina, who had supported the dead brother in his noble plans, now trapped in a tower prison, where she fearfully awaited the Sultan's amorous advances and political schemes.

Then came Reicher the hero, playing Herr—Mister would be more appropriate—Joseph Wesley-Smith, a rifle-toting English adventurer who had met and befriended the murdered prince. He arrives by steamship, with his bosom companion, at a rather modern port, where it is revealed that he was called to Zanzibar by the now dead man, only to learn that his invitation is now meaningless. Nevertheless, he sets out in a camel caravan for the capitol city, to find out what is going on.

After that the story got really interesting, I suppose, but I did not follow it as I might have. I knew it climaxed with the rescue of the Princess and a successful revolt, and along the way there were any number of frightful tortures and harrowing confrontations with the Sultan's thugs. I did not remember the details as I should, for I was riveted by the character of Bobby Mack, the somewhat comical companion to the hero. Bobby Mack was played by Calvin Hartmann, and I recognized him at once as the mysterious "Jones". His hair was not slicked back this time, but otherwise he had not changed.

I am not sure that he ever played the part as it was written. From his initial appearance he seemed to cast conspiratorial glances toward the camera, and his timing was off, as if he were not fully paying attention to the scene. He would be caught short when spoken to by others, and then react tardily, about a second too late. He seemed to have something on his mind, something which did not clearly connect to the events around him. Either that, or he played his generally light role in an unnecessarily brooding, introspective manner. An odd performance at

191

best, but I suspected more than that.

Bobby Mack (the titles always wrote out the full name) uncovered a plot to ambush and kill Wesley-Smith. He fled through the bazaar, the Sultan's henchmen at his heels. He took a knife in the back, but that did not stop him. He staggered to Wesley-Smith's apartment, where the hero had carried the liberated Princess, and dropped dead in a touching scene, not before he gasped out the whole story. Armed with this knowledge, hero and heroine departed to avenge their friend and save the kingdom from nastiness. Bobby Mack lay where he had fallen on the tiled floor, draped by silk curtains in a little alcove. The image should have faded to black at that point. It did not.

Now this night vaulted to the ultimate heights of weirdness. I saw what I am about to describe. I heard what followed, and I do not refer to music. It happened like this:

Bobby Mack stirred, his hand clutched at a curtain and pulled it aside. He sat up, stared straight into the camera, rose to his feet. He looked, fearfully, from side to side. He stepped partly out of screen to the left, then went and did the same to the right. He centered himself again, and faced me, and he spoke, and I heard his words!

I will not pretend to have memorized what he said, but I am not likely to forget the gist of it. The audio was clear and natural, as if he were in my room speaking to me face to face. He said:

"I am called Calvin Hartmann. That's what they call me. It isn't my real name. That—I'm not supposed to tell my real name—they don't like it, and anyway I'm not sure I remember it correctly any more. Think of me as Calvin Hartmann. That will do as well as any other.

"I'm talking to you. Yes, you, not the audience, or the camera, or the director; you. You know who you are. Somehow you can see and hear me as I really am. I sensed you out there, and I've been trying to reach you for hours. Are you listening? I think you are. I still feel your presence. Don't go away, don't fall asleep, don't kid yourself that this is a dream. I might not be much more than that now, but believe me, this is really happening. I may not have much time, and I have to tell you.

"I'm not an actor. I'm not somebody from way back when. I was just a regular guy, leading a regular life, nothing special about me, maybe a lot like you. I led a normal life, with a job, family, and friends, nothing out of the ordinary. I wasn't even into movies—I didn't know anything about this stuff—whatever made it happen, it wasn't that. I was there, in the real world—your world—and then I was here, in this place.

192

LATE NIGHT MOVIES

"I went to sleep one night, like I'd done a million times before, and I woke up here. I thought it was a dream. I told myself that at first. I told myself that for years, perhaps for centuries. Now I know better. I know next to nothing, except that it is real, and I don't know how to make it stop.

"I came to in this terrible fantasy land, where nothing is what it seems, where no one is what he seems. That includes myself. I was suddenly standing, wide awake, on a set, in the presence of complete strangers. The set, an interior scene, was bathed in blinding light. The lights were above me, and to the sides, dazzling in their intensity, and hot. It was like an oven in there. In front of me I saw the big movie camera, surrounded by darkness. Someone stood behind the camera, operating it. I couldn't get a good look at him. He stayed in the shadows at all times. Once, long ago, I peeked, tried to see who he was—

"Those others—the ones behind the scenes—came forth, ordered us to perform. We did. I did. I acted my part. I knew what to do, but I didn't know why I did it, or why I obeyed. There didn't seem to be any possibility of choice. I went through the motions, recited or mouthed the lines, made the designated movements. That's what it's all about. That's all it's ever been about.

"My fellow actors seem to be in the same boat as I. Apparently we all arrived here the same way. I can't be certain of the details, because we don't talk much to each other. It isn't allowed, between takes.

"It isn't so bad while the camera is running. Comparatively speaking, I mean. We act out these figments of someone's imagination, under duress, but there is no genuine pain or horror during a take. Retakes can be horrid. Those in charge don't like it when anything goes wrong. That makes them very angry. At least, I think it does. It's hard to tell with them.

"You see, those others—the ones who set the scene, who arrange the stage and give us our lines and cues—aren't human. They could fool you from a distance—they're passable imitations—but up close the little flaws betray them. They look like they were put together hastily. They would never step in front of the camera; that would give the show away. And it isn't wise to talk to them, for they will answer, and the mere sound of their voices unlocks the gates of madness. I can't stand to hear them. I try to anticipate what they want of me, so that I don't have to listen to their instructions any more than necessary. Oh, and I never argue with them. I've learned my lesson. The penalties are too great. They can be ferocious when they don't get their way.

"This place isn't just a stage. It is a world, with its own laws and rules, its natural order. I haven't seen much of it myself, but I've seen enough. From your vantage, you see only what you're supposed to see, a series of more or less normal, explainable images. It isn't really like that. It's all phony. Now, you're saying, 'Of course it is, it's a movie stage. What else?' I don't mean that. I mean it's phony even on those terms. There is a world beyond this set, but it isn't like anything you would expect.

"When the director calls cut, we don't step behind the backdrop to dressing rooms, we don't take a break in the cafeteria, or stroll the studio grounds. There's nothing like that out there. There's nothing sane or wholesome out there. Before I played this last bit, they changed the set. They don't build a new one, they just make it change. It runs like water; it liquefies, then they shape it like dough. While they're doing that, they drive us out, into the darkness. It is dark out there, always a dim, murky twilight, and yet I can discern a landscape. In the immediate vicinity I see filth, slime and rubbish, the refuse of filming and staging mixed with the foulness of this land. Flimsy walls and ceilings totter and sag under the weight of caked on mold; floors break through at a footstep, crumbling with rottenness; the chambers reek with putrefying trash. No human being could ever truly survive, much less thrive, among such chaos. I often wonder if the garbage generated by this endless production has been piling up here since the beginning of time, and will do so forever. Seen from outside, there is little sense of structure to the shooting area. It looks less like a building than a neglected dump. There I dwell, within that forsaken heap. Beyond the circle of disorder and decay I see rocks, reddish rocks, and a barren plain stretching in all directions to a black horizon. A sun never appears in the sky. I don't think there is one. The sky itself radiates feebly, without sun, or moon, or stars. Sometimes, far out across the plain, lights move and flicker, suggesting that there is more to this unspeakable realm than we will ever know. Something goes on out there. Does it have anything to do with us? The others must come from somewhere. Somehow this set must be maintained from outside, although I haven't the slightest idea how they do it. It seems eternal, self-contained.

"As do we. We don't eat, we don't sleep, we don't live. We simply exist, and perform. I hate it. This can't be the totality of my future—

this can't be my forever—only I'm afraid it is. What have I done to deserve this? I can't bear thinking about it.

"It's no use trying to run, although I have tried. We all have, once. I made a break for it, early on, fled across the plain as fast as my legs would carry me, in a straight line. I had nowhere to go, but anything was better than this. I ran and ran through the stifling darkness, for what might have been eternity. Dry, crusty soil crunched beneath my feet. Weirdly configured boulders loomed and receded. Nothing lived out there, nothing moved. There were no landmarks of any kind, and yet, for a period, it seemed as if the dim horizon itself approached. Of course that's impossible, like everything else here. Then I heard the whispering, coming from far off, from all directions. An inexplicable, indecipherable whispering, composed of countless low, inhuman voices. I didn't understand, but I feared. The mystery of the dark gave way to the terror of the dark, a palpable, tangible fear which rose up and enveloped me. Fear became the only fact of my being. When I couldn't take it any longer, when I felt my resolve ebbing and my brain disintegrating, I found myself back here. I may have run in circles, but I don't think so. Maybe every path leads back here. Maybe they brought me back. I don't remember. I was here again, that's all. I wouldn't try to run again.

"It's getting late. If they miss me... I have so much more to tell. The director—I mentioned him—I told you I looked. I wasn't supposed to do that; it's forbidden. He keeps to the shadows, with good reason. The other ones, the—the staff—they feign the trappings of humanity. He doesn't bother. There's no need. I saw him. I've seen who's in charge. I've wondered if he granted me that glimpse, once, just to make the point. Do you want to know who's running the show? Can I describe, with words, the blasphemous essence of horror, the epitome of all that is vile and corrupt? Mark my words, for I have seen. I tell you—"

At this point came a dirty cut, a bad splice or edit, followed by a jump to the next scene, already in progress. Reicher carried Miss Heim up a seemingly endless tower staircase, pursued by a horde of goons flashing swords. There was considerably more to the climax, but that was the last I saw in this one of Calvin Hartmann.

I did not awake with a start; I did not suddenly realize that my mind had slipped into reverie; I did not find myself in bed. I sat there, on the couch, surrounded by the debris of snacks, watching as *Rendezvous In Zanzibar* concluded. My sensations, my awareness of the world, felt quite real. Nothing could have—or has—convinced me that my experience was less than actual.

One more movie played before dawn, an inconsequential puff piece called *Mr. Mulligan's Holiday*, dating from the late Thirties. I was not familiar with it, nor did I waste much time on the story, which passed itself off as madcap comedy. I can not, at this time, recall who starred. I know that the name I sought on the credits did not appear. I watched it solely on the chance that something else of an unusual nature might happen. I think it did. There was one scene, when the stuffy Mr. Mulligan and his vivacious, ever laughing secretary were pressing through a crowded bus station, where I may have spied something. The extras surged away from the camera, as the main characters elbowed their way to the left. One extra struggled against the pack, toward the screen, desperately waving an arm in the air, before the mad throng bore him away and out of sight. I only saw his face for a moment. I believe it was Calvin Hartmann.

That was all. Dawn arrived, the spell broke, my life had to go on, regardless of the dire thoughts which mystified me. Nor have I learned anything since which would serve to explain or minimize the puzzle. I have not heard of anyone else sharing my experience. That was for me alone. Those movies are real enough, despite my initial doubts; I looked them up in guidebooks, read everything the authors considered worth mentioning. I discovered no overt indicators of fabulous mystery.

More to the point, I have seen *Rendezvous In Zanzibar* again. A company which specializes in golden oldies released it on DVD, and I snapped up a copy as soon as I heard about it. I still think it strange that I had missed this one before—very strange indeed—but I do not deem myself an expert, so I will let that pass. There is already a sufficiency of the weird in this matter, without seeking more.

In general it is the movie, even the same version, that I watched that night. It is a fine film. I would enjoy it better if it was exactly the same. Then I might pretend, somehow, that what happened to me was the product of a long forgotten cinematic joke. There is a problem with my personal copy. A minor plot element has been changed. The hero, Wesley-Smith, has no sidekick in this one. He travels to Zanzibar alone. There is a chase and death scene very much like the one I recall, but it involves a devoted native servant of the Princess. The character portrayed by Calvin Hartmann does not appear. Hartmann does not appear.

In fact, if my sources be accurate, there was no Calvin Hartmann.

LATE NIGHT MOVIES

The actor, the man, never existed. If my vision and memory be true, then I fear that the situation must be stated another way: he no longer ever existed. Such a concept defies my imagination. He was there, and now he is gone, and before he went he tried to communicate with me. I ask myself why he chose to contact me. There can be no question that he singled me out for special attention. That troubles me. That troubles me quite a lot. I try not to think about it.

About the author:

A degreed anthropologist, wilderness enthusiast, and photographer who makes his home in Arizona, Jeffery Scott Sims is a writer of fantastic and weird fiction. He is the creator of popular characters such as Professor Vorchek, the investigator of strange mysteries; Jacob Bleek, the questing medieval wizard; and the combative and colorful heroes of ancient Dyrezan.

His publications include the recent dark fantasy novel, *The Journey of Jacob Bleek*; the harrowing thriller *All Expenses Paid*; and many dozen short stories of the bizarre and the macabre. A number of these tales are set in the exotic and mysterious wilds of Arizona, or in imaginary lands at the ends of the earth.

Mr. Sims maintains a literary web site, *The Weird Writings of Jeffery Scott Sims*, which in addition to providing useful information on his works also offers an ever growing collection of entertaining essays devoted to unique or unusual topics related to the weird tale. This material may be freely accessed at http://jefferyscottsims.webs.com/index.html

www.ingramcontent.com/pod-product-compliance
Lightning Source LLC
Chambersburg PA
CBHW031334170626
46807CB00002B/700